STORMY Waters

DK MARIE

Cover by Avery Kingston First edition 2023

Previously published in Kindle Vella under the title *Stormy Waters*.

Author Note:

This story is a contemporary romance where love and hope prevails, but some topics might be troubling to some readers, such as the mention of physical and mental abuse. Readers who may be sensitive to these topics, please take note.

This is dedicated to all those who've suffered from
broken, false love.
May you find your happily ever after.

Contents

CHAPTER ONE

Eden Perez shifted her Mustang into reverse. The engine revved, and the tires spun, yet it remained stubbornly in place.

"What's wrong?" her daughter asked from the car's Bluetooth.

"I think I'm stuck." She shifted into park, opened the door, and groaned.

Her tires sat on—no, had sunk into—her muddy lawn instead of the gravel driveway. "Raven, I need to hang up. Figure out what to do."

"Okay, but you're still going to my basketball game tonight, right? We're playing against our rival."

The way her eleven-year-old daughter always double-checked their plans said she didn't believe Eden would show up. It made her heart ache. "Of course. Watching you crush the other team will be the highlight of my day. Te amo mi nieta."

Raven giggled. "What did you say?"

The last sentence had slipped from Eden's lips without a thought. She said it every time she ended a call with the only other person she loved—her abuela. But she and Raven didn't have a touchy-feely type of relationship. That was what happened when the mother spent most of her daughter's life over two thousand miles away.

But Eden was here now and would stay...as long as her fellowship went well, and Motts Children's Hospital hired her.

She cleared her throat. "I said, 'I love you' in Spanish."

There was a tick of silence, and in it time stopped as she waited for Raven's reply.

"That's so cool. I love when you speak Spanish. Will you teach me?"

Eden pressed a hand below her collarbone, near her wilting heart. "Yes, but your bisabuela—your great-grandma—would be a better teacher. I speak more Spanglish than Spanish."

"But she lives in New Mexico."

"I hope that'll change…"

If I get hired at the hospital, maybe I'll convince her to move to Michigan. Eden hated all the uncertainties.

Raven's dad, Asher, said something in the background, then Raven sighed. "I gotta go. Time for school."

They said their goodbyes and hung up. Eden grabbed her umbrella from the passenger seat and stepped from her car. The heels of her favorite leather ankle boots sank into squishy grass, and the scent of wet earth filled her nose. "April showers bring May flowers, my ass. In Michigan, it brings mud. Lots of mud."

How had she managed to forget the state's temperamental springs? Since returning in May, she'd once again experienced all the seasons, getting a crash-course reminder in the 'Great Lakes State' moody weather.

She tiptoed around puddles to the car's rear. *Dammit.* The tires were buried in muck up to the rims. There wasn't time for this delay. She had a million errands before picking up Raven from school. And skipping an afternoon with her daughter wasn't going to happen.

"How is it I'm able to operate on infants with perfect precision but can't back out of my driveway without ending up in my front yard?"

After a few calming breaths, she walked to the passenger's side since it was still on the gravel driveway. She retrieved her phone from the center console, hoping the only repair shop in this tiny town also had a tow truck because she had no one to call.

Her elbow smacked into the door's window, and she cursed as her ancient cell phone tumbled from her hand. It landed in a shallow puddle with an ominous crack.

"No, no, no. Please, no."

Grabbing it, she groaned. The screen was shattered and black. She wiped it on her jeans, then held the power button. Nothing.

She sucked in a lungful of rain-soaked air and stared at the reason she'd rented this house—the lake in front of her. It wasn't large, but most of the surrounding land was owned by the government, so there weren't many homes. The patter of the light rainfall hitting the water was usually soothing. This morning, it mocked her.

Sighing, she looked at the only other house on the dead-end road. The family was kind but basically strangers. She couldn't bang on their door. It wasn't even seven in the morning.

She craned her neck toward the large restaurant atop the hill, aptly named The Hill. Its massive patio jutted like a stubborn chin from the steep bluff. She could walk there and borrow someone's phone. Maybe she'd get lucky, and one of the college kids would be opening the restaurant. They were nicer to her than the older ones who remembered the first time she'd lived in this small town.

Pressing her lips together, she pushed off from the car. Bemoaning her luck wouldn't check items off her to-do list. She could deal with whoever was there if it meant getting her hands on a working phone.

Making her way up the steep incline toward the restaurant, she toed around the nastiest potholes, wishing for a sidewalk. A gravel road combined with last night's storm wasn't ideal in a stiletto heel. She should've chosen a more reasonable shoe, but after five days in clogs, she'd wanted something feminine.

Less than halfway up the hill, after countless near falls, she regretted her choic-es—from her footwear to waking her neighbor. In retrospect, they had two little kids and were more than likely awake and starting their day.

Oh well, no point in turning back. Eden was almost at the restaurant. And her jeans were already mud speckled, and her equally dirty boots were probably destroyed.

After too many more minutes of struggling up the muddy hill, she stepped onto the worn wooden floor of the massively long metal-covered porch of The Hill. She sighed. Mental and physical weariness tugged at her. She'd have to add changing out of her ruined clothes and getting a new phone to her already growing to-do list that wanted to eat up every moment of her day off from the hospital.

She pushed through the entrance, and a ding echoed through the large, empty restaurant. Well, empty except for one man. Tate Siren, the new owner of The Hill—and her landlord—stood behind the long bar with a laptop in front of him.

It had been easier dealing with the old married couple who used to own the restaurant and two homes at the bottom of the long gravel driveway she'd just walked and now despised. Her stomach never did an excited flip at seeing them, as it did now, looking at Tate. Nor did they sneak into her late-night fantasies.

And he was a handsome distraction that was one-hundred percent off-limits.

His beautiful mouth pulled into a smile. It always surprised her how genuine it appeared. She almost believed it.

However, Tate's sister, Lilith, was Asher's girlfriend. The very same Asher who was Eden's ex and the father of their daughter. And while her ex was a kind man, Eden had screwed up enough with her choices that she could only imagine the stories Lilith—or the town gossips, told Tate.

"I hope you aren't too hungry. The morning cook doesn't arrive for another hour." Tate pointed to a carafe. "But I have coffee. Want a cup?"

She shook her head even as her caffeine addiction screamed yes. "No, I was hoping to use your phone."

"Is everything okay?"

"No. My car's stuck in the mud." She held up her cracked cell. "And I just broke my phone. Could I use your phone to call a tow truck?"

"I'll do you one better." He closed his laptop. "I have some boards behind the restaurant that I've used to help a few customers who'd had the same problem."

She stepped to the bar, moving between two stools. "That's okay. Letting me use your phone is more than enough. I don't mind waiting." She did but hated being indebted to someone even more.

"The reason I started helping customers is because the single tow truck in town is owned by one of the slowest men in Michigan. I'd bet good money a sloth would beat him in a race."

Her chest tightened, and she crossed her arms over the pressure. There went her beast of a to-do list, but that was better than being beholden to Tate. "It's fine. I'll wait."

He squinted his gray eyes, but instead of calling her out, he said, "My morning is shit. I could use the fresh air."

"I—"

Holding up a hand, he shook his head. "Listen, it's partly my fault you're stuck. I didn't realize until the snow melted that I needed to have your driveway graded. Let me take a look. If your car's going the way of the poor horse from *The NeverEnding Story*, we'll call for professional help."

Surprised laughter bubbled from her, popping some of her stress. "Guess I wasn't the only kid in love with that old eighties movie," she said.

"Kid? I watched it last weekend with Chloe. Bawled like a baby during that scene," Tate joked.

A twinge of jealousy pinched Eden. Tate was closer to his niece than Eden was with her daughter.

His phone dinged, drawing her attention to where it lay on the bar between them. The name Katrina appeared on the screen. Tate flipped his cell, muttering, "Christ."

He didn't say more, but it seemed as if her cloud of stress had transferred to him. "Everything okay?" she asked.

"Fine. Great." His tone and frown told a different story.

But he wasn't any of her business and didn't give her time to pursue the topic, anyway. He came around the bar, walked through the dining area, and stepped toward the main doors. "Come on. Let's see if I can help you get unstuck."

She followed, relieved the rain had let up for the moment. Looking from the sky to Tate's back, she took in his faded black Henley. The way it showcased his broad shoulders and defined biceps was lovely. Her gaze fell to his butt. Perfection. *Stop. Look somewhere else. Think of something else.*

Her mind drifted to the missed phone call. The name Katrina was vaguely familiar. A face flashed in Eden's mind when they reached the long driveway. A pretty blonde with cupid lips and cornflower blue eyes that had a sharp edge to them, Tate's girlfriend, Katrina. Were they together, or had they broken up when he moved?

Again, it wasn't her business, yet she blurted, "Are you and Katrina still together?"

"No." He didn't turn around, but it was obvious in the stiffness of his reply and how his broad shoulders tensed that the question upset him.

She was such a thoughtless jerk to ask such a personal question. This was probably why she'd had very few friends. "I'm sorry. That was nosey and rude." The hill was progressively becoming steeper, and her calves burned with the effort of not tipping or sliding down the mud-slicked driveway.

He turned just as her right foot slid forward. She locked her leg muscles, barely managing not to fall. Though, she suspected, moving might change that.

"Shit, Eden." He dropped the boards he was holding and hustled forward, helping to get her into a standing position that didn't hurt. "Those heels are dangerous on this surface."

"Shit, Tate. Had I known how my morning would be, I'd have worn hiking boots. Scratch that. I wouldn't have gotten out of bed."

Ugh. She was being rude again. Looking up to apologize, she found him grinning. And so close. He really did have an exquisite mouth.

Keeping hold of one of her arms, he shuffled around until he was behind her. "Let's walk the rest of the way like this. Then I can catch you when you slip in those ridiculously high heels. I'll come back for the boards when you're at the car."

She wasn't a damn damsel in distress, but the fear of breaking an arm or fingers more than halfway through her fellowship, had her accepting his help. "My hero," she drawled, and began walking, his soft chuckle making her smile.

Not even two steps later, Tate grunted. Gravel shifted behind her, and she was on her back, looking at the gray sky in a blink. Her heart pounded, and she waited for the cold, wet, and pain to sink in. Instead, there was deep laughter from under her. Under her?

Oh. Tate was under her, his arm around her, his big hand splayed on her stomach, keeping her in place. "Are you okay?" he asked.

She took stock. Nothing hurt. In fact, his warm, firm body along her back felt rather nice. "I think so. You?"

He sat, adjusting her onto his lap. "Just my ego hurts."

But you smell wonderful, like an outdoor adventure.

She shook her head. The inexplicable reaction of desire for him was becoming a nuisance. Holding onto his firm thighs, she pushed up. He gripped her waist, giving her the boost she needed. Turning, she looked at his black Converse, smirked and offered her hand. "Let me help you the rest of the way down the hill. We don't want you falling in those ridiculous shoes."

"My hero," he drawled in the tone she had used moments ago. She laughed and it mixed with his.

Wiping his palms on his jeans, he stood. "Let's walk next to each other. Help whoever falls next."

"Good idea."

Her playful mood lasted until they reached her car a few minutes later. Tate stood next to Eden, staring at her Mustang. "Damn. It looks like the mud is trying to swallow your car whole."

"Told you." Suspecting he regretted his offer, she gave him an out. "Ready to loan me your phone?"

Tate retrieved the boards he'd brought from the restaurant and aligned them with the rear tires. "Nah. Let's try this first. Start your car and reverse really slowly. I'll get the boards tucked so the wheels will stop spinning, and then you can back out on them."

She got inside and did as instructed. Slowly pressing on the gas, the tires caught and crawled backward. After she'd moved a couple of inches, he hollered for her to stop and switch into drive with the wheel turned all the way to the left.

The direction was simple, but her follow-through was a disaster. Her mud-covered boot slipped while she pressed on the pedal. The car shot forward, and Tate's startled yell echoed across the lake.

She slammed on the brakes as her heart crashed into her throat. Had she hit him?

No, she was driving forward. But what if he'd somehow fallen under the rear wheels??

Shit. Shit. Of all the people to hit, it had to be Lilith's brother. *Like the woman needs another reason to dislike me.*

Jamming the car into park, she jumped out. Relief pressed into her. Tate stood a few feet from the back of her car. His jeans and black Henley were covered in slime and muck. His gorgeous auburn hair was more a, well, muddy brown. There were even flicks of dirt in his close-cropped beard.

Even more surprising, he was laughing. She rushed to him. "I am so sorry."

"Well, you know how to make a man forget his problems."

"What? By giving you new ones?"

He snorted. "Yup."

"Will you have to time to go home and shower before opening your restaurant?"

"Depends on when my cook arrives. If he arrives on time, I can get home and back before the early lunch rush."

"Does he normally show up late?"

Tate nodded, not looking the least bit annoyed.

"And that doesn't bother you?"

"He works as a security guard to make ends meet. Sometimes he oversleeps."

Eden scoffed but kept her negative comments to herself. He seemed to hear them anyway and said, "If he needs a few extra minutes of shut-eye to make it through the day, I don't mind."

"You give people an inch, they'll take a hundred miles."

Tate cocked a brow. "Isn't the saying, 'a mile'?"

"It's always more. A lot more."

He opened his mouth, then closed it, seeming to study her. She hoped he wouldn't try to change her mind. It wouldn't happen, and she didn't have time for a debate. Her to-do list was waiting.

To her relief, he only said, "Not always." Then he tapped his muddy shirt. "Thankfully. I have a change of clothes in my office. I'll wash up in the bathroom sink."

She glanced at her tires. They were no longer stuck. She could be on her way. Her gaze moved to Tate. He was looking up the steep hill toward his restaurant as a violent shiver shook him. Knowing she was the cause wrapped her in guilt. She couldn't leave him cold and covered in mud.

"How about I get your clothes while you can take a shower at my house? Then you won't have to open late or spend the morning finding mud in odd places."

Even though the offer had left her mouth, it surprised her. She needed to pay him back for his help, but her nearly neurotic need for privacy meant she didn't have company often. Her only regular visitor was Raven.

Yet, the thought of Tate inside her home didn't bother her in the slightest. Unlike most people, his presence soothed instead of agitated her.

"You sure?" he asked.

"Tate, you're covered in the worst parts of spring because of me. It's the least I can do."

"Since a clump of something just slid into my jeans and down my ass crack, I'm not going to refuse your offer."

Walking to the porch to unlock the door, she teased, "Please don't use my loofah to clean your behind."

"No way," he said, following her. "My ass is much too delicate and sensitive. I'll use your face towel instead. Those are much softer."

She snickered, pushing open the door. "Gross. I'm going to hide a few bathroom items before I get your clean clothes," she joked, removing her ruined boots. "There're fresh towels and washcloths in the linen closet."

"Is that a hint to stay away from the ones you're using?" His lips twitched, then broke into a smile that made her heart flutter.

She couldn't help returning it. "Maybe."

He told her where to find his clothes, and after driving to the restaurant to get them, Eden knocked on the bathroom door. "Where do you want me to leave your stuff?"

"Would you mind setting them on the sink?"

Heat crawled up her neck to her cheeks. "But you're in the shower."

"Would you rather me stroll out in only a towel? And I have the water so hot the glass in your living room is probably fogged. You won't see anything."

She took a deep breath and stepped inside, keeping her eyes fixed on the counter. Setting his stuff on it, she grabbed for his muddy ones. "I'll soak your clothes and wash them this evening with mine."

"Thanks. And, hey, what's with the control panel in here? I feel like I'm in a carwash."

"The previous landlord had approved the upgrades," she replied, a tad defensive.

She *had* gone overboard, but after a rough shift at the hospital, her sauna shower was worth every damn penny.

"Believe me, I'm not complaining. I'm scheming ideas of how to shower here every day."

Laughing, her gaze drifted in his direction, and she froze. His back was to her, and the glass was fogged, but she saw a massive, colorful tattoo through the steam. Tracing its outline on his broad shoulders and most of his back, she then moved to his wet, tapered waist. He was exquisite.

"Eden?" He glanced over his shoulder.

She jolted. "I'm sorry, um, I didn't know you had such a big tattoo on your back."

He smirked as if to say, "That's not the only big thing I have." *Don't think about his dick size. Look away, woman, look away!*

The hiss of water cut off. "I'm finished. But you're welcome to stay for the whole show."

She ripped her gaze from him. "Dios mío, sorry! Sorry! I'll give you privacy." Her pulse raced faster than her legs as she left a very fine naked and dripping Tate in her bathroom.

CHAPTER TWO

Eden patted her flushed cheeks, moving quickly through her house. She couldn't decipher if the heat was from desire or embarrassment that Tate had caught her staring at him like a damn perv. Although, she hadn't been totally lying, his tattoo *had* caught her attention. She didn't know he had any, let alone one that spanned most of his back. She'd love to see it clearly, without the steam blurring the image. Maybe even run her fingers along the lines, explore him.

Whoa. Slow it down, woman.

But it was hard to forget his broad shoulders, firm ass, and muscular legs—all pleasing to the eye and hard—so hard—to ignore. "Ugh." She shook her head. "Keep your mind out of the gutter or he's going to scc it on your face."

In the kitchen, she grabbed a mug from the cupboard and placed it under the spout of the coffee machine, hitting the brew button. She closed her eyes and listened to the beans grind, followed by the click and drip of a cup being filled. She inhaled the comforting scent, letting it calm her.

And it worked until Tate's deep voice filled the kitchen, asking, "Could I have some?"

Her heart tripped and sped up, but her nod was calm and collected. Needing a reprieve before meeting his eyes, she got him a cup, and busied herself making him coffee, training her gaze on the liquid falling from the machine. When it was finished, she asked, "How do you take yours." Not wanting to show she was a little rattled and too affected by him, she schooled her features and looked at him.

"Some cream would be great." His expression was neutral, all calm.

Why did disappointment sink into her? *Idiot*.

His hair was damp, so it was a little darker, more brown than red. The longer part on top, usually up and off his face, flopped onto his forehead, making him appear almost boyish. She wanted to brush the strands back. See if they were as soft as they looked.

Seriously, what the hell was wrong with her? She needed to stop thirsting after him.

It had been a long time since she'd been with anyone, but she barely noticed the absence. Her busy life didn't allow room for dating and sex, which rarely mattered to her. Now she couldn't stop thinking about it—not dating, but sex... and with a certain hot restaurant owner.

After getting the creamer from the fridge, she added some to his coffee then handed him the warm mug. "Thanks," he said, taking a sip and watching her over the rim. That mischievous glint had returned to his eyes. "So..."

She scrambled for something to talk about before he could make her blush again. "You mentioned earlier you were having a bad morning. What happened?"

"My afternoon bartender had a family emergency and had to call off for the week. I'll have to cover for him and the only drink I know how to make is a Whiskey Neat." Tate slouched against the counter behind him.

"Wow." Eden laughed. "Yeah, that could be a problem."

He held his thumb and index finger a centimeter apart. "A little bit."

"Do you have a sub? Or can't another one of your other bartenders pick up a double-shift?"

"My fill-in is on vacation. In Texas. I've asked my two evening bartenders. One takes an evening college course and the other's married to a police officer who works at night, so he has to stay home with their kids."

Eden sipped her coffee, resting a hip on the opposite counter. "What's your backup plan?"

"I don't have one."

Dread on his behalf trickled into her. She massaged her throat. "I don't think I could fall asleep each night if I didn't have the following day mapped out. And with my career, I have plans for my plans, then backup plans for both of them."

Though, except for her plans with Raven, the other ones she'd made for today were becoming less important the more time she was around Tate. And that was the other problem with him. Eden enjoyed talking with him too much. And not just today. If a shift at the hospital was particularly difficult, she'd find herself at The Hill, pretending it was for dinner, but really, she was secretly hoping he'd have time to stop at her table. Their conversation always lifted her spirits.

"It's one of the reasons I left my old career for this place. It's less rigid," he said.

"You did something with money, right?"

He nodded. "An Investment Fund Manager. I liked the challenge, but being chained to a desk wasn't for me. I like this better. Talking to the locals and tourists is my favorite part, but switching from cook, to waiter, to manager keeps me from getting bored. Each day and its problems are different. It keeps things interesting."

It sounded like purgatory to her. The unknown, winging it—would give her an ulcer.

"Except this week might be too interesting. Corporate life didn't prepare me for mixing drinks. When you showed up, I was looking up easy drink recipes, planning to watch some how-to videos." He frowned, pulling at the collar of his T-shirt. "The problem is, I haven't owned this place long enough to know the customer favorites—which ones I should learn to make. Hell, I don't even drink enough to know what people love in general."

Eden tapped her foot on the tiled floor. She'd been a bartender in college. Helping him would mess up the morning's schedule, possibly tomorrow's, and those were her only days off from the hospital. But settling the debt she owed him would make the inconvenience worth it.

"Thank Christ it was my afternoon guy and not my evening bartender." Tate tipped back the mug, finishing his coffee, then set it on the counter. "Anyway, I better get back and learn some drinks."

Mentally shifting around her to-do list and finding it doable, she said, "I'll help you."

"Um, you're a surgeon who operates on kids, right?" He rubbed the back of his neck. "I feel like an asshole having to double check since we've talked about your fellowship."

"You're right, I'm a pediatric surgeon." Did he find it odd that she took care of other people's children but hadn't been around for her daughter's early years? She couldn't explain to him why operating for ten hours or more on a baby was less stressful and scary than the chaos of motherhood. She cleared her throat. "But during medical school I was a bartender."

"Babies and booze, huh?" Tate asked. "It's an odd combination. Then again, I've babysat when my niece was in her colic phase. By the time my sister returned to pick up Chloe, I needed a few drinks."

She loved his playful reply. It didn't echo her shortcomings. Although, part of her heart ached at the reminder she'd missed those precious early years with her child. Suppressing her regrets, she said, "Thankfully, I had a scholarship, but mixing cocktails helped pay for housing and textbooks."

Tate tilted his head. "Asher mentioned you went to Stanford. Is that right?"

She nodded.

"I had a friend who went there," Tate said. "I thought they didn't give out scholarships for medical school."

"They award need-based scholarships and grants." Her voice was smooth, but her insides rioted. Talking about her past always made her queasy. She didn't want his concern or pity. Shifting to their original topic, she said, "I can look over your current drink menu and teach you the easy ones. You could offer a small discount. That should quell most customer complaints at mistakes made."

"That's perfect for me, but weren't you heading out for the day? I wanted to help get you unstuck, not have you stuck with me all morning."

She gave a slight shrug and took a sip of her coffee. "I don't want to owe you."

"Why would you owe me?"

"For helping me."

"No repayment necessary. I'd have helped anyone in your situation."

That rang true. From what she saw of Tate, he was the first to offer a helping hand. Didn't he know people would take advantage of him?

She wouldn't do that to him but was compelled to warn him. "You should have boundaries, or people will use you."

"You wouldn't."

"How do you know? From our sporadic conversations? Or are you one of those people who can judge a person's character from the first time they meet?"

He broke eye contact and sagged. "No. In fact, I'm terrible at it. But your goodness is hard to miss. And you're a friend." She stared at her coffee, hiding her surprise. "And friends don't keep score," he finished.

Everyone keeps score.

She smirked, hoping to hide her sharp, cynical edges. "And here I thought you tolerated me because our connection to Asher. And because you're my land-lord—"

"And you're my sister's boyfriend's baby-mamma."

She snorted. "I was going to say Raven's mother, but your description works too. Even if it makes me sound like I belong on a daytime talk show where the guests get into fistfights and the audience cheers them on."

He laughed, and Eden loved the deep rumble and how often and easy he was with humor and happiness. It seemed to flow from him. Hers was rare and restrained, much like her laughter.

"I'd put my money on you," he said. "You're a surgeon, known for being good with your hands and knives."

"And I know how to make some excellent drinks too. So, let me pay you back."

He pushed his hair off his forehead. "It must really bother you, this belief you owe me. Do you ever ask for help?"

"Not if I can help it."

"Why?"

She ran a finger around the rim of her coffee mug. "Most of the time it's easier, simpler, to do things on my own, my way." It also alleviated the risk of disappointing others or having them disappoint her.

"That seems lonely."

Alone isn't lonely; it is safe. "I find it efficient. Anyway, I have the experience. You need help. Why not take mine?" She grinned. "For a man who offers help easily, *you* seem to hate accepting it. You might be as stubborn as me."

He held up his hands. "Fine. I'm desperate. But *now* I owe *you* big time." Picking up his empty mug, he asked, "Since I'm now in your debt, could you add another coffee to my tab?"

"Sure, but this makes us even." Her fingers slid against his as she took the cup. The simple, accidental touch warmed her belly. And lower.

Eden swallowed as one problem solved turned into another. She'd no longer owe him, but what would she do with the giddiness rising within her—how her body hummed in anticipation of spending more time with him?

CHAPTER THREE

Since Tate had taken over as owner of The Hill in February, he'd see Eden stop in after leaving the hospital about once a week. Sometimes they'd chat, and other times it was a simple wave. She always looked one hundred percent the surgeon. And it wasn't the doctor's scrubs but her manner. Competence and efficiency was Eden Perez. Even now, behind his bar, studying his liquor collection, she appeared confident and sure of herself. Eden was a chameleon.

He was the opposite in every way—fumbling through life, burning bridges and people, switching careers when most his age were getting comfortable and settled in their profession. Sure, he was better suited as a restaurant owner than a marketing manager, but he'd mortgaged everything for his new dream. The fear of failure taunted him.

Shaking off the unhelpful introspection, he asked her, "How long did you bartend?"

She grinned. "Are you checking my credentials? Worried I might not be helpful?"

"Nope." He chuckled. "Don't forget, my previous teacher was randos from the internet."

Setting a bottle of vodka and ginger beer on the worn bar top, she said, "I did it on and off through medical school and my residency. So, about five years. I'll teach you the easy classics that never go out of style."

Twisting off the cap of the ginger beer, he took a drink. "You're giving away more time and effort than I did for your car unstuck. I owe you. Let me give you a bottle of my best whiskey."

"I don't drink." She took the ginger beer from him. "And that's for the Moscow mule I'm going to teach you how to make."

"No drinking, huh?"

"Nope." Her tone said the topic was closed for discussion.

"Okay. No booze. How about I give you my soul?" Or *my body?*

Eden's throaty chuckle filled the restaurant. It drifted straight to his libido, which until this morning had been hibernating. He was hit on often while working, especially by the rowdy weekend crowd, and it never did a thing for him. However, catching Eden's gaze washing over him when he'd been in her shower had woken his sleeping sex drive, and now it was hungry.

"A soul might be useful." Eden's voice pulled him into the present. "But we agreed, we're even after this. Plus, how do you figure you owe me? I almost ran you over and *did* drench you head-to-toe in mud."

"Yes, but your spa-retreat shower made up for that." He leaned against the bar, crossing his feet at the ankles. "Though... I did let you ogle me for free."

"I was not ogling you." Her reply was so prim that Tate couldn't help laughing.

Eden's lips twitched like she wanted to join in but wasn't quite willing to give him the satisfaction. That was fine with him. Earning her laughter would make the sound all the more sweeter when he heard it.

"Do you normally charge people to watch you shower?" she asked.

He pointed to the wood-paneled walls painted an ugly orange-ish brown. "I need to update my restaurant. Those renovations won't pay for themselves." He wiggled his brows. "Why? Are you willing to pay?"

"Depends."

"On?"

"How steamy the shower stall will be."

Holy shit. Is Eden flirting with me? Disbelief and desire spread through him.

Her eyes widened as if she'd surprised herself. Clearing her throat, she pointed at the vodka and soda. "Do you want me to show you how to make the drinks or just write down the recipes?"

"Writing them down is fine." He grabbed a spiral notebook from under the bar and handed it to her, pretending he was relieved they'd switched to work. He should be—it was safer. But he couldn't deny that he liked spending time alone with the mysterious Eden.

They weren't strangers. That was impossible, given she was Raven's mom, whose dad was dating Tate's sister. However, chatting at a few busy family gatherings wasn't the same as one-on-one. Today he was seeing a different, more relaxed side of Eden. Her humor and intelligence were sexy.

Not that he was interested in more than being her friend. There was a time he'd have loved to date someone like her—smart, capable, and hot. But that was before Katrina.

Now all he wanted was peace. The chaos of intimate relationships held no appeal.

He glanced at Eden. She was intent on the notepad in front of her. His stupid, kamikaze brain wanted to ask her if she was dating anyone. Or if the rumor that she was still hung up on Asher was true. Neither was appropriate, so he asked, "Does Stanford not have a pediatric fellowship?"

"They do." She didn't look up from the notebook. "But I wanted to come here."

"Is UMich's program better?"

"No. Stanford is slightly better." She looked up from her notes. "Are you asking in a roundabout way why I'm here?"

Subtle wasn't his way. He'd only been making small talk. Tate had figured her return had something to do with her daughter. And possibly Asher.

Before he could answer, she asked, "Do you believe the town gossip? That I came here to win back my college sweetheart?"

He'd heard people say that exact thing, but it was an unfair assumption—unkind to Eden and Raven. "No, I—"

She huffed, tapping the pen top in her with force. "Why are people so willing to believe I'd endure Michigan winters for a college fling, but not my daughter?"

He held up his hands, wanting to calm the agitation clearly simmering in her. "Because people like to make up stories, the more sordid the better. Or, if we want to think kindly of the town gossips, we can say it's because we live in a small town. Those are supposed to be filled with hopeless romantics who love second-chance stories, right? At least, that seems to be the case in romance books," he joked.

Eden beautiful smiled reached her eyes. "What do you know about romances?" she asked.

"I have a sister who's obsessed with them." He shrugged. "I might have read a few."

At the mention of Lilith, Eden's gaze returned to her drink list. "The only second-chance relationship I'm interested in is with Raven."

Was she setting him straight? Letting him know the flirting a few minutes ago was empty? Disappointed twisted around him, but he shook it off and nodded, telling her without words that he got the message.

He tapped her sheet of paper that already had a few drinks listed. "Could you keep it around ten? And simple? I like things easy. Something quick and satisfying, that'll leave my customers happy."

Eden's lips twitched. "Are you still talking about drinks?"

"*Tsk, tsk,*" he shook his head, grinning. "Are you still dreaming about me becoming a shower sex worker?"

She snorted. "You wish."

He should consider the morning a shitshow. An important employee had called off for the week. Tate had gotten two calls from his ex. One he'd mistakenly answered that had turned ugly when he politely told her not to call him. The other he'd let go to voicemail when Eden had first arrived at the restaurant. Soon after that, he was covered in mud—all before his second cup of coffee. Yet, instead of being upset, he was feeling pretty damn great.

"Hey, Tate. How's it going Bri—" Gus skidded in his tracks. His gaze bounced between Eden and Tate.

Tate looked at the old clock on the equally ancient, paneled wall. Damn, the restaurant would open in less than an hour. Time raced when he was with Eden. "Brian had a family emergency. She's giving me a crash course in bartending." He pointed with his chin. "You know Eden, right?"

Of course Gus did. Since Lilith moved here almost a year ago and Tate followed a few months back, he'd learned everyone knew everyone. Gotta love small towns.

"She's helping you? Why? How?" Gus asked.

It probably seemed odd to him that Eden knew anything about mixing drinks. "She—"

"Here's the list." She handed the notebook to him, her movements stiff as her voice.

The sudden, cold shift in her had him taking the notes in silence. He shouldn't be so disconcerted. It was how she sounded when talking to pretty much anyone but her daughter. Still, the tone hadn't been there all morning.

Finding his voice, he asked, "Everything okay?"

"Why wouldn't it be? I fulfilled my debt. Now I have to get on with my day." She left without looking at either of them.

What the hell? Was she fine helping him when there was no one to see it? Guess the high and mighty surgeon was too good to be seen slumming it with the dive bar owner.

"She's an odd woman," Gus said, eyeing the door Eden had exited. "Hot, but icy as hell."

No doubt about the hot part; she reminded him of a younger Salma Hayek, but so what? He'd get a print from a favorite artist if he wanted to look at something pretty. Hell, an original. The cost would hurt less than chasing after a complicated woman. He'd learned that painful lesson with his ex.

Tate shrugged, trying to shake off his annoyance. "She's alright."

Gus's eyebrows nearly reached his receding hairline. "I know you're a monk, but are you blind too?"

Fucking nickname. His employees loved to tease him about his lack of interest in the customers who were too interested in him.

"She looks like trouble to me," Tate replied mildly.

"Tempting trouble…"

"If your wife heard you talking like that you'd be in huge trouble," Tate joked.

"Shiiit." Gus wiped imaginary sweat off his forehead. "She'd kick my ass."

"Then get started in the kitchen before I call her and tattle," Tate joked. "And after you get the grill and grease heated, help me with a little day-drinking. I need to test my menu."

And forget about Eden's smile.

The entrance door dinged. Without looking, Tate said, "Sorry, we aren't open yet."

"I'm sure you can make an exception for me." His dad sauntered in.

Tate grimaced, then released his tightened jaw. Great. First, Eden's sudden cold-shoulder crap. Now his dad would shovel on more. This day would be a shitshow after all.

CHAPTER FOUR

Tate's dad slid onto the stool directly in front of him. "Why are you behind the bar? It's a little early for a drink, don't you think? Then again, maybe you've just realized all your terrible life choices and needed something strong."

Not even a good morning before he starts in on me. "I'm fine with my life choices." Tate glanced at the notebook where Eden had written the recipes. Would the proud surgeon have left his side as quickly if he still had his corner office and custom suits? He flipped the notebook closed. "I'm covering for the day bartender," he said.

"I didn't know you knew how to bartend." Dad twisted around in his stool, stood and grabbed a ceramic coffee mug from a nearby table. "But what do I know about my son? I thought he had more smarts than to leave a great job for this dive."

"This place isn't a dive." Sure, Tate always called his catch-all resturant one, but he said it with affection, not disdain. "And I guess I'm full of surprises."

Dad leaned his elbows on the bar top. "When will they be good ones?"

Fuck. He loved to toss jabs that left a mark.

Tate rolled his shoulders. "You know, for someone who hates my restaurant, you spend a lot of time here." His dad stopped by at least twice a week for a meal. "And you don't exactly live around the corner."

"I don't like that you gave up a great career." His dad grinned, tapping his empty mug on the bar top. "But I love your cooks."

"Did you hear that Gus?" Tate shouted as he reached for the coffee carafe and filled his dad's cup.

Gus's shaved head, brown eyes, and broad smile appeared behind the line. "What?"

"My dad complimented your cooking, and this man hands out compliments about as much as Ebenezer Scrooge gives away money."

"Harrison Siren, sir," Gus pointed with a spatula, "You are getting the breakfast special *and* an extra order of the best slices of bacon I've got."

Tate's dad gave Gus a thumbs-up. Reopening the notebook, Tate stared at Eden's nearly indecipherable writing. He squinted at the scribbles. Had she written lime or lemon? Damn, he should have had her type these out.

"What's that?" His dad tapped the page with a blunt finger.

"A friend who used to be a bartender helped me with a few drink recipes."

"Was it the Mexican walking to her car when I arrived? Raven's mom?"

"Really, Dad." Tate dipped his chin. "'The Mexican'?"

His dad held up his hands, palms showing. "What? I didn't mean anything by it. She's a good-looking woman." That was probably what he considered the most important thing about her—that she was attractive.

"Her name is Eden Perez. And she's a pediatric surgeon doing her fellowship at the top hospital in Michigan. She's more than a pretty face."

"So you *do* think she's pretty." Tate held in a groan as his dad kept talking. "Do you two got something going on? What does Asher think about it?"

Tate scoffed. "Why would Asher care?"

"She was his woman."

"Over a decade ago." Why was he even arguing? Eden wasn't interested in him. And he was on a hiatus from dating.

"Doesn't matter. Asher isn't a stranger or acquaintance. He's your good friend and your sister's live-in boyfriend." He shook his head like he disapproved of the arrangement. "Moving in on his ex—that he had a kid with—is wrong."

Tate waved a hand as if brushing away the conversation. "I'm not making any moves. She and I are friends."

"Why not more?"

This time Tate couldn't hold in his groan. "What the hell? You just said Asher has dibs on her for life. Now you want to know why we aren't dating?"

"Fine, not her. But you need to find someone. You aren't getting any younger. It's time for you to settle down and give me some grandchildren."

"You have Chloe. And Raven."

"They are great girls—the best. But I want more. And a grandson would be nice."

Tate liked kids but didn't have to have them. And definitely not now. He was still getting over the blow of Katrina pretending she was pregnant when he'd broken up with her. He'd known it was bullshit—she had been on her damn period when she'd made the hysterical claim. It was the idea of him trapped with her that had sat like tar in his blood. And he would have been trapped because she'd have made sure the only way he'd ever see his kid was if he was with her.

"Sorry to disappoint you. Again," he muttered.

As if thinking about Katrina reminded his dad of her, he asked, "Why'd you end things with the pretty little blonde? She was a good woman. You could've done the long-distance thing. It had worked for Asher and Lilith. The distance is about the same."

Tate snorted. Yeah, well, they had a good relationship. Real love—the exact opposite of him and Kat. Hell, just hearing her name aloud had dread pooling in his veins.

Dad tapped his knuckles on the bar. "What?"

Tate considered, then decided to be honest. "I didn't end things for no reason. She and I weren't good together."

"More like you grew bored. Like you did at your old job." Dad made a clicking sound with his tongue. "You're like your mom, jumping from one shiny thing to the next—hobbies, jobs, relationships."

Tate wanted to tell his dad that Mom had a right to build a life that made her happy. Maybe remind him that she'd met and married Ted a few years after the divorce, and they were still together. But saying any of this was pointless as the previous topic of Eden.

"A single, divorced old man is the perfect person for relationship advice. Tell me, Romeo, when was the last time you even went on a date?"

"Don't get lippy, young man."

"Young man," Tate scoffed, trying not to be amused. "I'm almost thirty, not thirteen."

His dad chuckled. "Shit, where does the time go? Speaking of time..." He looked behind Tate and said louder, "What happened to my breakfast?"

"Don't get your britches in a bunch, Harrison," Gus called from the kitchen. "Give me two minutes."

Not wanting the conversation to return to his personal life, Tate pushed the drink list toward his dad. "Can you tell me what this says?"

He pulled a pair of reading glasses from the breast pocket of his flannel and picked up the notebook. "Hell, son, is this even in English? I'd ask her to come back and read it to you."

"Yeah, sure." Tate had no intention of calling Eden.

This morning's little rollercoaster was enough for him to know all he needed about her. He'd let one temperamental woman drag him through hell. He wouldn't willingly walk that path again.

CHAPTER FIVE

Tate scanned his email, regretting he'd checked it. Playing bartender yesterday hadn't been easy, even with Eden's helpful list. Once that was over, he'd had to cover for two sick servers in the evening. A long night and an early morning were a terrible combination—add the five messages in his inbox from Katrina, and he was left wondering why he got out of bed.

He rubbed at the annoyance bubbling in his chest. Leaning into his chair, it creaked as he stared at the cracked ceiling tile in his small office. When would this shit end? Not work complications. Those were expected, and he could deal with them, but Katrina was like a virus—unwilling to leave and a pain-in-the-everything that could become a huge problem.

"Anyone here?" called a woman's voice, and for a horrible second, he thought it was Katrina. Then he recognized it as Eden's.

"I'm in the back," he said, closing his laptop. "I'll be right there."

He told himself the lightness in his chest was because it wasn't his crazy ex crashing into his new life, but he'd never been a good liar. Walking down the narrow wood-paneled hallway, he reminded himself Eden was the woman who'd brushed him off less than twenty-four hours ago. Hell, it was better that she had—it helped extinguish his inconvenient attraction toward her.

Stepping into the open dining area of the restaurant, he found her in front of the row of mirrored beer and liquor signs lining the wall near the entrance. "What's up?" His question had sounded clipped, almost angry. She didn't need to know yesterday's slight had stung. He removed all emotion from his tone and asked, "Is your car stuck again?"

She shook her head. "Why aren't you open?"

"I don't serve breakfast on Tuesdays and Thursdays." He eyed her. "Not to be rude, but why are you here?"

He really wasn't trying to be a jerk, but Eden rarely stopped in the restaurant in the mornings and never on her days off. And she couldn't be heading to the hospital because she wasn't in scrubs. Today, she wore burgundy leggings and a long, fitted cream sweater that hugged her in all the right places.

"I finished a paper for a medical journal, so I decided to get some fresh air. I do enjoy the stroll up here more when it isn't raining and I'm not in heels. How was bartending yesterday?"

"You care?" He wanted to eat the question when it slipped from his tongue, especially when her smile faltered.

"What do you mean?"

"Never mind."

A flare of heat flickered in her eyes. "No. Explain."

"You insisted on helping, but then took off." Out loud, he sounded like such an ass, and going by her expression, she'd agree.

"Did you expect me to toss my whole day aside?"

He was being the egotistical jerk his ex had always accused him of, letting his feelings run his mouth. But since they were now out in the open, he should at least explain them. After apologizing.

"You're right. I'm sorry." He scrubbed his palms on his face. "It wasn't so much that you left, but the abruptness of it..."

"Gus looked appalled that I was here," Eden said, thankfully looking less upset. "Many of your customers would react the same. I wanted to help, not hurt your business."

He opened his mouth and then closed it, unsure how to reply. Then found his words. "Gus wasn't appalled—startled, maybe. Dr. Perez behind the bar was probably a strange sight." That was mostly true. He didn't see a reason to bring up his cook's comments about her being frosty. "As for the lunch regulars, why would they care?"

"Because most of the locals dislike me," she said flatly. "I'm the heartless bitch who abandoned her daughter and a great guy. And to make the sin worse, I did it for my career."

Shit. Guess he didn't have to worry about his bluntness bothering her. She was even more direct than him.

And he'd heard the gossip. It was true some of the townsfolk didn't like her. A handful didn't because of her past choices, and others called her a snob. They said she thought she was too good to befriend anyone in their small town.

However, after learning about her reason for leaving yesterday, Tate suspected the lack of friendships was from the cold-shoulder reception since moving back and her busy schedule, not a pretentious attitude.

As for her decision to leave after Raven was born, he'd always stayed out of those gossipmonger debates. The busybodies liked to toss around words like 'abandonment' or 'deadbeat parent.' Neither fit Eden. According to Asher, while she was living in California, she called Raven frequently and visited during every break. Eden had even flown in for important events, spending time with her daughter and then hopping on a red-eye to make it to classes.

"Fuck them. This isn't a town of saints and angels. People talk crap to make themselves feel better." Tate grinned. "And if you're sitting behind the bar to keep an eye on my crappy mixology skills means less customers, I'd probably still come out ahead financially. I learned something about myself yesterday. I'm awful at talking and mixing drinks. It's embarrassing how many I had to give away because I messed up."

Eden chuckled, leaving her post by the door and moving closer to him. "Wow. That bad?"

He held up a hand and tilted it back and forth while stepping behind the bar. "I had a surprise lunch rush where everyone wanted to chat about their shitty week while getting their midday drink on. Plus, I had to guess some ingredients."

"Why?" Crossing her arms, she leaned on the bar top. The position pressed up her full breasts in her V-neck sweater.

He strained to keep his gaze on her face and the conversation. "I should've had you type out the recipes. Never ask a doctor to handwrite *anything*."

"That stereotype is true for me." She laughed, and the husky sound wrapped around him. "Yet, another reason my scribe is so valuable."

"A scribe? Sounds medieval. I'm picturing parchment paper and bloodletting with leeches."

"Ew." She shuddered. "Nope. No way. Those blood-sucking worms creep me out. I won't even walk in a lake without water shoes in case one's hiding between the rocks and sand." She ran a hand along her arm as if brushing off invisible creepy crawlies. "And sorry, a medical scribe isn't like the ones in *Game of Thrones,* though mine is just as invaluable to me. Amy, my scribe, records all my patient's information in real-time. She accompanies me during hospital rounds and meetings, giving updates before visiting each patient and makes any and all necessary changes in their files. Oh, and she uses a laptop, not a scroll."

Tate snapped his fingers. "Damn, *Game of Thrones* hospital edition could be interesting."

"Indeed. And I won't mind having my own dragon."

"Same." He pointed to the kitchen. "I made some coffee when I first arrived, want a cup?"

She nodded, asking for light cream. He returned a minute later with two full mugs and took the stool next to her. They swiveled in their seats to face each other. Their knees brushed, and he tried to ignore how much he liked her near.

"Did you manage to cross off everything on your to-do list yesterday?" he asked.

"Yup. All the important stuff was completed. I had to push aside the personal reading time and order my groceries online, doing curbside pickup instead of going in. I even managed to buy a new phone and research where Raven and I would go for dinner." She blew on her coffee, then took a sip. "We went to a new Cuban place in Ann Arbor. It was fantastic."

Damn, next to Eden, he was a disorganized bum. "What is personal reading time? Why do you have to schedule it?" he asked.

"It's reading that has nothing to do with my job. If I don't schedule it in, all I end up reading is medical journals."

"What do you do if the book is really good, and you can't put it down?" He was a night reader, and the days that followed binge-reading were rough.

"Hmm." She looked at the ceiling, then back at him. "I can't recall that ever happening. I set aside a certain amount of time and stick to it. Well, except for yesterday. That was the first time in a long time I deviated from my plans."

Gratitude plucked at his heartstrings. She had made an exception for *him*. "Well, I hope you didn't have to give up a page-turner you've been dying to get back to, on account of me."

Her cheeks reddened.

"Wow, that's some color," he said. "I'd love to see the books on your nightstand. Do they feature tattooed men, dripping wet from a hot shower?"

"You're never going to let me live that down, are you?" She groaned around a smile.

"Nope. Not when I can't stop thinking about the heat I saw in your eyes." *Shit*. That last part of honesty wasn't supposed to be said aloud. He was staying away from trouble and the chaos of relationships. That meant no flirting or acknowledging an attraction. Rubbing the back of his neck, he stood. "I'm going to refill my cup. Want more?"

"No, thanks. Mine's still full."

So was his, but he needed space from her and his admission. And from the way she was suddenly staring intently at her mug, she might need it too.

When he returned, he sat on a stool next to her, and she asked, "What do you like best about owning a restaurant?"

"I like how every day I do something different. Sometimes it's keeping up on orders and employees to make sure things run smoothly. Other times, I'm a cook or waiter. I also like that I spend very little time in my office at my desk. I much prefer being out here." He opened his arms to encompass the main area of the restaurant." Talking with the customers is great. But… maybe not while I'm mixing drinks. They really don't like when I get to chatting and forget some key ingredient, like say, alcohol."

She waved a hand. "I'm sure with your charm, no one was too upset."

He sat straight and grinned. "You think I'm charming?"

She pushed his shoulder lightly. "Hush, you know you're charming. I'm sure you're one of the reasons your parking lot's always full."

Her compliment shined through him. "Damn, I wish you had stayed yesterday. I'd have loved for my dad to hear what you just said. He takes it as a personal dig that I left my old job for this 'dive'."

"What did you do before?"

"Marketing manager."

She sipped her coffee. "That is a big change, but I could see how it could help with owning a restaurant. Do you miss it?"

He usually answered with an immediate no. He second-guessed himself enough and didn't want to give fuel for others to do the same. However, he answered honestly. "Sometimes. I miss the stability of it, and the regular-ish hours and pay. But, like I said, this suits me better. And as a bonus, I don't have to see the same people day in and day out."

"But the ones you do see the most, you have to manage them—hire and fire them."

"True, but I pick my employees." Tate held up his index finger. "One of my job requirements is that they aren't assholes."

"Ugh, must be nice to have that option," she sighed.

He agreed. His last job taught him toxic people are soul-crushing. However, presently her tone had him forgetting his past. "Are their people you can't stand at the hospital?" Tate asked.

She nodded. "Every year Michigan Medical picks two doctors for its fellowship program. This year it was me and the pompous Dr. Leeday. He's such a prick." She tapped her chin. "Or maybe he's a nice guy but is acting like jerk toward me because we're vying for the same surgical position when our fellowships end.

Anyway, he's trying to paint me as incompetent. My Amy told me Leeday's spreading a rumor that the only reason I was selected for the fellowship was because I'm a Mexican-American woman and the hospital needed to fill a minority requirement. Asshole."

"He does sound like a prick." Tate set his mug on the bar top. "And wow, I'm impressed."

"About what? That I haven't punched him yet?" Her eyes flashed with humor as she made a fist, then shook it out. "It's only because I don't want to hurt my hands. I need them for the job."

Tate laughed. "That's impressive too, but I was referring to you getting the fellowship at Michigan. One of two openings. You must be a helluva of a surgeon."

She straightened. "I am." He loved how she said it without arrogance but with confidence and conviction. After a moment, some of it dimmed. "Which is why I better get the job instead of Leeday."

"I'm sure you will." He tapped a finger on his mug's handle. "But if he weasels his way into your job, is there another position in the hospital for you?"

"Not for the surgeries I want to perform. I could apply to Children's Hospital in Detroit. But with that much distance, I'd barely see Raven. If it wasn't for my abuela, I'd do it in heartbeat and make it work. But she lives in New Mexico, and in the last year, she's had health issues that worry me. I need to be closer to her, to take care of her. She uprooted her life for me once, leaving Mexico to raise me, asking her to do it again, so I can work two hours away from Raven seems unfair."

"Christ. That had to be fucking stressful." He rested a comforting hand on her knee and wanted to leave it there. Removing it, he said, "But you'll get the job over Dr. Prick. And then the move will be worth it for your abuela. She will get to be close to you and Raven."

Eden offered a weak smile. "She would love to spend more time with her great-granddaughter. But what makes you so certain? Have you seen me operate? Do you have the ability to jump into the minds of those who are in a position to hire me?"

"Nope, but you're going to give me a description of Dr. Prick, and I'll wait for him to leave the hospital and then I'll break all his fingers. In two places," Tate joked.

Her smile turned genuine and joined with her sexy laughter. It was rapidly becoming his favorite sound.

She started to reply, but Gus pushed through the front door. Disappointment filled Tate. Now Eden would book it.

His cook stopped mid-stride and faced Eden. "Are you here to rescue Monk *and* our customers from his terrible job as bartender?"

"Monk?" Eden repeated.

"Ignore him. He's an asshole." Tate's cheeks grew warm. It'd soon reach his neck.

Eden's grin widened. "I thought you didn't hire assholes."

Tate chuckled. "Everyone makes mistakes."

Gus laughed and started toward the kitchen, pushing through its double doors. "Don't listen to him. He loves me."

"No, I love your cooking," Tate called before turning to Eden, hoping he wasn't the color of a tomato. "Are you taking off?"

She eyed the main doors like it was her escape to freedom. It shouldn't matter—couldn't matter—but it did, and he had to clamp his mouth shut. He wouldn't ask her to stay.

CHAPTER SIX

Eden should go home and double-check her paper on minimally invasive robotic surgery. She should go home and take a cold shower. She should go home. Tate made her want things she didn't need or deserve.

Instead of doing what she should do, she did what she wanted. "I'll stay," she told Tate. "I feel partly responsible for your failure."

"Ouch. Failure is harsh. Besides, those who got the free messed up drinks didn't seem to mind." His grin warmed the cold edges of her heart. Her desires too.

"I'm sure they didn't, but you might when it comes time to replace all that liquor you had to give away."

"Hmm. Good point. Maybe I'll slim my temporary drink menu down even more." He held up three fingers and grinned. "Beer, wine, and shots."

His sexy smile made her nerves race in warning. She should stay in her comfort zone; entering Tate's was dangerous. Yet, the thrill of it coursed through her in a deliciously warm and exciting way.

"No need," she said. "I'll help during your busy time. When would that be?"

"From the lunch rush until about two-ish. But it really depends. Some days I serve only a few drinks. Other times, like yesterday, it seems everyone needs something to wash down a work week." He waved a hand. "It doesn't matter. I'm not going to ask you to waste whatever free time you have today. You've already done too much."

It was rare she had two days off. She wasn't even on call. That was a near miracle. Her original plan was to finish one paper and start on another before picking up Raven from school...but one hour wouldn't make a huge difference, and being around Tate was a fun distraction.

"It's not time wasted when spent with you." The truth of the admission skittered through her veins. His combination of easy-going and bluntness appealed to her. Laughing, joking, and talking to him felt like a vacation. Still, she sounded a little needy and desperate, so to save face, she threw in, "Like you said yesterday, friends help friends."

"You're not worried I'll ask for a hundred miles?" Tate asked.

She laughed and shook her head. "But do me a favor."

"For you, anything."

Those three words were a cozy blanket to her soul. Granted, given the context, he probably knew her request wouldn't be serious. However, no one but her abuela trusted her enough not to ask about conditions first. That would change if Tate got to know her better, but she didn't let that diminish her current good mood.

"I'm no good with small talk. So, I'll pour the drinks." She pointed at herself, then at him. "You chat up the customers."

"You don't even need to make them. Just sit with me behind the bar and answer my questions or correct me when I make a mistake." He paused, drumming his fingers on the bar top. "Are you sure you're okay with staying?"

It dawned on her that he might not want her here. Customers would gossip when they saw her with Tate. "Would you rather I leave?"

His fingers stopped tapping. "Why?"

"People will talk."

"Let'em talk."

"Remember, many of them don't like me."

He came around the bar, stopping in front of her. "Ignore them."

"I try," she whispered, hating the vulnerability in her voice.

"But they've made you believe you don't belong here. You do."

His insight made her feel like she was standing naked before him. And not in a sexy orgasmic way, but under a bright light that magnified all her worries and insecurities.

He squeezed her hand briefly. "Find your people and the haters won't matter."

"I don't need people." She straightened her shoulders. "I have my career and my daughter."

"If you plan on staying here, it wouldn't hurt to make it more of a home."

He had a point, but she didn't know how to make it happen. Forging friendships didn't come as easily to her as biology, physics, and math.

As if reading her mind, he said, "I'll help you."

Pride had her crossing her arms over her chest. "What makes you think I need help?"

Thankfully, he was kind enough not to point out that she'd moved to Michigan around a year ago and didn't have a single friend. Well, until he'd informed her they were friends.

Instead, he said, "I'm sure you don't, but in my line of work I meet a ton of people. I can steer you clear of the assholes. Introduce you to people worth your time."

His kind offer had tears prickling behind her eyes. She picked up her mug and finished her coffee, hoping the warm liquid would burn away her fragile mood.

The brief pause and inflection reminded her she was in Michigan to fix her fractured relationship with her daughter. Not join book clubs and go on dinner-dates with friends or whatever-the-hell people did with their free time and friends.

She waved a hand. "I'm not worried about my social calendar. I'm worried hanging out behind the bar will hurt your business. It might be better if we toss out my illegible handwritten recipes, and I type them out for you, then I head out."

"If it's an issue for anyone that you're here, they can find another dive-restaurant to eat their lunch."

Again, his words made her feel things she'd rather not; growing attached to Tate was an unwanted complication. Disregarding her fluttering stomach, she looked around his place. It was outdated but not gloomy. Her favorite feature was the natural lighting. Instead of having a wall of liquor behind the narrow bar that ran along the restaurant, the bottles of booze sat below huge windows that overlooked the outdoor patio and the lake beyond. Inside were cheerful booths and a scattering of tables with checkered red and white table clothes.

"This place is far from a dive."

"Really?" Tate patted the scarred bar top, then pointed at the wood paneling that screamed nineteen-seventies. "I love her, but she isn't pretty."

Sure, the décor couldn't be called modern or stylish, but it had a welcoming vibe. There were old photos of Michigan and posters of the local bands that played at The Hill on Friday and Saturday nights. And a large, well-loved world map hung near the entrance. Tourists placed a pushpin on their hometown. All of it was interesting and unique. "I think it has great personality," she said.

His deep laugh rumbled through her. "Isn't that what people say when trying to talk up someone or something that's ugly?"

"Sometimes," she admitted. "But not always. Like your restaurant, you have a great personality and are far from unattractive."

He wiggled his eyebrows. "Are you saying I'm hot?"

"Do I need to get you a fishing pole for the compliments you're hoping to reel in?"

"Depends. How many will I catch?"

"Insufferable man," she muttered, but her huge grin probably gave away that she liked his playful banter. "Why don't you tell me what you plan on updating."

"I was talking to Paloma and Max. Do you know them?"

She nodded. "They're friends of Asher. Paloma and he were a thing before Lilith."

"Yup. Well, Max and Paloma recently started working together. She does interior; he does exterior. They have some kick-ass ideas." He rattled off improvement ideas with such enthusiasm she was swept away in his homey yet modern vision for his restaurant. Or maybe it was him that captivated her. Witnessing his drive and excitement was incredibly sexy.

His cell dinged, and tension crept into his shoulders and around his eyes. She found it odd but was distracted when his T-shirt pulled tight as he leaned back and straightened his jean-clad leg to remove his phone from his pocket. The man was fit; he had a flat stomach and fantastic biceps and triceps.

As he read the text, he visibly relaxed. "One of my afternoon cooks is running behind. I need to see if Gus can stay later."

Why would finding out a cook would be tardy be considered good news? She gave an internal shrug. Maybe any text at the start of a workday was a cause for worry.

"Would you mind keeping an eye on the bar while I talk to Gus?" He glanced at the clock on the register. "We open in two minutes."

"Sure."

It didn't take long for Eden to regret her impulsive decision to stay. Tate's company was great, but the side-eyes and whispers about why she was behind the bar had her holding in snarky comments—and fighting the urge to walk away without looking back.

She might have left if watching Tate in action wasn't so compelling. He was a master multitasker and had an ease with people she lacked. Every person who spoke with him ended up in a better mood than when they'd arrived.

She wished she could lighten up, be more like him. However, that was impossible. It wasn't in her. Tate was different; he was day to her night. He'd probably led an easy, charmed life. It was easy to be light and carefree when dark despair didn't weigh down a person's past or present.

"Eden, could you grab me a new bottle of Maker's Mark?" Tate asked. "They're behind you, on the lowest shelf."

"Sure." When she turned around, bottle in her hand, she saw her neighbor Olivia sliding a big box onto the bar next to Tate. They didn't talk much, but she was easy to recognize. One, because Olivia was stunning with thick black hair cut in a bob, impossibly long lashes, and huge brown eyes, and two, she and her family were renting Tate's other home—the only other house on the gravel road that dead-ended where the lake began.

Olivia squinted at Eden as if confused. "I thought you were a surgeon."

"I am." Eden gave a quick explanation, then pointed at the box. "What's in there?"

"Pies," replied Olivia.

"And they're the real reason my booths and tables are always packed," Tate said, coming around and picking up the box. Indicating with his chin a man in a checkered shirt, he asked. "Would you mind making him a Bourbon Sour?"

She made the drink, and the man took a sip, sighing. "All your bar stools would be filled if you let this pretty lady make more of my drinks." The stranger wouldn't be saying that if he were a local, but she smiled, pleased.

"You wound me," Tate said good-naturedly. He'd moved further down where the bar became the food pick-up station. Dividing the two was a small turn-style cooler, and he was loading it with pies from Olivia's box.

Eden's taste buds watered at the sight. "You made those?" she asked Olivia. She often ordered a slice with her takeout dinner. Hips be damned. The cherry and blueberry pies were too good to pass up. "They are the best I've ever tasted, and I've eaten a lot of them."

"Thank you." Olivia seemed to glow with pride. "Before moving here, I had a small bakery, but with Elijah traveling so much, and the babies, we've put opening one here on hold. Until then, I keep very busy supplying The Hill with my tasty treats."

After Olivia and Tate discussed his order, he returned behind the bar, stopping beside Eden. "My afternoon bartender will arrive shortly. You can walk back with Olivia, if you want."

Her heart pinched. Did he want her to go?

He gave a slight tilt of his head and mouthed, "Friend."

Heat infused Eden's cheeks, and she sucked in her lips. He was serious about finding her friends. Irritation and gratitude hugged her.

"That would be lovely," Olivia said from behind them, seemingly oblivious to the standoff behind the bar. "And if you're free, want to have a cup of coffee or tea? Elijah is actually home today and taking the girls to the park. I'd love to talk to someone over the age of two."

The unexpected suggestion startled Eden. She hadn't been invited for idle chatter in... was it since she was best friends with Asher's twin sister, Hope, back in college? Yup, and wow, that was over a decade ago. She was a sad sap. Maybe she did need Tate's help.

Pulling her cell from her pocket, Eden checked the time, and her pulse skipped. No wonder her social battery was flickering on empty—two hours had passed. Raven's school day was half over. Eden's paper was finished, but she was meeting with Dr. Abraham Muller, her fellowship director tomorrow. She should be at home preparing for it, not watching Tate like some lust-sick teenager.

"Do you mind if I take a raincheck? I'm taking my daughter to an early dinner before her basketball game, and I need to prep for a meeting with my fellowship director."

Tate came closer. "Thanks again for helping me. I appreciate it."

"It was a nice break." But the pressure of what she should have been doing was pressing into her. She turned to Olivia. "Ready?"

She nodded, reaching for her box. Eden faced Tate. The urge to hug him was tremendous. He took half a step closer, then stopped, pressing his hands to his sides. Did he feel it too?

Her need to touch him was so strong it nearly overtook her mounting stress to get home and tackle her conference work. She backed away from the too-tempting distraction in front of her, saying, "Good luck with the rest of your bartending shift."

As they headed to the door, Olivia leaned in. "Do you and our hot landlord have something going on?"

"We are just friends." Eden peeked over her shoulder and caught Tate checking out her ass.

She wanted to ignore the jolt of pleasure flowing through her. Or use it as a warning to stay away as her new mantra flashed through her: *Tate is a distraction I cannot afford.*

Yet her traitorous, disobedient thoughts were already conjuring ways to see him again.

CHAPTER SEVEN

"Are you ready to win?" Eden asked, getting out of her Mustang. She pressed the seat lever and then reached into the back, retrieving her laptop.

"Yup. But this team—" Raven had come around to Eden's side of the car, crossing her gangly arms. "Are you going to watch my game or do work?"

Eden glanced at her messenger bag, wet cotton balls of guilt and frustration settled into her chest. "I was going to glance over my notes for tomorrow's presentation before the game started...and maybe during intermission." It was already early evening. Tomorrow would be here in a tick of a clock, and the pressure of perfection was tightening around her.

Raven rolled her eyes. "Half time, Mom. Intermission." She shook her head and grinned. "Were you a theater nerd in school?"

Eden tapped her bag. "Just a nerd. My after-school activities were studying and tutoring other students. Though I was in science club."

"Wow. You really were a nerd."

Eden laughed, and they started toward the middle school's gym entrance. "Yup, but don't mock the nerds. They get shi—stuff done. They're ambitious, and usually get the colleges and careers they want."

"They also bring homework to their kid's games," Raven was still smiling, but her comment still pinched Eden.

"That doesn't mean your games aren't important—"

"But work is more important?"

Ouch. The question wasn't said with rudeness, just curiosity, which made it worse. This wasn't pre-teen sass but an honest question.

She opened the school door for Raven. "No. More that I have responsibilities that can't be put off. Kinda like—"

"Oh, there's Molly. I need to tell her something. Don't worry, Mom. It's okay. Just don't miss any of the baskets I score." She hugged Eden, then took off running toward a tall girl with short brown hair.

She wanted to tell her daughter a surgeon was who Eden was, yet her heart was Raven's. It was too late. The locker room door had shut behind her. That was fine. Words were weak. Actions left their mark.

Eden rubbed near her collarbone, where a tattoo covered an old burn scar. She knew this truth firsthand. But *her* actions would heal, not hurt.

Turning right, Eden powerwalked through the open gym door, determined to blast through her notes before the game started, then review her paper during the break. She took a seat halfway up the bleachers and opened her laptop. She'd made it through a quarter of her notes when someone sat beside her.

"This reminds me of your college days when we used to come to Hope's soccer games. You always had your trusty computer and notebook," Asher said.

Eden hit save and closed her computer, swallowing her aggravation. It wasn't aimed at Asher. She liked chatting with him. It was more that she hadn't stuck to her to-do list and was paying for it in the form of stress. She plastered on an easy, false smile, asking, "Does your sister still play?"

"Hope coaches little kids on a community travel team."

Eden nodded, not sure what else to say. She and Hope had been best friends in college until Eden left Asher. He was way more forgiving than his sister. In her eyes, Eden was still enemy number one—the bitch who abandoned everyone in the Crowley family. And Hope was right.

It was a good thing Eden was a workaholic nerd because she was a disaster at everything else in her life.

But she was trying for Raven and herself. And as Tate had said, that meant planting roots in her, hopefully, new home. Asher wasn't only the father of her child, but someone she considered a friend, which meant chatting with him at their daughter's game instead of sticking her face in her work.

"Raven told me today; you took her sailing over the weekend."

Asher leaned back, resting against the bleacher seat above them. "Really, it was my friend Max who took her. He has a two-person sailboat. I think Raven found a new obsession."

"I got that same sense too. She talked non-stop about it."

"Speaking of new hobbies. I heard you picked up a new one."

Eden shook her head. "A new hobby?"

"Bartending."

"Oh." Her confusion cleared. "I work part-time as one in California. Tate helped get my car unstuck, so I repaid the favor by giving him a few pointers since he has to cover for his absent daytime bartender."

She hoped her attraction toward Tate didn't show. She was positive Asher wouldn't give two turds who she dated...unless it were Lilith's brother. Not that it mattered because Tate was staying firmly in the friend zone. This afternoon's stress made it clear she didn't have time for anything more.

Asher nodded. "That's right. I remember you mentioning you worked at a place called Ocean Dreams. I'd thought you were a waitress. I didn't know you were a bartender. I also didn't know you and Tate were friends."

"More like acquaintances," Eden didn't like how the lie tasted on her tongue. Tate had called her a friend, and she was distancing herself from him because it was easier than trying to explain her conflicted feelings for him.

"Asher!" called a man from the sidelines of the court. "My assistant coach can't make it. Will you fill in for him?"

"Sure," he yelled back, then turned to Eden. "I better get down there. I'm taking the team for ice cream after. Do you want to join us?"

She started to say no, thinking about her morning meeting but stopped. The purpose of moving here was to be in Raven's life. Sharing important *and* simple moments with her—like getting ice cream after a game.

"Yes, I'll go," she told Asher.

It was fine. She'd peek at her work when Raven wasn't on the court. Go out with her after. Maybe skip an hour of sleep to prep more for the meeting.

"Great. Talk to you after the game," he said.

Eden watched him go, wishing she could parent like him. He was involved and present with their daughter since day one. Work and life balance seem to come easily to him.

Reopening her laptop, she was determined to keep her eyes on the screen but her ears on the game. She wouldn't miss any moments when Raven was on the court.

Though by half-time, she was internally cursing the ref's whistle. Did he have to use it every thirty seconds? It was damn annoying. And distracting.

Eden huffed, her annoyance shifting to herself. Her daughter's game wasn't a distraction. She was being a shit mom, preoccupied with work. She shoved her laptop in her bag and focused on the game, only glancing at the notebook she'd retrieved, jotting notes for her next research topic.

Raven's coach called for a time-out, and the teams huddled on separate sides of the court. The score was tied, and the game had only three minutes left. Eden stared at the temporarily frozen clock on the scoreboard. Something about the red-pigmented number unlocked an idea, and she began scribbling them in her notebook.

As she wrote, cheers and clapping erupted. Her pen jolted on the page, and she looked toward the court. They were hugging and clapping her daughter on the back. Eden's gaze raced to the scoreboard. Raven's team won. And going by her team's reaction, she'd made the winning shot.

Eden had missed it.

She dropped her chin to her chest. Then chucked her notes into her bag, not caring when a sheet got stuck in the zipper and tore. Ignoring the thickness in her throat, she stood and made her way toward the team and her daughter.

"Did you see?" Raven asked, hopping from foot to foot. "Did you see?"

"Yup," Eden lied because what else could she say? Admit she was a failure as a mom? *I'll fake it until I make it.*

A not-so-quiet fear chattered she'd never 'make it' as a mom, that Raven was better off if Eden stayed in the far background, letting others, like Asher's girlfriend, take over. Lilith was a natural caregiver.

No. Eden would do better—had to do better.

"Come on," she said, resting a hand on Raven's shoulder. "Your dad mentioned something about ice cream."

Raven's grin widened. "You're going too?"

"There's nowhere I'd rather be." At least she was finally telling the truth.

CHAPTER EIGHT

Eden took a deep, cleansing breath, letting the scent of antiseptic and bleach soothe her. The weekly meeting with the fellowship director Dr. Elizabeth Muller and other fellow, Dr. 'Prick' Leeday was going smoothly, even if fatigue hung from Eden.

She'd rushed home after ice cream with Raven and reviewed her notes and research paper twice, ensuring everything was perfect. It had meant less sleep, but it was worth it. Talk of her completed research and the upcoming conference had gone without a hitch.

"Okay, let's move on to patients." Muller tapped her pen on the papers in front of her. "Perez, do we have an issue with the family in Room 502?"

"Problem? Amy, would you pull up the file?" Her scribe nodded. Eden kept her facial features natural, but under the table, she fisted the hem of her white coat, trying to piece together how her difficulties with the patient's parents had made it to the fellowship director. And in what way. When she'd checked on Janie this morning, the shy five-year-old was recovering on schedule and was in high spirits. The parents had nitpicked and questioned her, but that was nothing new.

Leeday cleared his throat. "The Smiths were worried about the care their daughter was receiving." He left off 'by you,' but Eden heard it in his pompous tone. "They asked me to doublecheck everything when I stopped in yesterday during rounds. I had to make a few changes."

Ah, so that's how it got to Muller. Leeday was king of passive-aggressive tactics to make Eden look incompetent. She was also positive little Janie's parents were delighted to have the white male doctor at their daughter's bedside while Eden had had a couple days off.

She wished she'd taken the time to look through her patient's files. She crossed her arms over her stomach as knots of bad decisions pulled tight. There had been ten minutes between rounds and this meeting. She'd spent them texting Tate.

When his message had first dinged, she'd planned on ignoring it until her lunch break. But a photo of a nearly full tip jar had caught her attention, and the next thing she knew, they were texting back and forth, and her cheeks were hurting from smiling.

"They often ask for a second opinion." She sighed, taking the tablet with Janie's file on the screen. "They're difficult, but I didn't notice any changes on the patient's chart."

"You must have been in a rush when looking over her care." *Asshole.* Leeday clucked his tongue. "And I'm not sure what you mean about her parents. I had no issues with them. They were receptive to all my advice."

Eden pressed her tongue against her teeth to keep from saying, "No shit. If I had a penis or lighter skin, they'd have done the same."

Both the husband and wife were dismissive of her and mocked the male nurses. She'd bet every penny in her bank account if she'd given one of those nurses her white coat outside the room and let them speak for her, the parents would've followed all instructions without question. But there was no sense in sharing her insight with Leeday or the rest of the room. He would huff under his breath about her being a *sensitive woman.* As if both were a disease.

Amy tucked a lock of her pin-straight black hair behind her ear before running her finger over the screen to highlight a section. She tapped on it. Eden read the indicated area. It was as she suspected.

"Yes, I see the change here on the chart." She glanced at Muller, then focused on Leeday. "The patient was constipated. You ordered a stool softener."

His mouth pressed tight, his thin lips disappearing. He nodded stiffly, then changed the subject to his recent research publication. Eden ran her knuckles along her breastbone, focusing on the sensation so she wouldn't laugh. To her left, Amy coughed, and it sounded a little like a giggle.

The meeting ended ten minutes later, and with each step away from the conference room, the weight on Eden's shoulders lightened. "Glad that's over."

Amy pushed her glasses up her nose. "I can't stand Dr. Leeday. His humble-brags about himself and his 'excellent' work ethic makes me want to puke."

Eden straightened the lapel of her white coat. "He is a good surgeon. But I take issue with the way he belittles me."

"It's because he knows you're the better surgeon."

"Maybe. And I mean, maybe that's why he does it—not maybe I am the better surgeon." She smiled. "I *know* I'm better."

"That's the truth." Amy handed Eden a file. "I hope like hell you're hired, and not that jackass."

Eden loved her scribe. Her documentation was precise. She had a knack for answering questions before they were asked and sensed when Eden needed silence, a laugh, or something in between. Amy's dislike of Leeday was an added bonus.

"Me too." To work at her first-choice hospital and live near Raven would be a dream. "Which is why I need to publish more papers than him, have flawless surgeries, and happy patients and parents."

"Yeah, yeah, I caught your hint. When I finish typing the notes from this meeting, I'll proofread the paper you sent me last night." Amy swiped her ID against the scanner, and the doors to the pediatric floor opened. "I can't believe you're already finished with it. Do you sleep, like at all?"

"I'll sleep when my fellowship ends and the hospital hires me," Eden replied as her lab coat pocket buzzed. She glanced at the message.

Tate: How'd the meeting with your director go?

She was touched he remembered: Leedway was there so about as fun as surgery without anesthesia.

"Mmmh," Amy hummed, snagging Eden's attention.

She looked up. "What's wrong?"

"I've never seen that look on your face."

"What look?" Heat crawled up Eden's neck, and she was thankful for her olive skin. Maybe her blush would go unnoticed.

"Happiness."

Eden dropped her phone back into her pocket. "More like mild amusement." None of her thoughts or feelings about Tate were mild.

"Who amused you?"

"My friend."

"Does this friend have a name?"

Eden hesitated. Amy was very open about her personal life, but Eden didn't talk about hers. Mainly because outside of her daughter, she didn't have one.

"His name is Tate," she said.

"Oooh, the friend is a *he*." Amy did a little shoulder shake. "Is he single? Cute?"

"We're friends. What do his looks matter to me?"

"Maybe I wasn't asking for you. I'm single and looking."

Eden took in Amy's delicate stature and bubbly personality. She would be perfect for easy-going, fun Tate. Eden's happiness curdled in her stomach.

She swallowed the growl threatening to escape. "Forget about Tate and let's talk about the meeting."

Amy stuck out her bottom lip. "Damn. Professional Perez is back."

"I need her. I won't lose my focus. Men, friends, and dating aren't important. Getting the position over Leeday is."

"Okay, fine. True." Amy agreed, then winked. "Unless your friend is hot. If he is, then he deserves a little more attention. From me."

Nope. She couldn't have him.

Christ, Tate isn't mine. Never will be mine.

If only the longing in her damn, lonely heart would listen.

His presence in her thoughts might lighten her mood and make her hungry for things she hadn't wanted in a long time, but none mattered. What did, was getting this job and becoming the mother Raven deserved. Now wasn't the time to lose focus. She took out her phone and pulled up his profile. With a sigh, she muted her handsome distraction.

CHAPTER NINE

Eden touched her toes, then stretched her arms over her head, glancing at the stars. She sucked in a lungful of the night air and had to admit she liked the fresh, earthy scent of the lake water over the briny ocean air of California. Jogging up the gravel road from her house, she slowed, spotting Tate's Bronco in The Hill's otherwise empty parking lot.

There was no reason to visit him. A week had passed since she'd stepped inside his restaurant. His bartender had returned, and Eden was busy with life. She'd even held back from returning most of his texts, so those had slowed—but not her thoughts about him. Those ran rampant in her mind and went down some rather kinky paths.

She rocked on her heels, rooted in indecision. Should she stay or go? It had been a long few days at the hospital, where she'd had to rise early and stay late. She had the day off tomorrow, but exhaustion would catch her soon. The intelligent thing would be to run off her stress and then sleep. She should *not* chase after the butterflies Tate had freed within her.

The last time she'd lived in Michigan, she'd done that with Asher. It had ended in chaos and pain, with her running toward her career and away from her heart—from her daughter.

The gravel whispered and crunched under her running shoes as she turned from the road toward Tate. She ignored memories and logic and moved toward him as if powerless to resist his pull.

The open sign was off, but the door wasn't locked. She pushed through it, and soft music greeted her from the speaker on the tiny stage crammed into the restaurant's corner. Tate sat at a table close to the bar with his feet propped on the chair across from him, a laptop in front of him. He was lifting a long-neck beer to his mouth when their gazes met. His lovely lips pulled into a genuine smile. Her heart expanded as if making room for him.

"You really should lock your door," she pointed with her thumb over her shoulder. "Who knows who'll show up at closing time."

"Since it was you, I'll call it a win."

Warmth spread through her chest, but she hid her delight with a joke. "As opposed to a wandering drunk demanding one more drink?"

"Since I'm no longer bartender he will be thrilled." Tate tilted his head. "But why are you out at this hour?"

"This hour?" She raised her brows. "It's only a little after ten. I'm surprised the restaurant is closed. *And* you sound like an old man."

"I only do late nights Friday through Sunday when there's live music. I might do it during the week too at the height of summer tourism, but now it isn't worth it. *And* some days, I feel like an old man."

"How old are you?"

He gasped theatrically. "You're never supposed to ask a man his age." After taking a sip of his beer, he said, "I'm twenty-seven."

"Really?"

"Yup." He laughed. "Why are you surprised? Do I look as old as I feel?"

"Depends. How old do you feel?"

"Tonight?" He looked at the ceiling as if calculating large numbers. "Eighty-five."

"No way." She grinned. "You don't look a day over eighty."

He clutched his chest. "You are ruthless, woman."

In truth, she'd figured him to be around her age of thirty-three, maybe even older, not because of his looks but his accomplishments. He'd had some high-powered business career before switching to restaurateur. And The Hill seemed to be thriving under his care. Oh, he was a great landlord too.

"Do you have more rentals than mine and Olivia's?"

He nodded. "I have my old condo in Royal Oak and two small starter-homes in Wyandotte."

All of this before he was thirty. Tate was a man of surprises.

Hmm. She was five years older than him. Did he date older women?

It didn't matter. He wasn't for her. Even if she had time to date, his relationship with Raven, Asher, and Lilith would complicate things.

"So, if the restaurant closes early, why are you still here?" she asked.

"It's *my* late day as I get caught up on inventory and paperwork." He dropped his feet to the floor and pushed the chair out. "Want to sit and visit? Or do you need to go and... you never did say what you were doing."

"Guess." She skimmed a hand down her torso to her thighs, indicating her black sports pants and red fitted hoodie.

His gaze slid over her, pausing at each curve. She'd never felt particularly sexy when running, but his perusal warmed her as if she'd sprinted a mile or two.

"Running from wolves?" he suggested.

She scratched her eyebrow. "Huh? You lost me."

He smiled, and it was nearly predatory. "Your black hair and the red shirt give off a hot Little Red Riding Hood vibe."

He thinks I'm hot. Warning bells clanged, but she ignored them, allowing the compliment to sink into her skin, wrapping around her desire for him.

"Do you have to run off, Little Red?"

Gripping the back of the nearest chair, she said, "Depends."

"On?"

She shouldn't say it, shouldn't flirt. "Will you be the wolf chasing me?"

Heat flared in his eyes, and he rumbled, "Do you want me to? Because Eden, I'll gladly devour you whenever and wherever you want."

His words and the hunger behind them had her hot *everywhere*. She tugged her bottom lip with her teeth. She should run, run away from him and the images now fornicating in her head. She cleared her throat. "I can stay for a bit."

Needing a little space from Tate and her desires, she walked behind the bar, filled a glass with ice water, and squeezed a lemon into it. The music switched to an energetic song by The Lumineers that had her pulse dancing.

Tate stood, rolled his shoulders, then stretched his arms over his head. He wasn't overly bulky, but she wouldn't call him lean either. Tapping her feet to the beat, she took in his lovely, muscular arms, then moved to his flat stomach, finally stopping at his strong thighs. Before he noticed her checking him out, she asked, "You don't have the body of a runner, but do you run?"

He quirked a brow. "What do I have the body for?"

To be naked and plastered against me.

She sucked in her lips, then released them. "I don't know. Maybe rowing or weightlifting."

"You're right about both. I row almost every morning. Also, before joining an MMA studio with my friend, Jackson—

"You say that like I don't know who he is," She teased. "He's been Asher and Hope's closest friend since they were little kids."

Tate mock bowed. "My apologies. Before joining MAA with Jackson—the man everyone knows and loves." She rolled her eyes. He grinned and continued. "I used Asher's kick-ass workout room at his and Lilith's house."

"Thanks for the thorough, smart-ass answers."

He chuckled. "Anytime. Do you like dancing?"

The question seemed off-topic until she took note of her body. Besides tapping her feet to the song, she was swinging her hips to the beat. She stilled. "Sure. Who doesn't?"

"Why don't you ever come here on the weekends when there's live music?"

"I'm usually working." And she didn't have friends to call for a fun night out.

"Well, that's a shame. I don't have a band, but..." Walking to the small stage, he fiddled with something on the side of the speaker, and the volume rose. He held out his hand to her. "May I have this dance?"

"Now?"

Just them on the dance floor, their bodies moving in rhythm together, that sounded like danger—and so damn enticing.

He nodded. "Yup. Now. It's best never to put off fun."

For years, that's all she'd done. But with him smiling at her and the music sinking into her bones, she no longer wanted to deny herself. Eden took his hand.

He twirled and dipped her on the chipped and scuffed dance floor as if it was the nineteen forties, and they were dancing to swing music. "Look at you. A man with moves." She fought the urge to swoon.

Grinning, he came closer, sliding a firm leg between her thighs, and they rocked to the song. "I like the way we move together."

She did too. Too much.

The song ended, and another began. It was popular and was playing nearly every time she turned on her car. It had a double beat that reminded her of Cumbia-style music.

She took a step back but didn't let go of Tate. "You can lead. But are you confident enough to follow?"

He lifted one thick, angular brow. "Where are you taking me?"

She bit her tongue, wanting to reply, to the bedroom. Counting to three, she said, "I'm going to show you a dance I learned when I was a teenager."

Tate was a quick study, smooth and playful. The empty restaurant disappeared as the pleasure of him holding her and the sensual rhythm took over. One song became another, then another. It didn't matter the genre; they kept dancing, shifting closer and closer.

Each time his body brushed against hers, it left behind a print of heat and an ache that reached between her legs, teasing and tantalizing her. Her spreading desire had her thoughts wandering back to the bedroom. Would he lead? Or would he continue as he did now, paying attention to her body language and anticipating what she wanted?

After too many songs and yet not enough of them, a slow ballad crooned from the speakers. He held his hand, palm out, while the other slid loosely around her waist. "Keep going? Or do you want to stop?"

She went willingly into his arms as they matched the slow tempo. The heat of his body thawed more of her reserve, and she held him tighter. His earthy scent of peppermint and masculinity wrapped around her. To stop herself from running her lips along his collar, she looked at his face, intent on asking some mundane question—anything to dispel her mounting hunger.

Their gazes snagged, and words fell away. He was watching her with starving eyes. She licked her lips, imagining how he'd taste.

"Can I kiss you?" he whispered so quietly she worried it was her wishes and not reality.

Looking into his eyes, she saw his question wasn't from her fantasies. She brushed her mouth against his. Bliss bloomed and raced through her as he deepened the kiss, but he didn't rush it. He nudged her lips apart, stroking his tongue lightly against hers. His savory taste of hops and hunger had her craving more.

Pressing into her, he wrapped his arms around her, eliminating all space between them. The feel of his hard chest against her breasts had lust pooling hot and heavy between her legs.

Needing more, she skimmed her hands down his back, gripping the hem of his T-shirt.

A woman's voice shattered the bliss. "Are you kidding me?"

The words hit Eden like a whip. She and Tate broke apart and turned to face the intruder.

Lilith stood before them, hate emanating from her. "You couldn't have my boyfriend, so you've moved on to my fucking brother? What is wrong with you?"

CHAPTER TEN

Shocked into silence, Tate stared at Lilith. He barely recognized her. She was a rigid statue next to the hostess stand, gripping a plastic container so tight her knuckles and nails were stark white.

Her eyes narrowed on Eden. "You should've been named after the damn snake, not the garden."

What the hell was going on with his mild-mannered sister? "Lil, stop. What's your problem?"

Her gaze swung to him. "Last winter, Eden tried to steal Asher from me. Told him she wanted him back."

Bullshit. Eden had flat-out said she wasn't interested in Asher. She wouldn't lie about it. *Right*? "No, she moved here for Raven."

Lilith snorted. "She asked Asher to give her—their relationship—another try."

Tate shook his head. "You're wrong."

"Ask her. Ask Asher." Lilith tossed the plastic container on the nearest table. It landed with a noisy thud.

He turned to Eden, the question on his lips, but she answered before he asked. "It's not that simple."

"But it is," he replied quietly. "It's as simple as yes or no."

Eden's lips pressed together, and she sighed as if disappointed in him. *In him.* "I don't owe you an explanation, *friend*. But it isn't what you think." Her gaze flickered to Lilith. "Or you."

He needed her to stop talking around it—to just give him a straight answer. She sounded so much like Katrina it hurt to listen.

"Please, Eden." He paused on her name, reminding himself she wasn't his ex, even if her words were so familiar. "Answer me. Yes or no."

"Fine, Tate." Eden's voice was frozen, all ice. "Yes. I asked Asher to give us a try. As a family. Me, him, and Raven. For Raven."

His gut twisted, and something in him shut down. When they'd talked about her reasons for returning to Michigan, they'd been little more than acquaintances. Why would she lie to him? Did she have to fabricate a story that made her look blameless? Or lie for the sake of lying—just like Katrina?

Was history repeating itself? No. He would *not* get tangled up with *another* manipulative, callous woman.

"What about my sister?"

"What is she to me?" she said in the same cool and smooth tone. All emotion had vanished from her. "I was thinking of my daughter."

He snorted. "That's a weak excuse. You don't need Asher for Raven."

"It's not an excuse—And I don't need one. Nor do I need to be having this conversation. Al diablo con ustedes, y al diablo con ella." Eden spun on her heel, but instead of storming out, she walked with way more dignity and grace than Tate was feeling.

When the door clicked shut with barely a sound, he faced Lilith. She was pale, the fight evaporating from her.

"I'm so sorry." She fell into the nearest chair like a marionette with its strings cut. "I was out of line." Tears gathered around her eyes.

Her explosion of anger was so unlike her. It rattled him. The quiver in her voice cut at his heart, already racing from the abrupt shift between him and Eden. He sat next to Lilith, rubbing her hand and searching for a topic change to help calm her—hell, calm him.

"To what do I owe this lovely late-night visit?" he asked.

"Sorry," she repeated, seeming to ignore his question. "I didn't mean to drag drama in with me. I should've kept my big mouth shut and left, but all I could think about when I saw her all over you," Lilith winced, "was how she's coming after another man I love. First, she tried to snake her way back to Asher. Now, you. It's weird."

"Well, I appreciate you trying to protect my virtue," he deadpanned without humor.

"I can't save what you gave away a long time ago." Lilith's joke fell as flat as his. "How did it even happen? At the family gatherings you two barely spoke."

Katrina had made sure of that. If he had given what she deemed was too much attention to Eden or Hope, Asher's twin sister, at holiday get-togethers, a huge fight always followed. He'd kept his distance and, therefore, the peace.

"She's been helping with a bartending issue, and she'd stopped by to see how things were going. We started dancing." He shrugged.

Lilith's lips pulled into a frown. "Bartending issue?

He waved his hand. "It isn't important. It was taken care of." What was important was that Lilith had interrupted and inadvertently reminded him of his oath to stay single. He shook his head. One incredibly hot kiss, and he'd been ready to toss it aside. "Any reason you stopped by?"

Lilith sighed. "I have some good news I kinda overshadowed with my tantrum. And..." She picked up the container she'd tossed on the table. "I know it's your late night and you never ask the staff to cook for you, so I brought Asher's veggie tacos you love."

"Thank you, but I'm a big boy. I would have managed." Maybe. He hadn't eaten since lunch, and his stomach rumbled when he took the container from her.

"The lion roaring in your belly is telling a different story." She sat in the chair next to him, patting his knee. "I'm sorry, li'l bro, I could have handled that better, but you don't want to get mixed up with that woman. The only person she cares about is herself... and her daughter," she conceded.

"Yeah. I get it."

Honestly, he wasn't sure he did. He couldn't reconcile the guarded, sweet woman he'd just danced with and kissed to the one Lilith saw—a conniving temptress. Which one was the real Eden?

He closed off his appetite for Eden and focused on the one in his stomach. After eating two tacos, he asked, "What's new with you?"

"Besides making a fool of myself this evening?"

"Don't worry about it. Really." If he didn't redirect her, she'd tunnel into a path of self-flagellation and remorse. His sister was too damn hard on herself. "I shouldn't have been kissing her. I'm taking a break from women."

"Why?"

He shrugged, breaking eye contact. "Do you want a taco?"

"I already ate too many. They're all yours."

His gaze settled on her, and the food in his stomach hardened. He knew her too well and could read her face as easily as a child's book—questions were coming. She leaned her elbows on the table and asked, "What happened to you and Katrina? Why did you break up?"

"We weren't that great together. I didn't see any sense in trying it long distance when I moved here."

"That's it?"

"Yup."

Picking up a napkin, he pretended to wipe dinner crumbs from his mouth. It was a lie. And he hated to tell them to his sister, but he'd already kept so much from her concerning Katrina, he didn't see the point of upsetting her now that it was over.

Grabbing for another topic change, he remembered her mentioning she had good news. "That was your happy announcement?"

Lilith smiled, and it was genuine. "Asher and I are getting married." She showed him her left hand. On her ring finger, shone a beautiful art deco ring that was one hundred percent his sister's style. "We want to have the wedding in October of next year."

"That's great." He leaned over and hugged her. He forced his happiness for his sister to the surface, shaking off the whiplash at how fast things had gone to shit with Eden.

"Soooo," Lilith hedged.

"That sounds loaded." Tate took a bite of his taco.

"Will you be my Man of Honor?"

He choked on his swallow. After getting it down, he repeated, "Man of Honor?"

"It's like a Maid of Honor, but a man."

He rolled his eyes, "Thanks, Sis, there's no way I'd have figured that out on my own."

She poked him in the ribs. "Shut up."

"Is it allowed?"

"It's my and Asher's wedding. We can do whatever we want." She took his hand. "It has always been you and me. You're my best friend, so I want you as my Man of Honor."

He squeezed her hand. "I'd be honored." They'd been through a lot together. He was lucky to have her as a sister. "Who am I walking down the aisle with? Jackson or Hope?"

Lilith cleared her throat. "We wanted to ask Hope if she'd marry us."

"Hope's a minister?"

"No but getting ordained is as simple as filling out a form online."

"That's cool." It was a great idea. Asher was close to his twin sister, and Lilith and Hope were also tight.

Tate quirked a brow. "So, me and Jackson, huh?"

"Does that bother you?"

"No." He held up a hand. "Unless you expect me to wear a dress and heels."

Lilith laughed. "I think finding either of those in your size would be difficult. I'll have to settle for you in a tux and oxfords."

He snorted. "I am so thankful for my big feet."

Checking her phone, she stood. "I have to pick up Chloe."

"It's after eleven. I'm surprised you and Asher let her stay out this late on a school night." They were fair but were not laissez-faire parents.

"Special occasion. Today was the last track meet, and one of the girls broke the school record. The team's celebrating at one of the runner's homes."

"You could've called me. I'd have gotten Chloe on my way home. We're neighbors, but I'm getting all the benefits." He indicated the tacos. "Let me help you too."

"I should have, probably would have, if I wasn't worried about you skipping dinner." She tapped the chair she'd just vacated. "And I wanted to ask you in person about being in the wedding."

"I'm glad you stopped by."

She scoffed. "Oh, I'm sure you are. Who doesn't love being interrupted while making out by shrieks from their sister?"

"We weren't making out."

She gave him a yeah-right-look. He ignored it.

"It was a mistake. It shouldn't have happened."

"That we can agree on." She kissed his cheek. "I'll see you later, little brother."

"Bye, Sis."

She waved and left, leaving Tate alone in the quiet restaurant with his loud thoughts.

He shoved the sweet memory of Eden's lips and her soft body against him in a dark corner of his mind, forgetting about the enticing woman.

Tonight, was a splash of reality. Some things mattered, like the success of his restaurant. And some things didn't, like getting trapped by another manipulative woman.

CHAPTER ELEVEN

Eden leaned on her front porch railing and stared at the lake in front of her, letting its hypnotic sway soothe her. The scent of wet earth and blooming trees tickled her lousy mood, lightening it a little.

Steps crunched and shifted on the gravel to her left, threatening her moment of peace. She faced the sound and saw Olivia walking their steep shared road, carrying the now familiar pie box. She was nearly between their houses and turning toward hers. Eden's initial reaction was to retreat before being noticed.

The incident last night with Tate and his sister didn't have her in the mindset to reach toward a possible friendship. Then again, Tate—the asshole—was right about one thing. If Eden meant to stay in Michigan for Raven, she should try to plant a few seeds that might give her roots in this small town. Her kind neighbor didn't seem like a bad place to start.

"Wow, you're already restocking pies? Tate." Eden paused as the bitter taste of his name stung her tongue. "He wasn't kidding that your pies help keep his restaurant's doors open."

Olivia swiveled toward Eden. "Hey, neighbor." She wiped her brow with exaggeration. "Baking for The Hill keeps me almost as busy as my little girls. I was in my kitchen well before the sun rose, filling Tate's latest order. My back and feet are weeping."

Eden rubbed her hands down her slacks. "D-do you want to come over? Take a break? I have a new tea I got from my favorite shop in Ann Arbor."

Jesus, she was such a dork. Her heart was pounding, and sweat prickled under her arms. She was acting like a teenager asking out her first crush instead of an adult inviting her neighbor over for a drink. Where was all this nervousness coming from?

But she knew the answer. Putting herself out there for rejection was never easy, but on the cusp of Tate's rebuff didn't help. *Asshole*. But she refused to let him hold her back.

"That sounds wonderful. Let me pop inside." Olivia pointed at her house. "I'll let Elijah know where I'll be."

Eden nodded and sat on her porch swing. Then she stood and paced. Should she wait here or go inside and boil the water for tea? Thankfully, Olivia returned within minutes, saving Eden from her painful, unexpected insecurities.

When she reached Eden's steps, Olivia held up a pie with a perfect golden crust. "I tried a new recipe, strawberry rhubarb. Tate mentioned he loved it as a kid. I'm going to surprise him with it but want to sample it first. To make sure the recipe is perfect."

"I am all for helping you with that task." Next to her abuela's conchas, pies—all pies—were her favorite dessert. "We're having an actual, real spring dream day. Do you mind if we sit on the porch?" Eden asked.

It was far from a California or New Mexico spring, but her job had her indoors too much. On her days off, she layered up and spent as much time as possible outside.

Olivia glanced at the sky. "Good idea. April loves to play with us. We need to soak up some of the warmth in case it snows tomorrow." She looked toward her house, biting her lip. "Do you mind if we sit on your back patio, where my kids can't see me? If they spot me out here, they'll fuss to come over. I love them with every beat of my heart, but my husband has been gone for two weeks. And is leaving again this afternoon." She inhaled, then exhaled with a whoosh. "I need a break."

"I get it." Eden lied. She didn't know the exhaustion of parenthood. And it hollowed her; having reasons for leaving didn't fill those regrets. Opening her front door, she motioned Olivia inside. "And as an added bonus, I have two cherry trees in full bloom out back. They're stunning."

Cutting through the living room, Olivia paused at the floor-to-ceiling bookshelf between the kitchen and bedroom entrance. "Oh, I love books. Mind if I take a look?"

She did because a lot was revealed by what a person reads. However, refusing would be rude, so Eden said, "Go ahead."

"I'm a huge fiction reader." Olivia ran her fingers over the spines. "I see that you're not. There are so many books about pediatric surgery. And about parenting..."

Was that judgment in Olivia's voice? The possibility set Eden on edge. She'd read every damn book about parenting if it made her a better one.

Olivia pulled out a book. "Have you read this yet?"

The parenting book had been a favorite, very useful. Eden pressed her lips together to keep any unpleasant words from tumbling out and nodded.

"Did you like it?"

Eden offered another stiff nod. Would her parenting style be under the microscope all afternoon?

"I have this book on hold at the library, but the waitlist is miles long. Would you recommend buying it?" Olivia asked.

Oh. A tingling swept up the back of Eden's neck, spreading to her cheeks. Olivia wasn't judging, merely curious. She felt better about Olivia but crappy about herself. Did she always have to assume the worst of people?

She wiped away her unfriendly frown and said, "I highly recommend it. But you don't need to buy it, you can have mine."

Olivia held the it to her chest. "Are you sure?"

"Yes." Eden referred to the book constantly, but she'd get another one.

"Thank you." Olivia's gaze returned to the bookshelf. "Do you read any fiction?"

Eden pointed to the bottom shelf. "I have a few." But I haven't read them yet. Maybe after my fellowship."

Olivia hunched, surveying the titles, and tapped one. "Oh, *Taste of Passion*, that is one of my favorites. I love that it takes place in Michigan. Let me know what you think when you read it."

"My scribe—work colleague—gave it to me. But, um, I will." However, she doubted Olivia would want to meet again. Eden couldn't stop acting so damn awkward. She cleared her throat. "Did you want to try the tea? Or do you want something else? Lemonade? Sorry, I don't have alcohol."

Olivia grinned. "Given it's a little after nine, I'll manage. But, seriously, I'm not picky. Whatever you're having is fine with me."

Right now, Eden almost wished she had alcohol. A little of that soft buzz that seemed to chill most people would be nice right about now. She exhaled. This was ridiculous. She could handle hours of intense surgeries, shrug off the passive-aggressive Dr. Leeday, and give talks to panels and students. However, chatting with her kind neighbor reduced her to hesitations, stumbles, and nerves, wishing for a cocktail before noon.

Last night's argument with Tate seemed to have really kicked her confidence in the gut. It pissed her off.

She squared her shoulders and tried on an assertive smile. "I picked up a new tea blend."

"That'll be perfect," Olivia said.

Eden grinned, "But I didn't tell you the blend yet. It could be something gross."

"I'm not sure a gross tea exists. And, honestly, I'd be happy with tap water. I'm here for the adult conversation."

"Then I will give you conversation and Butterfly tea." In the kitchen, Eden filled the electric kettle and then pointed at the sliding glass door just outside of the kitchen. "You can head to the patio, if you want."

"Is there anything I can do to help?" Olivia asked.

She gestured to the washcloth folded neatly on the sink's faucet. "Would you mind wiping the bistro table?"

"Not at all."

Once Olivia was outside, Eden leaned on the counter and exhaled. What in the hell were they supposed to talk about? Olivia was a stay-at-home mom with two adorable kids and a handsome husband. Eden was a workaholic, trying to be a good mom, and had absolutely no love life.

Once again, Tate flashed in her mind. She shoved him aside.

After steeping the tea, there wasn't a reason to delay. She placed mugs, utensils, and the pie on a tray, then slid open the door with her elbow, saying, "I forgot, I have to pick up Raven soon. But we have just enough time for pie and tea, I think."

It was the truth—sort of. Soon was after basketball practice, five hours from now. But Eden needed an out if she became even more awkward. Which, at this point, seemed a given.

"That's perfect as I only have about an hour. I have to take Elijah to the airport." Olivia stood. "Let me help."

"I got it." Eden set the tray on the bistro table, then poured the tea.

They sipped, and she stared at the blooming trees, tapping her fingers on the ceramic mug, searching her mind for a conversation starter. In the near distance to their right, the jutting corner of The Hill's patio peeked through the mostly bare branches. Was Tate there now, holding onto his righteous, erroneous misconceptions?

"Is everything okay?" Olivia asked. Eden startled at the question.

Damn, was last night's blowup with Tate scrawled all over her? "Yeah, I'm great," she lied. "What makes you think something is wrong?"

"You seem distracted."

"Sorry, I'm terrible at small talk. But, hey, chatting with your toddlers might not seem so bad now," Eden joked. Mercifully, Olivia laughed.

"No worries." She sliced into the pie and handed Eden a piece. "Ask my husband, once I get started, I can talk enough for the both of us."

Eden bit into the desert and moaned. The sound was embarrassingly close to the noise she made when climaxing. But she didn't care; her mouth had been transported to a tasty heaven. The tart rhubarb was the perfect companion to the sweet strawberries, and she ate every bite. Even the crust was delicious.

"Dang, woman," Olivia giggled. "I'd say this recipe is a hit."

"It is exquisite." Eden closed her mouth tight to keep from licking her fork. And plate.

"Have another slice. You're eyeing it like you eyed Tate that day I stopped at the restaurant." Olivia winked. "I can tell you're craving more...pie."

"Yes, you're right." Eden cut another slice for each of them. "Pie—and only pie—is what I want."

After last night, she could say that with complete honesty. She didn't need Tate's laughter or sexy smiles. Not when it also came with accusatory, stony judgment. Sure, her suggestion to Asher had been stupid, but she'd done nothing wrong. Not that Tate had let her explain. Or that he deserved an explanation.

"Did you grow up in Michigan?" Olivia asked.

Ugh. The getting-to-know-you questions. Eden fiddled with the handle on her coffee mug. "No. New Mexico. Did you here?"

Olivia tilted her head. "Not one to talk about yourself, huh?"

Shit. Redirection hadn't worked. But like earlier, when asking about books, there was only curiosity in her voice. Eden sucked in her cheeks and then released them. "I'm boring."

"I doubt that." To Eden's relief, Olivia took a sip of tea and moved on. "I'm from Michigan. Dearborn. My dad moved here from Lebanon during the civil war. My mom's American."

She went on to tell Eden about life in Dearborn and traveling to Lebanon as a kid. And how she met her husband Elijah at Wayne State. Their conversation naturally moved to college life.

Olivia was right; she could talk but didn't drone. It was light, fun, and captivating, especially when they'd moved on to stories of her travels. They filled Eden with wanderlust. Once her father passed away, the family vacations ended. And when she became an adult, her school breaks were spent flying to Michigan to visit Raven. Or to New Mexico for her abuela. So, it was exciting to hear about Olivia's adventures.

"Where was your favorite place?" she asked.

Olivia tapped her chin. "The most unexpected delight was when we rented a tree house on one of the tiny islands in Lake Nicaragua—" Olivia's phone trilled, and she answered it.

The call was brief, but Eden could tell it was Olivia's husband, and she'd have to leave. Eden glanced at her cell resting on the table. Wow, over an hour had passed.

"Sorry, I have to run. I didn't realize the time, and Elijah needs me to take him to the airport shortly." Olivia smiled. "Let's do this again. And soon."

"I'd love that," Eden replied, buoyant after making a connection in her small town. And somewhat vindicated. She didn't need Tate's flimsy friendship and traitorous kisses.

CHAPTER TWELVE

Tate sat on his balcony, staring at the tiny whitecaps playing with the warm breeze on the lake. It was a beautiful false spring afternoon, but its serenity didn't touch him.

His stomach rumbled, but he was too full of regret to eat. What had happened with Eden yesterday gnawed at him. He wasn't sure if it was because he was attracted to a woman hung up on his sister's fiancé – damn, that was a fucked-up combination—or because disquiet was beginning to simmer in him. Maybe he and Lilith read the situation between Asher and Eden wrong. As time passed, he became less and less sure that she was the villain they thought her to be.

Tate groaned, scrubbing his palms against his short beard. All he knew from last night's confrontation was that he wasn't ready to date. It had dredged up a lot of unpleasant memories and feelings he'd rather forget—reminding him he was still too screwed up, thanks to his ex.

"Hey, Tate," Asher called from his dock next door. Lilith waved with too much enthusiasm. "We're going out on the boat. First time this year. Want to come with us?"

Tate never regretted leaving behind his old career or city life to buy his sister's lake house. But some days, he'd rather wish they were not neighbors, especially when she was being nosey. And there was no way the invite was just about a simple boat ride. He could tell how they were trying—and failing—to sound natural.

He waved them off. "Thanks. Maybe next time."

"Get your butt down here and come with us," Lilith shouted. "We need to talk."

"That request makes me want to come with you even less," he replied.

She put her hands on her hips. "It wasn't a request."

He snorted, amusement breaking through his worry and agitation. "You're not my mom," he teased-taunted.

Even from a distance, he saw her exaggerated eye roll. "I have tomato basil soup in the crock-pot. I'll give you some if you grace us with your presence."

"Are you making those red pepper sandwiches too?" he bargained. He might be full on guilt and unease, but damn, those sandwiches were good.

"Jesus, fine," Lilith groaned. "Now, come on."

He made his way to their ski boat and climbed aboard. Dinner better be worth the *discussion* he'd have to endure.

Asher was already at the steering wheel, cramming a baseball cap over his dark blond hair. "I'll try not to be offended that Lilith had to bribe you to hang out with us."

"Nothing personal. But you heard what she said."

"Yeah." Asher shuddered. "'We need to talk.'"

Lilith huffed. "Fine, I meant, let's talk. Like, you know, chat."

Tate wasn't buying it. Her body language and tone shouted she had something to say, and it wasn't idle chatter.

Once they were in the open water, Tate closed his eyes and leaned his head against the seat cushion, letting the weak sun warm his face. As they glided over the smooth lake, he was glad he'd come. Being under the summer sky with the waves rocking him lifted his mood.

The bench seat dipped, and Lilith's soft hair tickled his cheek as she rested her head on his shoulder. "I'm sorry for yesterday. I overreacted."

Tate groaned, some of his grouchiness returning. "Lil, you sound like a broken record. Let it go. It's not a big deal." He cracked an eye open. "At least not for me. I'll admit after finding out about the stunt she pulled, I'm surprised you still have her over for holidays and shit. Aren't you afraid she'll try something again?"

"I trust Asher. Plus, she's Raven's mom. And—"

"Okay, sure, I get not barring her from the house, but she just spent Easter dinner in your home, acting like everything was fine. Like she hadn't recently tried to steal your man from you."

"The incident wasn't recent." Lilith cleared her throat. "And when she came to him with her idea, he technically wasn't 'my man'."

Tate settled deeper into the boat's cushion as disquiet crawled up his spine. "What do you mean?"

"She made her *suggestion* during the brief time I'd broken up with Asher."

In the winter? Like six months ago? He faced his sister. "You said, 'she tried to steal Asher from me.' As in, you were together."

"That's what it felt like." Lilith looked at her hands that were knotted together in her lap. "But it isn't the technical truth."

He digested this new information. It made a difference.

Lilith looked at Tate. Her eyes were heavy with remorse. "I'm so sorry."

He was annoyed but also understood. "It's fine. It has to be difficult to have a woman hanging around who wants your fiancé."

"She doesn't," Asher and Lilith replied simultaneously.

"I was wrong," she said.

He sucked in a tired breath. Last night, he'd ended his friendship with Eden—and the possibility of more—all over miscommunication. Fuck. But he couldn't blame his sister. He'd been the one unwilling to listen to Eden.

Still, he had to know. "How were you wrong?" he asked.

"In every way possible."

He made a get-on-with-it gesture. "Stop being vague."

"When I went home yesterday, I was still worked up that Eden had come-on to you."

He'd been the one to make the first move, asking to kiss her. But that didn't matter for this conversation, and Lilith seemed determined to say what she'd lured him on the boat for, so he didn't interrupt to correct her.

"I asked Asher what exactly Eden had said when she'd suggested they get back together."

"Wait." Tate held up a hand. "Why was last night the first time you talked about it. It happened *months* ago."

"At the time, all that was important to me was that Asher wasn't interested. Plus, if he'd told me that Eden was still in love with him all these years later, I'd have a hard time with her in our lives. I figured it was best to bury and forget about it." Lilith sighed. "From the way I acted yesterday, it seems I haven't forgotten. Or forgiven."

"And I *had* pretty much forgotten because I knew her offer had nothing to do with me," Asher said. "Eden doesn't love me. She never did. We were so young and hadn't been together very long when we had Raven. Eden had suggested the idea one hundred percent for Raven."

Regret twisted and knotted in Tate's stomach. Eden had *told* him her reason for moving back to Michigan was for Raven. And she'd admitted the town's treatment toward her hurt. She'd been vulnerable with him—something he was certain she didn't do with many people. Then he'd acted like them—hell, he was worse than them because he knew her, and she'd trusted him.

"She thought being together as a family would be good for our daughter," Asher continued. "And since we got along and weren't seeing anyone, she thought it a logical solution. Eden is very logical—maybe too much. I don't think her heart enters into many of her choices and decisions."

Tate disagreed. Her heart *had been* in the suggestion—but not for Asher, for Raven. He slouched, the vinyl seat squeaking. "I was such an asshole yesterday."

Lilith leaned against him. "It's my fault. I am so sorry."

"No, it isn't." He knocked his head gently against hers. "Okay, maybe a little. But she and I have been talking a lot lately, and she basically told me everything Asher just said, well before you showed up with all your righteous and misplaced anger." He tickled her side to show he didn't blame her reaction or his actions on her. "And I chose not to believe her. Not to listen to her."

"I hold more than a little blame. You acted on what I told you. I'm your sister, of course you'd jump to my defense. As I would for you. Especially over a near stranger." After a loaded pause, she said. "Well, maybe not a stranger. Strangers don't kiss like you two..."

Tate groaned, rubbing his palms on the heat spreading on his cheeks. Though she was right, Eden hadn't tasted like a stranger. Her kiss had been like finding his way home.

Asher tapped the steering wheel with his palm. "Listen, it doesn't bother me, you two dating."

"Or me," Lilith cut in.

"If you like her, go for it," Asher said.

Tate shifted, resting his elbows on his knees. "Didn't you say she was too logical for love?"

"Who knows?" Asher shrugged. "You two could be good together. Maybe you're the guy who can chip away at her walls."

Tate tugged with his ear. "I doubt that. Besides the fact she'll probably never talk to me again, we have little in common."

"That's not true. You're both blunt. And workaholics." Lilith rubbed his back. "And oh-so pretty," she goaded.

He snorted. "I prefer rugged, masculine, or handsome."

"Just because you prefer it doesn't make it true," she muttered.

"You two are worse than Raven and Chloe," Asher teased.

Lilith narrowed her eyes, but her lips twitched. Asher reached for her wrist, pulling her onto his lap. He said to Tate, "Anyway, about you and Eden—call it a hunch. I sense stuff. My middle name should've been Eros instead of Hendrix."

"Hendrix?"

Asher smiled. "My parents met at a Hendrix tribute concert."

"My turn to drive," Lilith told Asher.

Nodding, he patted her hip. She stood, and he left the driver's seat, sitting next to Tate.

Asher squinted. "Are we done talking about our feelings?"

"You tell me. You and Lilith dragged me out here for this heart-to-heart," Tate threw back, then muttered, "I deserve three red pepper sandwiches for this shit."

Chuckling, Asher slouched, crossing his feet at the ankles and checking his watch. "The girls had a half day today. Eden picked them up from school to go shopping in Ann Arbor. She'll be dropping them off anytime now. If they're home and skipped eating for more mall time, you'll be lucky to get a sandwich."

"Well, shit," Tate groused, but he didn't really care.

His thoughts were on Eden. If she was there when they got back, maybe he could convince her to go to his place so they could talk things out. If they weren't there, he could wait until she arrived with the girls. He needed to apologize, but "I'm sorry" didn't feel like enough. She'd been a friend, and last night had offered a taste of more. He'd thrown it all back at her. He'd judged and condemned her without proof, just like everyone else in this one-light town.

He stared toward the shore, hoping his second chance was waiting there. He had to win back the friend he'd wronged.

...But when they arrived at the house, he only found the girls waiting—no sign of Eden. He'd have to wait a little longer for his second chance.

CHAPTER THIRTEEN

Eden hummed a tuneless melody while gathering milk, queso fresco, and sour cream from the fridge. Asher had mentioned a few days ago that Raven had recently taken an interest in cooking—a hobby Eden also enjoyed. Some of her best memories were cooking with her abuela. Eden set the food-prep items on the counter. Raven would be here any minute. They had a culinary date—the whole day together.

A few minutes later, Raven called to Eden from the front room.

"I'm in the kitchen." She glanced at the digital clock on the stove. It was two minutes after nine in the morning. They'd have plenty of time to make the large batch of Chiles en Nogada.

"Could you come here?" Raven called in a slightly stiff tone.

"Um, sure." Eden laid her knife on the cutting board and walked into the living room, pausing over the threshold.

Lilith stood on the foyer's welcome mat—a very unwelcome sight. Christ, hadn't she gotten enough bites in at the restaurant? Was she hungry for more? Eden had been relieved that Asher and Lilith were on their boat when she dropped off the girls since her plan was to avoid Lilith until her annoyance faded.

That didn't seem to be an option. "What do you need, Lilith?" She kept the irritation from her tone because Raven was in the room.

"H-Here. I brought you a coffee." Lilith thrust a travel mug toward Eden. Coffee sloshed from the small opening in the lid. She wiped it with her hand. "Sorry."

What the hell? Instead of taking it, she focused on Raven. "Would you mind crumbling the queso fresco?"

Raven hesitated. "Umm..."

"The white cheese," Eden clarified.

Raven nodded and headed for the kitchen. Once certain she was out of earshot, Eden asked, "What is it, Lilith? What more could you possibly have to say?" This time she let her annoyance lace every word.

"Just that I'm sorry."

A bark of laughter escaped Eden, and she tilted her head. "You're full of apologies this morning. Why?"

"Because I was wrong. I shouldn't have said the things I said when I walked in on you and Tate."

The searing memory of his perfect kiss scorched through her, immediately followed by his imperfect words, amplifying her exasperation. "You're right. You shouldn't have but thank you for the apology."

Ignoring Lilith's outstretched hand still holding the coffee, Eden turned away—too discombobulated with this odd turnabout to accept the gift—but then changed her mind. She glanced at the logo on the to-go mug. It was a damn excellent brew.

She twisted around and took the cup. "Thanks," she said before giving Lilith her back.

Walking toward the living room's bookshelf, Eden heard the front door close. She inhaled deeply, savoring the delicious, fresh scent, then sipped it. *Mmm. That's how coffee's done.* She had to admit the smooth and rich flavor washed away some of her bitterness toward Lilith.

Shimming her shoulders, she mentally moved away from the unexpected visit. She connected her phone to the Bluetooth speakers on her bookshelf. After pressing start on Raven's favorite playlist, Eden stopped in the laundry room between the living room and kitchen to grab clothes from the dryer. She paused halfway through the task and stopped her quiet humming. Was Raven pounding on something, or was it the music? The bass and drums were aggressive in the current song.

Grabbing the basket of clothes, she stepped into the living room and, with her free hand, turned down the volume on her phone, then headed to the kitchen. "Are you knocking on something?"

Raven shook her head. She stood at the counter with white cheese stuck to her finger and a small pile in front of her. "Did I do it right?"

She looked so much like Eden, but what she loved the most was Raven's eyes. Not because they were hazel like Asher's, but because they shone with happiness instead of fear as Eden's had at that age.

"You did great," Eden set her clothing basket on a kitchen chair. "Let's brown the ground meat, and then I'll show you the next step.

"When it's done, can I take some home?"

"Sure. Take all you want." Eden wished her place was also home to Raven. She glanced at her work bag resting on one of the kitchen chairs. When hired, she'd have all the time in the world to prove herself to her daughter.

"What do we do next?" Raven asked.

She pointed to the saucepan. "Do you want to cook the meat or cut up the vegetables?

"Can I cook, you cut?"

"That works."

Eden got the small stepping stool from the side of the fridge so the flame wouldn't be close to Raven's upper body. Standing side-by-side, they worked on the meal. The simple moment between them held so much precious peace. Contentment settled over Eden, and she held tightly to the soul-deep happiness. It gave her the nerve to ask, yet again, the question Raven always answered with a no. "Do you want to stay the night?"

She shook her head. "I like waking up in my bed. And Chloe and I are finishing a science project due on Monday."

Her answer was expected, but it still twisted Eden's heart. Worse, it was her fault. She couldn't expect her daughter to be close when they'd always lived so far apart. For most of Raven's life, she only saw Eden two or three times a year. The rest was phone and video calls. That wasn't conducive to creating a deep bond.

The pounding came again, and she easily recognized and located it this time. Why would they go there instead of the front door?

She moved toward the sound. "I told you I heard something."

"I thought you were hearing things in your old age," Raven teased.

"Hey! I'm only thirty-two." Eden knocked gently into Raven, then started toward the patio door.

"You're practically a Boomer," Raven quipped. "I hope it's Olivia and she brought her babies. They're the cutest."

Eden agreed, and it probably was her neighbor. Who else would it be? She and Raven were the only people who visited. Well, besides Lilith's surprise this morning—and that didn't count.

Turning the corner, she stopped short. Tate stood on the other side of the sliding glass door. *What is this? Sister and brother tag team today?* She was tempted to close the blinds.

He'd called her friend, kissed her like she was more, then treated her with spite and accusations. He was like everyone else in this damn small town.

Before deciding what to do, Raven said from behind, "Uncle Tate, what are you doing here?" She stepped around Eden and opened the door.

Huh. He's an uncle to her.

Eden didn't care for him much right now, but she liked that he was an uncle to Raven. She deserved as much family as possible, through blood or heart.

Tate scratched the back of his neck. "I stopped by to apologize to your mom."

No shrinking and side-stepping with this man. Her traitorous heart swooned.

Eden's gaze swung to Raven. Her furrow line had returned. "Why?" she asked.

"For a misunderstanding," Eden said. "Could you check on the sauce while he and I talk?"

"Okay." Raven fixed Tate with a glare. "You better be nice to my mom. Grovel until she forgives you."

Eden's whole body tingled and sparkled in the glow of her daughter's protectiveness. It lit up every corner of her heart.

"I plan on it," Tate replied.

As Raven left, Eden moved back, and Tate stepped inside. She crossed her arms over her chest. She appreciated his apology, but his face still pissed her off. "I take it you talked to Lilith."

"Yup, but—"

"Glad you're willing to listen to her." *But not me.*

Tate winced, sliding the glass door closed. "I deserve that. But I'd planned on apologizing before talking to her. After, I realized I needed to beg for your forgiveness." He shook his head. "I overreacted. Said shit I shouldn't have."

His straightforwardness was nice, and she could forgive, but forgetting wouldn't be so easy—not for her. "Yes, and you did it right after saying you didn't care or believe what people in the town thought of me."

He opened his mouth as if to argue, but Eden held up a hand. "Maybe you *think* you don't, but your *actions* say you do." Tears burned behind her eyes, but she wouldn't let them fall. "I thought you were my friend. I expected more from you."

"I am."

"Not a very good one."

He flinched. "I deserved that."

She nodded. "You were willing to believe the worst of me without even letting me explain."

"I was convinced whatever you said would be an excuse. A story. A lie."

"Because you're like everyone else in this town. Thinking the worst of me."

"No—"

"But you're worse than them. You call me your friend. Kiss me," she whispered the last part in case Raven was eavesdropping, "then flip a switch, treating me like I'm some conniving bitch."

"I swear, it's not because of town gossip." He rubbed the back of his neck. "Really, it's not you at all."

She scoffed. "It sure felt personal.

"I can give you my excuses and reasons, but in the end that's all they are—excuses. I was an asshole." He took her hand, running his thumb along her wrist. "I'm sorry. Will you forgive—"

"Uncle Tate." Raven came from the kitchen, her gaze landing on their clasped hands.

They let go, and he asked, "What's up?"

"We're almost done with our epic lunch." She looked at Eden. "...Um, what's it called again?"

Eden smiled. "Chiles en nogada."

"Yeah, that." She pointed at Eden, then Tate. "You should stay. Eat with us."

"Thanks, kiddo, but I should get back to the restaurant. Are you here all day?"

Raven nodded. "Dad's picking me up around dinnertime."

"You two should come by before then. I want a rematch at pool." He faced Eden. "Your daughter's a shark."

Raven laughed. "No, you're just bad at pool. But we can come by for a rematch before my dad picks me up." She poked Tate in the arm, grinning at him. "So you can lose again."

He snorted and tugged lightly on her ponytail. "Maybe you can give me some tips."

She shrugged. "Maybe. But I think you're hopeless."

Tate clutched his heart and stumbled back as if shot. "Ruthless."

Raven giggled, then asked Eden, "Can I finish cutting up the vegetables you didn't do yet?"

"Sure."

When Raven returned to the kitchen, Tate rested a hand on the patio door handle and faced Eden. The seriousness returned to his eyes. "Will you forgive me?"

Some of her hurt remained, and she clung to it. But should she? The muffled thump of the knife on the cutting board filled the heavy silence between them. She wanted her daughter's forgiveness. Perhaps she should offer the same to Tate.

"Maybe." A small smile tugged at the corners of her mouth. "Your apology was decent."

CHAPTER FOURTEEN

Eden didn't want to go to The Hill. Try as she might, she wasn't ready to completely forgive Tate, let alone spend the evening near him. Even if he was busy working, his presence would be felt. He had a pull that was hard for her to ignore—even if she should.

But Raven was giving her pleading eyes. "Come on, Mom, it'll be fun. Let's go for a little bit." she begged, weakening Eden's resistance.

Raven held up her cell. "What if I promise not to even glance at this while we're there? We can play pool. Or pinball."

Asher finally relented and gave Raven his old cell at the start of the school year. She was slightly addicted. The Hill had a decent-sized room at the back of the restaurant with fun, old-school games. Getting Raven off her phone to play them would be nice.

And between her daughter's pleading posture and hopeful tone, Eden had no choice but to cave. "Fine," she groaned.

Raven jumped up from the couch. "Yea!"

"But all I'm good at is pinball. I've never played pool," Eden warned.

Raven's eyes widened. "Never, ever?"

"Not once." Eden stood. "Let's go." She'd spend the evening with her daughter and worry about her mixed feelings about Tate another time.

However, as soon as she stepped into the busy restaurant, her gaze snagged on Tate standing behind the bar. Why did he have to be so handsome? His smile could melt February frost.

Raven walked around Eden, looking toward the game room. "Crap. Nothing's free," she huffed, then perked up. "Uncle Tate's at the bar. I bet he'll make me a root beer float. Maybe even get me an order of chili cheese fries."

"I don't know how you can even think about food after all those chiles en nogada we ate." Eden patted her stomach, pretending to be full.

In truth, they'd eaten hours ago, and the restaurant smelled good. And the chili cheese fries were amazing. However, she wasn't ready to talk with Tate.

She glanced around. The place was packed with high schoolers, all wearing matching team jerseys. "Do you—" She stopped when noticing Raven was halfway to the bar. Sighing, Eden followed and took the stool next to her daughter, who was already working on Tate for a float.

He looked at Eden. "Is it okay?" His eyes seemed to be asking about more than the float.

"No," she said, then turned to Raven. "When I told your dad to meet us here instead of my place, he mentioned something about taking you out for dinner."

Raven's shoulders slumped. "Fine. What about a regular root beer?"

"That's fine," Eden said.

Tate poured a glass from the soda fountain. As she sipped, a girl around her age called from near the game room. "Raven, come play air hockey with me!"

"What about me?" huffed a boy next to her. His similar nose and hair hinted he was the girl's younger brother.

"You suck. I want a challenge," she replied. The boy's face flushed red, and he stomped toward a table with a man and a woman, presumably his parents.

Raven looked at her with pleading eyes. "Do you mind, Mom?"

Ugh, who can say no to that face? "It's fine."

"Thanks!" Raven disappeared with the girl, leaving Eden alone.

With Tate.

As if answering her prayers, Jackson slid onto Raven's vacated stool. Nodding a hello to Eden, he said to Tate, "Shit, you're behind the bar again? I guess I'll take a Whiskey Highball then. Try not to mess it up."

"Screw you, dude." He laughed. "And I'm only here while my bartender takes a smoke break."

"Thank, Christ."

Tate's lips twitched. "Where's the confidence in your friend?"

Eden couldn't help smiling, and Tate zeroed in on it. "Would you like one of my drink specialties?"

"No, thanks. I'll have an iced tea."

"As long as it isn't a Long Island Iced Tea, we're good." Tate sighed. "I don't think I'm at that level of bartending yet."

"It doesn't even have to be sweet tea."

"That's because you're sweet enough," Tate winked.

Jackson snorted. "You are so smooth."

Tate ran a hand along the bar top, grinning. "Smooth as your favorite whiskey, am I right?"

"More like plonk moonshine." Jackson swiveled his barstool, facing Eden. "When a table's open, want to play pool?"

Well, shit. That would've been my perfect escape. "I don't know how to play," she admitted.

"I'll t—"

"I'll teach you," Tate said over Jackson. "Or we could play something else."

Did she detect a note of possessiveness in his tone? Going by Jackson's smirk, he'd heard it too. She sucked in her bottom lip, biting on it. Brushing off Tate was the smart thing to do...

"Mom," Raven called, running toward them. "Are you ready? A pool table's about to open."

"Wow. I didn't expect you back so quickly. Thought you might have ditched me for your friend," Eden teased.

"I wouldn't do that." The worry etched on Raven's face punched Eden in the stomach. She hated that her daughter was always anxious about her mother's mood, as if the wrong word would make her pack up and leave.

"I was kidding." She rubbed Raven's arm. "But I thought you'd be with your friend longer."

"Their food arrived."

Eden nodded. "I'm fine with playing pool, but remember, you'll have to teach me."

"Could we do teams?" Raven asked. "Me and Jackson. You and Tate. Then we can all give you tips."

"I like that idea," Tate said.

She glanced at him. Why did he have to look so hopeful? Like her forgiveness, her friendship actually mattered to him.

"Works for me too." Jackson ran a hand over his cropped dreadlocks. "Though watch your daughter the closest. Girls got an eye for the game."

Raven beamed. "Then it's settled," she declared. "You go with Uncle Tate. Me with Jackson. Once you learn Mom, we can break off and play winner."

Tate leaned close, a teasing glint in his eyes. "If I let you win, will you forgive me?"

"Let me win?" Eden laughed. "How about we see how well you take it when I whip you?"

Tate pulled in his lips like it was killing him not to say something. Or laugh.

She frowned. "What's so funny?"

"So, um, if I let you whip me...will you be in leather. Oh, or one of those sexy corsets?"

She smacked him lightly on his chest. "Whip you in pool, Tate. pool," she laughed.

"Aw, well, too bad. I'm sure you'd look amazing in either."

She shook her head, giving up on holding onto her grudge and deciding to enjoy the evening. Enjoy the way he made her see the fun side of life. She didn't have to trust him to like his company.

It didn't take long for Eden to get the hang of pool. She seemed to have a knack for it. After a quick lesson, they racked up and played teams. Tate rocked back on his heels. "I see where your daughter got her game-shark attitude. I thought you said—"

"Oh, here he goes again, telling me what I *said*..."

His grin faltered, and his gaze searched her face. When she smiled, he shook his head, chuckling. "You're brutal, woman."

"Too soon?" Eden wasn't worried. One of the things she liked about Tate was that she didn't have to soften her words. He was strong enough to handle them.

Raven sank the eight ball and whooped. "We win!"

"That was a lucky shot," Tate said. "Let's play one more."

"Luck." Raven rolled her eyes, pulling out her cell and looking at it. "I can't. Dad just called. I'll be right back." With her phone pressed to her ear, she moved to a quieter side of the restaurant.

"I need to head out," Jackson said.

After saying their goodbyes to him, Tate asked, "Why don't you break this time?"

She picked up the triangle. "Is there a trick to it?"

"Line it up. I'll show you." He set the end of his pool stick on the ground and leaned on it. "If you'd like."

Probably not. She'd watched enough games during her bartending days, but the opportunity of having him close, maybe even pressed into her, held tremendous appeal. "Sure."

He placed his hand over hers, correcting her hold. His chest was against her side, his seductive scent wrapping around her. It took her back to when they'd kissed—desire, slow and hot, coursed through her.

She glanced at him. They were so close she could see the flecks of blue in his grey eyes. Was that his hunger or hers reflected in them?

He blinked, then stepped away, asking, "You want to break? Or me?"

"You go ahead." Her body was bereft at the loss of his touch, but at least she managed to sound unaffected.

He moved to the opposite end to break. She chalked her cue, pausing when sensing someone close. Expecting Raven, Eden was startled to see an older man in her personal space. He'd been playing pool next to them. The tables were close enough that sometimes they'd have to wait on each other to shoot. But he wasn't lining up a shot. He stared at her with disapproval etched on every line and wrinkle on his face.

"Do I know you?" she asked.

He leaned in, and his stale cigarette breath assaulted her. "No, but I know Asher. He was a wreck when you left him and your baby. And what kind of woman leaves their kid?" His top lip curled. "Tate's a good guy. Leave him alone."

Guilt and shame pierced her heart, and the fight in her dried up. The crack of the balls breaking on her table diverted her attention. She stepped away from the man and turned toward Tate. He was straightening from the shot.

"Hey, Jim. How've you been?" Tate's easy-going gaze moved from the guy to Eden. His grin disappeared. "Is everything okay?"

"I'm just looking out for you," Jim answered.

Tate crossed his arms over his chest. "Oh, and how's that?"

Jim nodded toward Eden. "She's trouble."

Her gaze ran around the room. Relief flooded her when she saw Raven was still preoccupied on her phone. She didn't need to witness this harassment.

But it was time to go. They would leave. She would tell Asher there was a change of plans. Again. She focused on the red light of the exit sign.

A hand grasped her elbow gently. Tate. "Don't go. Please." He looked at the older man. "The only trouble I see is with you. You need to apologize to Eden."

The room went as close to silent as possible in a busy restaurant. Eden's skin prickled where people's gazes touched her.

"Son, I'm only—"

"You're only going to apologize to her. Or you're going to put down that pool stick and leave my restaurant."

"Tate, that isn't necessary," she said, even as her heart hugged his words.

"Yes, it is."

Jim shook his head. "If that's how you want to treat a paying customer who's looking out for you, I'll leave."

"Do that." Tate looked at the people closest to them, who were obviously eavesdropping. His gaze seemed to tell them that if they felt the same, they could fuck off too.

He watched Jim until he was through the door. After the man was gone, Tate turned to Eden and smiled as if nothing and no one was watching them. He pointed at the pool table. "You're stripes."

CHAPTER FIFTEEN

Eden looked from Tate to the exit and then glanced around the restaurant. Now that it seemed the entertainment was over, everyone returned to their own damn business. She shook her head, trying to recall what he'd said because what he'd just done took up all the space in her mind. How could it not—it was hot as hell.

He pointed at the pool table with his cue. "You're stripes," he repeated.

Oh, yeah, the game. She went on tiptoes and kissed his cheek. Returning her focus to the table, she sank the ball with the green stripe.

Maybe it was her lucky night.

She aimed again but hit the white ball too hard, and it shot past her target, bouncing off the table's side. Raven came up next to Eden. "Dad's on his way here."

"Okay. Do you want to take over, play my game until he gets here?"

"No. I'll play winner. He's coming here with Lilith for dinner." Raven smiled. "They wanted to know if you could stay and eat with us."

Nope. It wasn't her lucky night.

She didn't relish hanging around for awkward chit-chat even after Lilith's apology, but she wouldn't run. For Raven, she'd try to play nice.

Asher and Lilith arrived at the end of her game with Tate, and they took seats at one of the pub tables nearby. "Who's winning?" Asher asked.

"I am," Tate replied. "But barely. It's embarrassing, considering this is her first time playing."

"Didn't you tell me at Raven's basketball game you were a bartender during medical school. Aren't pool tables and bars a requirement?" he joked.

"Probably. But I never played where I worked." Eden rolled her cue between her palms. "Anyway, I'm learning quickly. Tate's a good teacher, has great form."

Looking at her, he grinned, posing in a way that pulled his shirt tight and enticing. "Oh, you like my form?"

His silly hotness had her caught between wanting to laugh and running her hands all over his solid *form*. "I meant you'd be a fantastic player if you weren't so impatient and would take the time to line up your shots."

"Oh, I can be patient..." His eyes flashed hot as if to say; *I can be patient with you—your body and your pleasure.* The man was temptation on legs.

Lilith's chair scraped on the floor, reminding Eden she was in a crowded restaurant. "As long as it isn't chess, checkers, tic-tac-toe..." his sister teased.

"Yeah, yeah." He shrugged, half-heartedly aiming for the corner pocket and missing. "I get strategic planning is great and all, but it's so fucking boring. I want action in my games."

"As opposed to thinking," Lilith teased. She turned to Eden. "But don't let him fool you. He was a money manager. I'm sure that required plenty of analytical thinking."

Her gaze was friendly, but it still unnerved Eden. She directed her attention to Tate. "Why'd you leave?"

His smile turned bitter, but his tone was light. "Should I refer back to my lack of enthusiasm for strategy and planning? Also, sitting behind a desk all day was making me slowly go insane." The heavy sigh that followed and the almost imperceptible slump to his shoulders whispered that there might be more to it.

"Raven mentioned you're staying for dinner. I'll eat with you," Tate said to Lilith. Then his gaze found Eden. "Will you join us?"

She clicked her tongue, pretending to consider it. "No, I'm going to head home after this game." She pointed with her stick. "Eight ball. Right, corner pocket."

His brows shot up. "When did you get your last two balls in?"

She sashayed to the other side of the table and bent, aiming her cue stick. "Pay attention. I'm surpassing the teacher."

"That you are," he chuckled.

"I'd love for you to stay," Lilith said.

Eden stiffened, missing her shot. She straightened, offering a smile as rigid as her spine. "Thank you, but I'm going to go home. I have to work tomorrow."

"You still have to eat," Asher reasoned.

Christ. Why were they all insisting? They'd be happier if she were gone.

Tate sank his last ball and then lined up the cue for the final shot. Half an hour ago, she didn't want the evening to end. Now she held in a cheer that the game was over.

"I don't want to intrude." She set her stick on the pool table. "I have a meal at home."

"Please, Mom. Stay." Raven popped out her bottom lip.

Eden held in a groan, tapping a foot. *Shit.* Relaxing on the couch with her latest parenting self-help book held way more appeal than hanging out with Lilith—the woman who was appalled at the sight of her brother kissing her.

Lilith slid off her stool. "Raven, why don't you play another game but with your dad? I can put in our orders. You want an Impossible Burger, right?"

"Fine." She hugged Eden. "Think about it. Stay."

She wanted to leave, but how could she say no? Forget pool; Raven knew how to play her mom.

Asher put an arm around Raven's shoulders as they strolled away. Eden swung her gaze to Tate. He was chatting with a guy who'd been playing pool with the older man Tate had told to leave.

Lilith rested a hand on Eden's arm. Ugh. Would this talk be as stilted and awkward as this morning?

"I get that you're tired and want to relax before returning to the hospital. However, if it's because you want to get away from me, I wish you'd give me a chance," Lilith said.

Fine. If she was willing to cut through the bullshit, Eden could as well. "You don't need to invite me out of obligation or guilt for the misunderstanding. It's kind of you, but unnecessary."

"It's neither of those." Lilith paused and smiled. "Okay, maybe a little guilt. I ruined your, um, moment with my brother."

Tate was walking past them and groaned. "Lil."

Eden glimpsed a light blush on his cheeks. It was cute.

"But mainly," Lilith continued, "I figured our lives will forever be entwined, so why not get to know each other better?"

Eden considered. Lilith had a point, and it would please Raven. It would make things smoother for her.

A pretty blonde server stopped beside them and pointed at Tate, who watched Raven and Asher's game. "He said you all need menus. How many?"

Lilith looked at Eden. "Five?"

She relented with a slight nod and then noticed they were a person short. "Where's Chloe?"

"With her dad. It's his birthday," Lilith said, sitting at the table.

Eden did the same. It seemed to signal the others to join because Tate, Raven, and Asher sat in the empty seats less than a minute later. Raven crossed her arms, kicking her chair with her heel.

The corner of Lilith's lip quirked. "Did your dad win the game?"

Raven nodded. "It's not fair. It's easier for him because he's so tall."

"He's as tall as me," Tate said.

She squinted and grinned. "Yeah, but your aim at pool is terrible."

Tate threw a straw at Raven. It bounced off her forehead. "Seems my aims not too bad."

She giggled and tossed it back at him. Warmth spread through Eden, watching everyone's easy interactions. A part of her lonely soul wanted to be part of it. Maybe she'd try, not just for her daughter, but for herself.

Turning to Lilith, Eden said, "Raven told me you and Asher have a date and place for the wedding. Congratulations."

"Thanks." Lilith leaned forward, excitement radiating off her. "We picked a place in Spring Lake. We're going to have the wedding on the beach."

Eden was happy for Asher. He was a good man and finally getting his much-deserved happily ever after.

Would she get one? Did she deserve one?

Next to her, Raven wiggle-danced in her seat. "Chloe and I are going to be junior bridesmaids. We are going to look sooo good."

"I'm going to be the Man of Honor," Tate said, gripping the back of Eden's chair.

She loved the untraditional twist. However, she couldn't resist teasing him, knowing she'd get to bask in the glow of another one of his gorgeous smiles.

"I bet you're going to look sooo good too." She turned, playfully eyeing his legs. "I can't wait to see you in heels."

He laughed, and his joy settled into her heart. His phone chimed from inside his pocket, and he pulled it out. "Then you're going to be very disappointed. I'm wearing a boring-old suit." Reading the message, his face clouded. "Fucking hell," he muttered.

"What's wrong?" she said at the same time Lilith asked who was calling.

He shoved his phone back into his pocket. There was a storm in his eyes. "No one. An insistent solicitor keeps calling and texting. I don't need an extended warranty on my truck." He smiled, but his expression looked as false as his words had sounded.

Understanding the need to sometimes bend the truth, Eden wouldn't question him. But she couldn't help but wonder who he was protecting—himself or someone else—and why.

CHAPTER SIXTEEN

Eden parked in her driveway. She turned and stared at the stars over the lake. Exhaustion pulled on her every limb. She hadn't had a day off in a week, and it had been a long one with too many emergencies and not enough sleep. She trudged to her house and flopped onto the porch swing. Grabbing the blanket she'd left outside last night, she covered her lap. The lush cushions and gentle breeze lolled her eyes closed, telling her the perfect place to sleep was her peaceful porch.

Her phone dinged with a text alert, and she startled from a light doze. Pulling her cell from her messenger bag, she read the message.

Tate: You still at work

Eden: Just got home

Tate: Hungry? I'll bring you dinner

Tempting. Eden: Too tired. I might sleep on my porch swing so I don't have to get up

Tate: Ok

She frowned, dropping her phone into her lap. Maybe they could see each other tomorrow, but probably not. Her show time was early afternoon, which meant another late night. Perhaps she'd have breakfast at his restaurant. They hadn't seen each other since they'd played pool—over a week ago.

Sighing, she took in the silhouetted trees with their barely-there budding leaves, moving to the moon reflecting off the water. Her eyes itched from lack of sleep, then blurred as she closed them. The crunch of someone walking on the gravel between the houses had them snapping back open.

Turning from the lake, she saw Tate approaching, holding what looked like a food container. Her breath caught as longing filled her lungs. She'd missed him. A lot.

Besides her abuela and Raven, she never missed anyone. Adding Tate to that shortlist made her heart squeeze.

However, when their gazes met, and he smiled, he settled into her heartbeats and filled her lungs with happiness—and her body with a dash of lust. Seriously, the jeans he wore should be illegal. They were straight-legged and worn, hugging him in all the right places.

He held up the container. "I'm dropping off dinner. You'll sleep better if your stomach is full."

Damn. Jean-porn, and he wanted to feed her. Was he trying to be irresistible?

As he stepped onto the porch, she said, "Bringing me food and looking good while doing it. How are you single?"

He paused mid-step and grinned. "Do I make a hot delivery boy?"

She laughed. "Indeed, you do."

He handed her the container. "I brought a salad with baked chicken. I figured you wouldn't want anything too heavy on the stomach since it's late."

"Thank you." She lifted the blanket and patted the space next to her. "Will you sit with me, or do you need to get back to work?"

"No, it's slow." He sat. "But if you want to eat, then crash, let me know and I'll take off."

"I might pass out once my stomach isn't screaming at me, but until then, I'd like to catch up with you." Now that he was in front of her, she couldn't bear to have him leave.

After handing her the food, he sat next to her and covered his legs with the blanket. "Not much to tell. The restaurant is steady, but the tourist season hasn't started. Gus worked for the previous owners, and he told me that will hit around

Memorial Day. So, I'm starting to prep for it." He patted her leg. "How has your week been so far?"

Instead of answering his question, she circled back to the one she'd asked him earlier, and he hadn't answered. "Why are you single?"

"Wow, you're really stuck on that." He chuckled. "Maybe no one is interested in dating me."

"Yeah, right." She opened the food container and inhaled deeply. The rich aroma of thyme and garlic filled her nose, making her mouth watered. The brine that Gus flavored the chicken with was amazing. "I worked at the bar with you, and women were constantly hitting on you. And that was the lunch crowd. I'm sure the weekenders are more aggressive."

He laughed. "Passing by the dance floor on a Saturday night can be hazardous. Some ladies are grabby."

That mental image soured her stomach, but she swallowed her toxic jealousy, studying the food.

"Why don't you date?" he asked.

She bit into the chicken and moaned. "Maybe I should date Gus. This is amazing."

Tate chuckled. "Too late. He's married."

"Well, damn." She knocked his shoulder. "And I asked you first. Why don't you have a girlfriend?"

"I was with someone for a while. Right before I moved here." He ran a hand through his hair and then traced a one-inch scar along his left eye with his thumb. "She was difficult. After her, I needed a break."

Eden vaguely remembered a petite blonde Tate had brought to Asher's Christmas dinner. The woman had given off an overly possessive vibe, turning sulky whenever he'd talked to anyone who was female and under sixty.

"What about you? Why don't you date?" he asked.

"How do you know I'm not seeing anyone?"

He leaned closer. His minty, warm breath teased her. "You kissed me the other day like there wasn't someone in your life."

Her cheeks heated against the chilly evening air, but she ignored the remark and focused on her food. She couldn't look at him. If she did, he'd see how much just thinking about their kiss affected her.

"I don't date because my career takes up nearly all my time. Any to spare is given to Raven." And even though it exposed her vulnerability, she continued. "Plus, it's messy. I haven't found someone worth the chaos." Or anyone willing to put up with hers if she ever let it escape her tight leash.

"I get that," he muttered, settling into the cushion.

After that, there seemed little else to say. She toed the porch swing, and it rocked gently as she ate the rest of her meal. He didn't seem to mind the silence, and for that, she was thankful. She appreciated a man who didn't need to fill empty spaces with useless noise.

She sighed in contentment, staring at the lake. "That was exactly what I needed. Thank you."

"Want me to go, so you can sleep?"

"In a few. I want to sit with the night and you for a little longer. Work up the energy to take a shower."

"Okay," he said.

The image of wet grass, sand, and inky lake, blurred before her. Then her head became too heavy for her neck. She kept jerking it upright as sleep pulled her under.

Warmth pressed into her side as Tate scooted closer. He put an arm around her. "Lean on me. I don't want your neck to snap," he teased.

His thick sweater was soft against her cheek. Sometime later, through a fog of sleep, Tate asked, "Where are your keys?"

"Front part of my messenger bag." She yawned. "Why?"

He brought her onto his lap, cradling her in his arms, and stood. "I can walk," she mumbled.

"Does this make you uncomfortable? Me holding you?" he asked. "If so, I'll put you down."

"I like it too much." She cuddled tighter into him, loving his firm body against hers. He felt so damn nice. And smelled like heaven. It made her want to sin. She nuzzled in his collar and dreamed naughty dreams of him. All too soon, she was being lowered onto something soft.

"Where are we?" she asked.

"Your bedroom," he told her. "Do you want to sleep or have me turn on the bath for you? You mentioned you wanted to shower."

"I'm too tired," she slurred, drunk on exhaustion.

He shifted, straightening, but she tightened her grip. "I'm not done cuddling with you. You're warm."

"Um, I can turn up the heat."

"It's not the same."

"That's the point," he chuckled. "I think when you wake in the morning, you'd rather have a warm house than some man in your bed."

"You aren't some man, Tate. You're my friend."

"Friend. Right," he muttered.

"Yes. One who was just naked in my dreams."

She heard him make a choking sound, but it barely registered in her sleepy brain. And the part that was working was busy conjuring up fantastic nude fantasies of the man holding her.

"What was I doing while naked?" he whispered.

"Everything I wanted." She pressed her lips to his throat.

He stilled, and she moved to his chin, then his mouth. Their kiss was fire, and she burned everywhere for him. She buried her hands in his soft, thick hair. Needing his hot skin against hers, she dragged her palms down his back, tugging at the hem of his shirt.

But then his magic mouth disappeared. He pressed his forehead against hers. His erratic breaths fanned her face. "We should stop."

She opened her tired eyes as her body wept. "Why?"

"You're half asleep." He rolled to his side. "I don't want to be your morning regret."

"My only regret right now is that you stopped." She wrapped her hands around the back of his neck, intending to bring his lips back to hers.

"You say that now" He sat up. "I should go."

"Please don't."

"I'm not going to sleep with you. Not until you're one hundred percent sure that's what you want."

"Fine," she huffed. "Lay with me for a few more minutes. Then I'll get in the shower...maybe you join me?"

He chuckled. The sound was deep and delicious. "I should head back to the restaurant. Close up. I'll come back in the morning, and we can talk."

She scooted closer, resting on his chest and yawning. "And then we take that shower together?"

He kissed the side of her head. "Sounds like the perfect plan."

CHAPTER SEVENTEEN

Tate was startled awake by his phone vibrating on a hard surface. He was on his side, fully dressed in last night's jeans and sweater, with his front pressed against a woman's delectable ass. She wasn't naked but could probably feel his hard-on through her thin cotton pants.

Through the unfamiliar open curtains, the sun was beginning to rise. The walls were stark white without any decorations. The squat dresser below the window was also empty except for a photo of Raven.

He was at Eden's house.

Shit. He'd fallen asleep. All night long. When was the last time that had happened?

His gaze fixed on the shiny black hair on the pillow in front of him. His plan had been to leave after she drifted off. For the last year, insomnia kept him company most nights, yet he'd fallen asleep in mere minutes with Eden in his arms.

Double Shit. He'd told his staff he wouldn't be gone long. That he was dropping off food for a friend. Then he'd disappeared. He needed to call his head waiter and make sure the night went smoothly and they were able to close up without him. Then he had to get his butt to the restaurant to open for breakfast.

And damn, how would Eden react when she woke to find him in her bed with freaking morning-wood.

"Are you trying to figure out how to sneak out before I wake up?" Eden asked in a voice laced with humor and sleep.

He chuckled. "No, but I might've been silently praying you recalled asking me to lie with you for a little bit."

"This is a little bit?"

There was still a note of teasing in her question, but he moved, putting space between them in case it was also a hint for him to get the hell out. "It was supposed to be... I was more tired than I realized."

"I wasn't asking you to leave." Before he could roll away, she squeezed the forearm he'd slung over her waist sometime during the night. Then she released her hold. "Unless you want to go."

He should check on his restaurant. "Nope. I'm good."

But what now? Should he talk about the weather? Or move aside her hair, exposing her neck, and kiss it? That sounded way more enticing than the weather. Even through his clothes, her warmth was heaven. *Damn it Don't go down that path, asshole.*

He squeezed his eyes shut, but that made it worse. Now he was picturing running this mouth along her perfect skin. *Shit.* Trying to be subtle, he shifted so his rock-hard dick wasn't pressed against her.

"What are you thinking about?" she asked, rolling to face him.

"I'm trying to figure out how to get rid of my boner," he admitted.

Her husky laughter filled the room as she crooked an elbow and rested her cheek on her palm. "Well, that was honest."

He smirked. "Too much?"

"No." She glanced south, then back to his face. There was heat in her eyes. "Just right."

He groaned, wiping a palm over his face. "Are we still talking about my honesty?"

"Is that what you want to be talking about?"

"Nope." He shifted onto his forearm and leaned toward her slowly, watching, waiting for any hesitation.

Her gaze fell to his mouth, and she tilted her chin, offering her lips. When his met hers, electric heat flooded him. He ran a hand up her back and into her hair, deepening the kiss.

She pressed him with her mouth and hands, then shifted on top of him. He gripped her hips and arched into the sweet heat between her legs. She rocked in a slow, languid thrust against him. He moaned into her kiss and clutched her ass, urging a rougher pace. She complied.

Her fingers skimmed along the waist of his jeans. "Do you want—"

His phone rang the chorus of Hozier's *Work Song*—the same tune that had woken him. The sound was a reminder he had responsibilities. He glanced at the nightstand, then back to Eden. But damn, he wanted her to finish her sentence.

He sucked her earlobe between his lips, reveling in her low moan. "Please finish your question."

His phone went off again. He glanced out the window. Gus would be arriving soon to get the kitchen ready for breakfast. And Tate had left last night and never returned. The Hill was his, and his staff depended on him.

"Sorry." He sighed. "I should see who's calling."

"Don't apologize. Your restaurant is important to you. So are those who work for you." Eden rolled off him, handing him his phone as the call cut off, going to voicemail.

He nodded, glad she understood. If only his body did too. His dick pressed painfully against his jeans. He adjusted himself before checking his phone. There were at least a dozen missed calls, voicemails, and messages. Yup. Nice, responsible boss.

Thankfully, he had great employees. The head waiter let him know the cash and receipts were in the safe. Gus had closed down the kitchen and locked up the restaurant before leaving.

He shot them a text, letting them know he was fine and that he owed them. Scrolling through the messages, he stopped at his sister's, and laughed.

"What so funny?" Eden asked.

"Just my know-it-all sister." He read the texts aloud.

Lilith: I called the Hill because you never answer your cell

Seems you delivered food to a certain friend at the end of the road & went AWOL

Did you stay for dessert ;-)

I'm not saying I told you so

But I told you so.

Running a finger along the collar of his T-shirt, Eden asked, "What was that last text about?"

"She and Asher are convinced you and I would be good together."

Eden shifted away from him slightly. "Hmm."

Something in her voice shifted his gaze from the phone to her. Her lips were pressed into a thin line. "What's wrong?" he asked.

"Nothing." But her tone said it was something.

Before he could press her for answers, his cell vibrated with an incoming message.

Gus: What happened to you last night? Did you melt the Ice Queen?

Irritation and dismay crashed into Tate. He clicked the side button, and the phone's screen went black. In its reflection, Eden's face smoothed out, all emotion disappearing. He'd lost her.

She scooted off him. "I'm going to take a shower. I can't believe I slept in my work clothes." Her tone was as blank as her expression.

His heart sank. Something in his sister's message had bothered Eden. And Gus's stupid, fucking comment had her shutting down.

"Eden, he didn't mean anything by that. He has stupid nicknames for every-one." He pointed at himself. "Remember, I'm Monk?"

"Fine. He can call me whatever he wants." She waved a hand while walking toward her bathroom. "I need to scrub off work."

Work or him?

She stopped at the bedroom door. "Help yourself to coffee if you want, but don't feel like you have to hang around."

Ouch. That was definitely a dismissal.

"What just happened?" he asked.

She half turned to him. "What are you talking about?"

"Why are you freezing me out?"

She stiffened. "When did I let you in?"

Tate shook his head. "What was last night? This morning in your bed? Are you telling me some stupid nickname has you walking away?"

"I don't care what he or anyone thinks of me," she scoffed.

"Then what is going on?"

"Didn't you hear me last night? I don't date. I don't have the time or want the chaos." She faced him fully. "I'm doing you a favor."

He muttered her words, trying to sort them out, to get them to make sense. "I don't get it. What's the favor?"

"I'm making sure things don't go any farther. Your sister and Asher are wrong. We wouldn't be great together."

Her words were a slap, and he flinched at their impact. "I don't agree. But if you're not interested, I'm not going to try to convince you."

"It's not—"

Heat bloomed in his chest, and he held up a hand, getting up from the bed. "You, but me. Got it. Eden, I don't need empty platitudes. My ego will survive your rejection."

Hell, maybe she was right and was doing him a favor. He'd left behind his old life for a fresh start. Getting entangled with another complicated woman wasn't a good idea. He was well aware of how quickly sweet could turn sour with them.

She came toward him, resting a hand on his chest. Her touch soothed him, which pissed him off a little. Did he have some damn defect that made him want women who weren't good for him?

Her fingers pressed into him. "But it's the truth. It *is* me. I'm a terrible person to date. An obsessive workaholic, married to my career. And I do like you, Tate. More than anyone in a really long time. But I will let you down."

He could see in her eyes that she believed every word, and his heart broke a little for her. She cared about him but was afraid of hurting him. That realization made him feel like shit, for his flash thought that she wasn't good for him. She was *too* good for him.

He took her hand from his chest. "I'm far from perfect. I'm impulsive, hard-headed. I get the hesitation to jump into a relationship. My last one was such a fucking disaster I haven't gone on a single date since we broke up. And haven't had a sliver of interest until meeting you."

Her eyes went wide. "Tate, I'm not the woman for you. I'm not relationship material."

"I'll I'm asking is for you to give us a try. Go on a date or two, see where it goes."

She sighed. "I can't."

"Can't or won't?"

"I don't want to try."

Really? He wasn't even worth exploring the possibility. A hollowness cracked within him. He nodded once. The lightness of the morning had fled, and he turned on heavy limbs.

Her hand slid to his waist, gripping his T-shirt. He gently removed her hold from him. "You've made yourself clear. Let me go, Eden."

"Please understand," she pleaded. "I don't want to lose our friendship. It's important to me."

The emptiness widened inside him. He'd miss her but had to make a clean break. "I can't be your friend. Acquaintance, sure, but not your friend."

Eden's nostrils flared. "Are you one of those guys who can't be friends with women?"

"I have plenty of female friends, but you can't be one of them."

"Did I read you wrong? Ten minutes ago, you were willing to sleep with me. But being my friend is too much of an effort?"

"Not at all. You're smart and funny, easy to be around. I love spending time with you, but we are way too attracted to each other to be only friends. Think about it. Every time were alone, we end up kissing."

Tate cupped her face, giving them one more try. "Eden, I honestly don't know where I want to take this, how much *I* can give you. But I'd like to give us a chance."

"I like you." She looked into his eyes. "As more than a friend. But I don't want to mess things up, and I always do. And when things fall apart between us, there will be consequences. I am Raven's mom, and Lilith will soon be her stepmom. We'll never be able to escape each other when we break up."

He tilted his head. "And you're certain we won't last?"

"It's a reasonable assumption. Most relationships don't work out, and I've never worked out with anyone. I'm considering all the angles."

"Only the shitty ones. What if none have worked out because they aren't me."

Her brows jumped, and a smile ghosted her lips. "You have a high opinion of yourself."

He chuckled. "No, I'm just considering the positive outcomes. Like, we get along great. Or we could amicably decide to stop seeing each other?"

"Possibly." He could tell she didn't believe it, and her next words proved it. "You'll eventually find me cold. Or I'll become fatigued at maintaining a relationship. *And* I need to focus on the most important one—the one with my daughter."

"Eden, you can have both."

"Maybe some women can, but not me. And I won't short-change my daughter again."

He dropped his hand from her face but didn't step away. "I won't pressure you into something you don't want."

She leaned into him. "I do want you, but I can't risk losing focus on fixing things between me and my daughter and also my fellowship. Perfection is imperative because when it's over, the hospital *has* to hire me. It's the only way to fix things between me and Raven. I don't have room for anything else."

He couldn't see why both weren't possible, but pushing the issue didn't seem like a good idea. Instead, he said, "Listen, let's take a breather." He ran a hand down her back, and her arms went around him. The simple gesture gave him hope. "You've told me before that you like to think things through. So, take your time. Think about it. Think about us. Will you do that?

She nodded against his chest.

"Okay." He brushed his lips lightly over her mouth and walked away.

Each step was a test of his willpower. She needed space, but he suspected she'd give into her fears, and they'd be over before they'd even begun.

CHAPTER EIGHTEEN

Eden scrambled a large skillet of eggs with machaca, tomatoes, and onion and slid them onto a small platter, practically skipping from stove to table. Raven had stayed the night. Yesterday, they'd made donuts and churros, eating them in front of the TV, laughing their butts off at a comedy Raven had selected. The evening had been perfect—a dream.

Setting the hot pan on the center of the table, she then grabbed the tortillas from the counter. "Breakfast is ready," she called down the hall to Raven.

A few minutes later, she shuffled into the kitchen, blurry-eyed and yawning. Sliding into the closest chair, she sniffed the air. "The food smells good. You should've woken me, I could've helped."

She handed Raven a plate. "It's an easy meal. But, if you'd like, I can give you the recipe. Or help you prepare it next time you stay the night." Damn, she loved that thought—Raven staying over becoming a regular occurrence.

It also made her think of the last person who'd stayed over. Tate. That had been a week ago, but it felt like yesterday. Probably because their morning together played on repeat in her fantasies. The press of his hard body against hers. His perfect mouth exploring her.

"What's this called?" Raven asked, grabbing a tortilla.

"Huh?" Eden blinked, focusing on her daughter.

She pointed at the food.

"Oh. Machaca con huevos."

"Most of the recipes you've taught me are Mexican dishes." Raven filled her tortilla. "Dad said my grandma was American and my grandpa was Mexican. Was he the cook in your house?"

Eden wasn't sure how she felt about Raven asking Asher—not her—questions about her family. Was she so standoffish about her childhood that even her daughter wasn't comfortable broaching the subject? Shame lodged in her throat, and she swallowed her remorse. Raven was asking now, and Eden would answer.

"Like you, I didn't take an interest in cooking until I was older—around thirteen or fourteen, living with your bisabuela. Most of what she taught me were Mexican dishes."

"That's cool." Raven tilted her head. "Maybe she can show me even more dishes while she's teaching me to speak Spanish. You remember, right? You said she'd teach me when she moves here?"

She looked so damn earnest it gripped Eden's heart and squeezed. Raven wanted to be part of her bisabuela's life. And Eden's. She didn't deserve her daughter's love, but she'd hold on to it, keep it close.

Raven took a bite, and around a large mouthful, said, "This is my new favorite breakfast. I want the recipe."

Sharing her favorite childhood breakfast with her daughter was a simple but perfect gift. A fuzzy, soft warmth filled Eden. Raven loving the meal made the moment priceless to Eden.

"Does most of your family speaks Spanish?" she asked.

It surprised Eden that Raven had so many questions. This was the first time the topic had come up, and she seemed intrigued, really invested.

"My family is yours too," Eden said gently.

"I know. But I've never met them. And the only one you talk about is your grandma." She paused. "My great-grandma."

Her words were another slap of failure that landed hard on Eden. "I'm sorry. I should talk more about them, but it makes me sad," she admitted.

"That's why I don't ask. Whenever I mention your parents, you turn gloomy." Her eyes filled will tears. "If you or Dad or Lilith died, I don't know what I do. And both of yours died."

Eden's stomach twisted, hearing her half-truth on her daughter's tongue. Her dad had died, but her mother was probably alive and still living in New Mexico. Eden rubbed the scar near her collarbone through her thin T-shirt. Her mother was dead to Eden and would *never* meet Raven. Therefore, there was no harm in speaking around the lie.

"But you should know about your family. Like your dad said, your grandfather was first-generation Mexican-American, but your grandma was American. She demanded we speak English in our home. Though when she wasn't there, Papa spoke to me in Spanish." Eden smiled. So many memories of him had disappeared, but she could still recall his deep, protective voice. It always held love and sunshine. "As I'm sure you saw during our video calls, bisabuela switches back and forth between the two languages. She likes to practice English with me but slips into Spanish if she forgets an English word or is too tired or angry."

"Did your abuela," Raven stumbled over the foreign word, but she kept going, "always live with you or just...later?"

"My parents had a duplex. Abuela stayed in the one above us when visiting from Mexico. Later, when I moved in with her, she found us a place closer to my school. She still lives there." Eden tapped her fork against her lips. "Do you remember meeting her in person? It was a while ago, right after you turned five. She and I came here for a quick visit."

Raven shook her head, frowning.

"Well, we'll have to change that."

Hopefully, she'd get the job at the hospital, and her abuela would move to Michigan. But until then... "I'll see if she's up for a Midwest vacation. She's terrified of flying, but if I go to New Mexico and fly back with her, she'll come."

"Or..." Raven smiled, and it held a mountain of adventure. "We could visit her. I've never been there."

The suggestion sparked delight and panic in Eden. She'd love to share some of her childhood with her daughter—but only pieces, like her papa and abuela. The rest was better off forgotten.

"We'll see. I'd have to talk to your dad and find out if it is even possible with my work schedule." Raven's smile weakened, so Eden quickly added, "If not now, we can visit after my fellowship." This was a lie. She wanted to keep her daughter and past far from each other.

"When does it end?" Raven asked.

Eden took a sip of her orange juice. "Soon. Middle of August."

Raven set down her tortilla and slumped in on herself. Eden tilted her head, pursing her lips. Why had the lightness and joy drained from her daughter? "What's wrong?"

"Is Tate your boyfriend?"

Eden nearly dropped her cup as fireworks went off in her chest. The shift in mood and topic gave her whiplash. And she had no idea how to reply. She definitely wanted him naked and in her bed. Might want to date him too. However, with her hectic work hours, she'd managed only a few quick texts with Tate in the last week. She had to talk to him before she could answer Raven.

She settled for the technical truth. "We're friends."

"Not *boy*friend?

Eden shook her head.

"Figures," Raven sounded more like a teenager than a kid. "Why don't you have a boyfriend?"

Because emotions are messy and I'm not good with them.

Men found her cold, and she didn't find them worth the effort. But she wasn't about to unload all that onto her child. "I'm busy with work. On my days off I'd rather spend them with you than some guy."

Raven glowed at Eden's words but looked like she was trying to hide it. "Uncle Tate isn't some guy. And you have no life."

"Ouch. I have a fulfilling job and a great daughter. What else do I need?"

"Friends. A guy...or a girl, if you like them too."

Eden choked on her orange juice. Did her *eleven-year-old daughter* just casually suggest her mom might be bisexual? She'd read in parenting books that encouraging open conversations about sex and sexuality was important.

She swallowed and waded into uncharted waters. "Um, if you have any questions about dating or sexuality, you can always ask me."

Raven clunked her elbows onto the table and stared at Eden across the table, appearing older than her years. "You're changing the subject."

"I'm not. What were we even talking about?" The first part was true, but not the second. She remembered; her dating life—or rather, the lack of it.

"We were talking about Uncle Tate," Raven said.

Eden pointed at Raven's plate. "Are you finished?"

"Yes."

She gathered their dishes. "Why are you stuck on him?"

Raven rolled her eyes. "I'm not dumb. You guys act all flirty around each other."

"I think you're mistaking friendliness for flirtiness." The lie slipped out before she could stop it.

Did it matter that her fib wasn't to deceive—more that it was unfair to make assumptions before speaking to Tate? He might have changed his mind about wanting to date her. So why risk confusing her daughter?

Raven stood, startling Eden. "Fine. Whatever." She grabbed her phone. "I'm going to the porch."

Eden closed the dishwasher. "Do you want to walk along the lake after I clear up the dishes?"

"No. That's boring." Raven started for the door.

"Wait."

She stopped but stared at her phone.

"What's wrong?" Eden asked.

"Nothing."

"Why are you mad at me?"

"I'm not."

Nervous energy thrummed through Eden. This disagreement would *not* go south like it always had with her mother. For one, Eden was sober. She inhaled, counting to five. "Yes. You are."

"Fine. I'm lying." Raven shrugged, scrolling through her cell. "I'm like my mom."

Her words punched Eden in the gut. "I don't understand why you're upset. Is it because I'm only friends with Tate? Why do you want us to date?"

"Because he's nice. Plus, you hate it here. If you're with him, you won't leave," Raven shouted.

A shock of cold spread through her, and she fell back a step. "I—I've been here for almost a year," she stuttered. "What makes you think I'm leaving? Or that I hate it here?"

"Because you hate the cold. And because you always leave." Raven twisted, heading toward her bedroom and slamming the door shut.

Eden followed Raven and knocked. "Talk to me."

Her only answer was a quiet shuffling. A minute or two later, the door swung open, and Raven stood in front of Eden in a pair of jeans and a green T-shirt.

"Talk to me," she repeated.

"I don't want to." There was a waver in Raven's voice that sliced Eden's heart "I'm going for a walk." She stepped around Eden.

"I'll go with you."

"No."

That one word was a bullet to Eden's heart. She pushed around the pain and asked, "Will you at least tell me where you're going?"

"To The Hill."

Eden trailed Raven to the edge of her driveway and watched her stalk up the gravel road. Once she stepped around to the front of the restaurant, Eden slumped to her porch and dropped onto the swing. She'd never seen Raven that upset. Heck, they'd never even argued before. And a teeny-tiny part of her rejoiced she hadn't lost control—hadn't turned into her mother when pushed by her daughter.

Sucking in a shaky breath, she went to her bedroom and grabbed her cell from the nightstand. She texted Tate.

Eden:Are you at The Hill?

Tate:Yup. What's with Raven? She looks upset.

Eden:We had a fight. What is she doing?

Her phone rang, and Tate's name flashed across the screen.

"She's playing one of the pinball games," he said after Eden answered. "Are you okay?"

"Not really," she admitted. "This is the first time we've fought. And I'm still not sure what set her off."

"She's almost a teenager. Isn't that reason enough?" Tate joked. "What started it?"

She cleared her throat; thankful they weren't talking in person. "You. She wanted to know if we were dating. Then it somehow steamrolled into her being convinced I'm leaving." Hopelessness nearly slammed her flat. "I can't...I don't know what to do."

"Give her time to cool off. I'm sure once she settles down, she'll let you know what's really going on."

"Do you mind if she stays there?" Failure suffocated Eden. She hadn't turned into her childhood nightmare but was still drowning in her inadequacies as a parent.

"Not at all. I'll keep an eye on her."

"Thank you. I'll be there in about an hour. Hopefully that will be enough time for her to cool down and hate me a little less."

"She doesn't hate you."

"Thanks, Tate." She hung up, unsure if she was thanking him for his gentle words, watching Raven, or being such a kind man. Whatever it was, it cracked some of the ice in her cold heart.

CHAPTER NINETEEN

Eden ended the call with Tate and let the numbness settle over her. It was better than the swell of emotions scratching and clawing at her fragile calm. The minute hand on the twin-bell wind-up clock on her nightstand ticked like the strike of a judge's gavel. She watched the numbers blur as they passed the three, the four, the five. After twenty minutes, she couldn't keep away from Raven any longer and left for The Hill.

Stepping inside, she spotted Tate talking to a customer at one of the corner booths. He waved at her, then pointed to the two pinball machines. Raven's back was to the room, her palms slamming against the side of the middle machine. Biting the inside of her cheek, Eden walked toward her daughter, stopping beside her.

Raven turned from the game. "I'm sorry. I was mean."

Her eyes filled with tears, and Eden wished she was the type of mom who was easy with her affections. She'd hold her daughter and know all the right things to say. Instead, she remained glued to the worn laminate. "It's fine." She sounded rigid.

"Is it, really?" Raven sniffed, wiping her nose.

Christ. She had to do better as a mother.

Lifting stiff arms, she brought them around Raven. She fell into them, and all the tension Eden had been holding vanished, making her temporarily weightless.

They held each other tight, and then Eden cupped her daughter's face. "Raven, "I'm not going anywhere. I applied for the fellowship at UMich to be with you."

"But what about when it ends?"

Eden's heart pinched. "First, I want to say, I don't need a man, job, or any other reason to be here except for you. *You* are the reason I'm here. Do you understand?"

Raven nodded, smiling, and dabbed her nose with her sleeve.

Eden ran a palm down her daughter's soft hair so much like hers. "I've applied for a permanent position at Michigan for when my fellowship ends. I want to stay. With you."

"You do? You promise to stay?"

She let go of Raven. Making promises was unwise. They often broke, and this one had fragile fault lines. First, she had to get the job over Dr. Leeday. Then she had to convince Abuela to move to Michigan.

Yet she needed to ease the pain and worry in her daughter's eyes and voice. "I promise."

Raven's arms wrapped around Eden again, hugging her so tight breath whooshed from her. Her strong embrace left her light-headed with relief. "I love you."

She hoped Raven believed her. If not, it didn't matter. She'd spend the rest of her life proving it. When they pulled apart, Eden floundered for something to lighten the mood. She did *not* want to cry in a restaurant full of people. The pinball machine trilled and dinged, demanding more quarters.

A mischievous grin lit Raven's face. "Let's make a bet."

"What are we betting?" A tingle ran up the base of Eden's neck.

Raven hip-bumped the race-car-themed machine next to them. "If I get the highest score, you have to take me to New Mexico."

Little fireworks went off in Eden's chest. She loved Raven's interest, but what would happen if her supposedly dead grandma showed up at their house in Albuquerque when they were there? She had recently been calling Abuela. "Want to go somewhere else instead? Your bisabuela will be moving here." Hopefully. "What about Oregon. I've always wanted to go there."

Raven bounced from foot to foot. "But I want to see where you grew up."

The noise in the restaurant swelled, and Eden sucked in air to calm her heart. When it slowed, she deflected. "What if I win? What do I get?"

"Um." Raven tapped her chin. "I'll leave my phone at home next time I stay the night."

A bark of laughter escaped from Eden, even as her happiness swelled at the mention of Raven staying over again. "Wow! Are you sure you're willing to take that risk?"

She nodded and steepled her fingers, pressing them into her lips. "Sooo... are we betting?"

They shouldn't but dimming the hope in Raven's eyes felt cruel. Plus, Eden had already made a promise of staying in Michigan and it might not be possible to keep. What was one more to add to her pile of hope? There was time to figure out both.

She held out her hand. "Deal."

Raven's grin was worth the stones of anxiety in Eden's stomach. She jingled the change in her pocket. "Let's play."

A tingling filled her limbs, making her buoyant with contentment. She let it settle into her soul. She'd argued with her daughter, but they'd come out the other side stronger, not broken. Maybe they wouldn't end up like her and her mother.

Her serenity lasted until she scanned the bar, and her gaze landed on Tate. He was another who made her feel too much—too many dangerous emotions. She pinged from lust to happiness to hope, then ponged to fear, worry, and possible loss of control.

A near-silent hope whispered that her daughter had just proved she didn't need the façade of perfection. Maybe Tate wouldn't expect it either. Perhaps she could loosen her tight hold on control and hold *him*.

The pinball machine trilled and flashed, and Raven whooped and spun in a quick circle. "That was three-hundred points!"

Eden slid quarters into her machine. "Enjoy the lead while you can, because you're about to lose."

Before pulling the ball's lever, she looked over her shoulder, stealing another glance at Tate. He was still watching her with those beautiful eyes. They told her she might win everything if she was brave enough to believe in him—in the possibility of them.

CHAPTER TWENTY

A knock on Eden's front door pulled her from an article on navigating pre-teen emotions. She glanced back at her computer and considered ignoring the visitor. The day with Raven had been draining, from the fight, the make-up, then losing at pinball—and what the loss could mean for her. Eden sighed. Hopefully Raven would forget about the bet.

All of it had her emotionally empty, and she wasn't up for small talk. But...what if it was Tate?

She closed her laptop, even though him visiting was unlikely. Besides her phone call this afternoon and a quick greeting at his restaurant, they hadn't spoken. And he hadn't stopped by her place since he'd asked if they could be more than friends.

But on her next day off, they would talk. They had to because Eden was nearly certain she knew what she wanted—him.

She backtracked to the bathroom for her robe. After leaving The Hill and dropping Raven off at her dad's, Eden showered and dressed, skipping all her undergarments. Whoever was waiting on her porch didn't need to be welcomed by her nipples poking a hello in her thin pajama shirt.

Unless it was Tate on her stoop, then the greeting was perfect.

Her breath caught when she opened the door. An hour ago, a storm had blown through, leaving angry splashes of blue and pink clouds in the darkening sky. But the true beauty was Tate standing before her like cozy comfort and delicious sex.

"Wow," she exhaled.

He glanced behind him at the lake and the setting sun. "Was that for me or the view?"

"Both."

"Damn, I should visit more often. You're good for a man's ego. And my view is damn spectacular too." His gaze had drifted to the vicinity of her chest.

She glanced down. Her robe had fallen open, and, yup, her nipples were as happy to see him as the rest of her.

He returned to her face, and his eyes shifted from lust to concern. "Anyway, I just wanted to check on you. It seemed like you had a rough day."

Why did this man have to be so sweet? She was fast discovering she had a kink for kind, sexy men.

She leaned against the door frame. "Raven and I are good, but damn, the drama wore me down. I feel like...I was going to give some analogy, but I'm too tired to think of any."

"How about; girls and their mood swings are a rough rollercoaster to ride." His lips twitched, telling her he was teasing, but she *had* to push back.

"Oh, please. Girls? Men's feelings and egos are as delicate and easily hurt as your testicles."

Tate's laughter bounced across the lake. "You might have us there." He backed up. "Anyway, if you're exhausted, I'll go. I just wanted to check on you."

He should leave, but that was the last thing she wanted. "Want to watch the sunset?" She pointed to the porch swing.

He gripped the back of his neck. "Last time we sat together on that swing, I ended up in your bed."

She rubbed the rough texture of his Henley. "Did you mind?"

"I most definitely do not," he said, walking to the swing and sitting.

Leaning inside her foyer, she grabbed the thick throw used for the swing. As she sat beside Tate, he asked, "Did you find out what really upset Raven? I get I'm an awesome catch, but there has to be more to it than us dating."

She bumped his shoulder, laughing. But recalling her fight with Raven hollowed out a little of Eden's heart. "Basically, it comes down to me being a crappy mother."

He turned sideways, facing her. "How are you a crappy mother?"

"Are you kidding me?" she scoffed. "I left my daughter for medical school. I put myself first." *Let my fear own me.*

"What makes Asher's career goals more important than yours. He could have come with you to California."

She shook her head. "His parents were training him and Hope to take over the family's construction company. He would have been letting them down. And—"

"*And* you'd been accepted to one of the top medical schools. He could have taken over the family business after you finished."

She shook her head again. "As I'm sure you know, back then, he was on probation and wasn't allowed to leave the state."

"Ah, yeah. That's right." Tate scratched his trim beard. "You were both in an impossible situation."

"Maybe, but I didn't even try to make it work. I gave away my daughter and ran, too afraid to stay."

He studied her, seeming to see way too much. "What were you afraid of?"

"Giving up my career." She fidgeted with the blanket, using it as an excuse to break eye contact.

"What else?"

"Being a mother." *Becoming my mother.*

"Makes sense. You were so young."

"Yes, that's part of it." The only part she'd share with him. Reaching under the collar of her shirt, she felt the old burn scar covered by a beautiful marigold tattoo. "But also I feared that if I gave up my dream of becoming a surgeon I'd resent Raven. Maybe take it out on her. So, I left."

He took her hand. "You left the state, but not your daughter. Asher said you called all the time and visited on school breaks."

Eden raised a brow. "You and Asher talk about me—about what kind of mother I am?"

"No. Me and a friend from Crowley Construction were over Asher's. The guy is recently divorced, and his ex was moving to Chicago with their two kids. He knew you'd lived out of state and was asking Asher questions on how you two make it work with Raven."

She blinked from Tate's handsome profile and her past to the lake and sky. Darkness had fallen quickly, and a few stars were already twinkling. "We missed the sunset."

"Watching you was better."

Amusement flickered through her. "That was smooth."

"I know, right? I impressed myself." He grinned, settling deeper into the swing. Resting an arm around her shoulder, he tucked her into his side. "Is this okay?"

"It's more than okay." She pressed closer into him. His warmth and earthy scent soothed and excited her.

"Good. With the sun gone, it's cold and I don't want your desert blood to freeze."

She turned to him. He was a breath away from her lips. Her pulse climbed up her throat as the decision to stay friends or become more hovered like a kiss between them.

Swallowing, she bridged the distance and pressed her lips against his, begging to see where he'd take it.

And her.

CHAPTER TWENTY-ONE

It seemed Tate was ready to take her wherever she wanted to go. One of his hands slid into her hair as he deepened the kiss. Need shot through her, killing all restraint. She shifted onto his lap and straddled him.

Needing to see this gorgeous man naked—and this time, not through a foggy shower stall, she tugged at the hem of his shirt. He obliged, gripping the back of his Henley and pulling it over his head before tossing it aside. The dim glow from the moon offered little illumination, and she briefly considered turning on the porch light. Instead, she used touch to see him, running her palm from chest to stomach, savoring firm muscle and the delightful dusting of hair.

He teased one of her nipples with his thumb through the thin cotton of her shirt. She moaned. Desire owned her, and she arched into his palm while shamelessly rocking against him, demanding more friction. He hissed against her neck and stood, gripping her ass. She wrapped her legs around his waist, relishing how his hard ridges pressed into her soft curves.

"I need more space for the things I want to do to you," he said.

She nodded as her mind whirled with all the possibilities. Kissing her, he walked toward the door. Once inside, she felt and heard him kick it closed. Then they headed toward her bedroom. He stopped in front of the California King, letting go of her bottom. Her legs slid to the ground. In two quick moves, she removed her shirt and lounge pants, standing naked before him.

He cursed. "No bra or underwear." He ran a hand down her side, stopping at her hip. "I want to touch and taste you everywhere. I don't know where to start."

She reached for his belt, unbuckling it. "Start by getting as naked as me."

He removed his boots and socks. Then his jeans. The man was glorious. From his firm chest and flat stomach, all the way to his magnificent thighs. Her gaze snagged on his impressive erection. Her mouth watered, and her body throbbed for him.

Stepping closer, he encircled her in his arms and kissed her in a carnal but somehow affectionate way. His touch almost reached her heart, making it trip in trepidation. She wanted to sleep with him but not think past their mutual satisfaction—the future was too daunting to consider.

Focusing on sex and pleasure, she said, "I have condoms in my nightstand."

He nodded, walking around the bed. Damn, his ass was perfection. Her gaze involuntarily shifted to his back because the tattoo that had caught her attention all those weeks back in the shower was in full view. It was stunning. There was a tree with vibrant green leaves at the very edges of the branches. The thick, gnarled trunk traveled down his spine with twisting roots spreading along his lower back. Hmm... it turns out she was a woman turned on by tattoos, at least when they were on Tate.

As he pulled a foil packet from the drawer, she watched him, sliding a hand between her legs. She moaned as pleasure sparked through her. His gaze bounced from her busy fingers to her face as he put on the condom.

"That is the hottest fucking thing I've ever seen." He stroked himself a few times then crawled up her body.

Making love to her mouth with his lips, he gently pushed aside her hand and took over. And holy hell, the man had been paying attention. He touched her just the way she loved.

He stopped before she fell over the edge of bliss, shifting away. She gasped at the loss of his touch. Then he kissed down her body, and she slid her hand through his hair. He stopped at her hip and bit. She jumped and laughed at the tickle torture.

"Keep going?" he asked.

"Um, you stopped with your magic fingers right before I came." She arched her hips. "Yes! Keep going."

His husky laugh brushed against her heat before his mouth covered her. Within minutes, his tongue and lips had her orgasm building once more, but he slowed his pace and pressure again before it could crash.

She groaned and considered pressing into him and taking what she desperately needed. Her gaze slammed into his, and she saw the hot mischief in his eyes. Realization dawned on the horizon of her lust.

"Are you withholding my orgasm?" she asked.

His wicked grin was all the answer she needed, but he said, "I want you to come so hard you become addicted to my touch."

She tilted her head. "Why? You worried you'll be addicted to mine?"

"I already am. Your touch. Your smile. Your quick brain. All of it. All of you."

Her heart fluttered, and her smile faltered. Hearts shouldn't be involved in what they were doing. This should be only about pleasure.

"Are you okay?" The concern in his eyes melted something within her. His combination of sweet and sexy was a dangerous mix.

She needed this to be sex. Only sex. That's all she could handle right now. Wiggling her hips and gripping his chin playfully, she said, "No. I'm worried your teasing might kill me."

He laughed, moving up, his tongue drawing lazy circles around her right breast. "What doesn't kill you makes your orgasms stronger."

Settling between her legs, he thrust *on* her, but not *in* her. The friction took her almost there. She was so aroused that the need to climax was as crucial as breathing.

Wanting him on edge as much as her, she pushed his shoulder. "Flip onto your back."

He obeyed, and she couldn't deny that it turned her on more. She straddled him, taking him in slowly, watching with satisfaction as his eyes glazed with hunger.

"Fuck. You feel good," he grated.

"Just good?"

He opened his mouth, probably to reply, but she rolled her hips, and his only word was her name on a moan. She rode him until his breath became choppy and his fingers dug into her waist. Then, with an enormous helping of willpower, she stilled and leaned down, kissing him.

He greedily accepted her lips, but she broke their connection when he thrust. His loud groan of frustration made her giggle.

"Woman, you're cruel," he said, tickling her sides. She loved how he was playful inside and outside of the bedroom.

She nibbled along his jaw, palming his balls. "I don't know what you mean. I'm just making sure your climax is fantastic."

His reply was between a chuckle and a grunt. Eden squeaked in surprise as he flipped her and slid back inside her. She couldn't stop her hips from meeting his pace. When his thrusts became deeper, her orgasm coiled around her.

"If you stop now, I'll...I don't know what I'll do, but you won't like it," she panted.

His strained laughter vibrated against her lips. "I have no intention of stopping. You feel too fucking good."

He kissed her, swallowing her scream of bliss as her climax slammed into her. As shockwaves of pleasure pulsed through her, he began to shake. She held him tight as he groaned her name through his orgasm.

His plan had worked. She was addicted to him.

CHAPTER TWENTY-TWO

Tate couldn't remember a morning when he'd awoken feeling this good. A night of fantastic sex and then waking to use Eden's miracle shower was the ticket to paradise.

Wrapping a fluffy towel around his waist, he left the bathroom. Entering Eden's bedroom, he found her already dressed in dark blue scrubs and brushing her hair. The downward motion through her silky strands was mesmerizing.

Damn, she made a sexy surgeon. She'd fit in on those popular hospital TV dramas.

She pointed to the dresser. "I poured you coffee."

"Thanks." He kissed her before taking the mug.

Her gaze ran over him. A hot and hungry look simmered in her warm brown eyes. "You need to get dressed before you distract me and make me late for work," she said.

He picked up his discarded jeans from last night and tossed his towel on the bed. "How much time do you have?"

"For what I want to do to you..." She embraced him from behind, her hand traveling south and cupping him. He hissed, his dick already standing at attention. "And you to me. Not nearly enough time."

"Woman," he groaned as she stroked him once, then moved to her dresser. "You're killing me. When's your next day off?"

She grimaced. "Thursday, but hopefully, some days will be slow so I can leave when my shift actually ends."

"That'd be nice," he said, pulling up and zipping his jeans.

Actually, it'd be fucking fantastic, but he was playing it cool. They were new, and she'd hesitated to give them a try. He didn't want to come on too strong and scare her off.

"Where's my shirt?" He hoped it didn't smell like stale restaurant food and sweat.

Eden's eyes widened. "On the front porch."

"Shit. I bet it's covered in dew."

"Maybe, but you can toss it into the dryer." She wiggled her brows. "Or arrive at work shirtless. That might get you some good tips."

He laughed, then kissed her neck as she applied an enticing shade of red lipstick. Grabbing his coffee along the way, he went to the porch to find his shirt.

His Henley was dangling half off the swing. And, yup, damp with dew. Picking it up, his gaze was pulled to the lake. Fog clung to the shore and surrounding trees, giving off a calm and eerie vibe. He sipped coffee taking in the peaceful hour.

"Morning, Tate!" a woman called.

He cough-choked on his swallow, glancing around. Olivia sat on her porch with her hands wrapped around a mug with a huge smile on her face.

"Morning." He waved, only to remember he was holding his shirt in that hand. He quickly lowered his arm. Maybe she hadn't noticed he was shirtless.

Olivia's grin widened. "Did I ever tell you how glad I am to have found this place?"

"Uh, no. I'm glad you like the house."

"Yeah, it's fine." She winked. "But I like the view more."

He snorted, shaking his head and turning to go inside. "I'll see you this afternoon. Remember, I need two extra blueberry pies."

"Got it. Oh, tell Eden I said good morning, and I'm *really* looking forward to having lunch with her on Friday."

He nodded, his nerves tingling as he pushed open the front door. Olivia was a sweet woman but a talker. His being here, this early in the morning and with only half his clothes on, was bound to travel fast.

Eden stepped from the kitchen, a travel mug in one hand and a breakfast bar in the other. "What took you so long?" she asked.

"Olivia was on her front porch. She saw me." He indicated his bare chest. "I'm sure she'll have a great time busting my balls this afternoon when she drops off my pie order."

Eden's shoulders stiffened. "I don't need her gossiping about who I slept with last night."

He sucked his lips into his mouth, biting on them and his disappointment. "Was last night a one-off?"

"I don't know what this is." Her tone sounded like she was speaking to an errant child. "We slept together once. I need time to process."

Process what? Either she was interested, or she wasn't. Tate inhaled deeply. He wouldn't let his wounded ego get in the way. Not this time. "I see. Okay. You better get to work. When I see Olivia today at the restaurant, I'll ask her to keep quiet about me being here."

He shook out his Henley, seeing if it was too wet to wear. The idea of hanging around while it tumbled in the drier had lost its appeal.

"Tate." His name came out like a tired sigh. She came around and stood in front of him. "I'm sorry. I'm not mad, and definitely not with you. Just the suddenness of it. We spent a single night together, and now we have to announce to the town's busybodies we are seeing each other."

That was harsh. "Olivia likes to talk, but she's also kind. If you don't want her to say anything, she won't."

"I didn't mean her, but if she mentions it to anyone or teases you at the restaurant, the gossipers who don't like me, will talk and judge. Don't you remember that old man? The night we were playing pool. And all we were doing was playing pool."

"Who cares? All that matters is what we think about us." He searched her eyes. "And how do you feel about us?"

She rested a hand on his chest. "I want more of you."

A heaviness on his limbs lifted. "Are you sure?"

"Yes. Honestly, I'd wanted a few days to process. That's just how I work." She sighed, leaning into his chest. He wrapped his arms around her. "Plus, I'm nervous because our lives are entwined, and I'm worried about the fallout when it ends."

"There you go again, having us over before we've barely begun." He held in an aggravated groan. He liked Eden a lot, but her doomed outlook was discouraging.

"I'm being realistic. Relationships don't last with me. I don't have time for them, and usually they aren't worth the effort." She hugged him tighter. "But you are, and I want to try with you."

Wow, she had a talent for offering hope and hopelessness in equal measure. It was brutal and honest. And he loved it. She might crush his heart, but at least she'd warned him instead of treating it like a toy store trinket.

"Damn." She sounded defeated.

He leaned back and looked at her. "What's wrong?"

"Yesterday I told Raven that you and I are strictly friends." Eden chewed on her bottom lip. "Now she's going to think I lied to her."

"I'm sure if you asked Olivia not to say anything until you've talked to Raven, she'll do as you ask. She may tease us, but she'd respect your wishes."

Eden nodded. "Yeah, you're right."

"As for us," he said, running his hand up her arms and resting them on her shoulders, "No PDA until you talk to Raven."

"Thank you for understanding." Eden stood on her toes and kissed him. He deepened it.

His phone chimed from her bedroom, breaking the moment. Guilt filled the space between them. "I'm sorry for getting a little pissy with you. I'm an asshole sometimes," Even though he was relieved that she wanted to date, he shouldn't have pushed and just let her process.

Was he kidding? Even when he was clearly frustrated, he'd be calm and kind. "You?"

"Um, yea. I've been told that I'm your typical clueless, impatient man."

"Tate, whoever said that is the clueless one." She kissed him as his phone trilled again. Then again. And yet again. She backed toward the front door. "Stay. Dry your shirt and call back whoever clearly needs to talk to you. Your family and friends seem rather protective. If you don't answer, they might send out a search party."

It was probably Lil. She and him were supposed to go to their dads for dinner tonight. He kissed Eden one more time before she left. Going into her bedroom, he grabbed his phone and swiped up on the screen. The call was from an unknown number, but as he read the first text, the caller became crystal, sickening clear.

This is Katrina.

You didn't reply to emails and blocked my number

Real cute

Asshole

Stop ghosting me

Be a real man and answer

Call me. We need to talk

I'm sorry, babe. I miss you and it makes me emotional

I love you and I'm worried about you.

Call me. I need to know you are ok. I just need to know you're ok

Please reply. I miss you. I love you.

Tate hesitated. She did have panic attacks. Bad ones. Maybe he should let her know he was fine. *No.* He didn't know which Katrina he'd get. The sweet, calm, and understanding woman or the irrational, manipulative one.

He deleted the texts and blocked the number but couldn't erase his unease. This was the fifth unknown number he'd blocked from her, and he lost count of the emails he'd deleted unread.

Dread clogged his chest. While dating, Katrina visited Asher's house several times for holiday gatherings. If she came looking and found him, what trouble would she bring? Would she tire of calling and emailing and start physically looking for him?

Fear replaced dread, not for himself, but for Eden.

One time he'd gone out to lunch with a female coworker. Autumn had left work later that day to find her car keyed and all the air out from her tires. The next day, he'd mentioned it to Katrina. She'd called Autumn a whore and told him to stay away from her. He'd laughed, figuring she couldn't be serious. She'd thrown the TV remote at him, striking him in the side of the face. Later, she told him the remote had slipped from her hand. She'd also denied doing anything to the car. Both had been a lie.

And that was all because he'd gone out to eat with a *friend*. What would happen if she saw him with Eden?

CHAPTER TWENTY-THREE

Eden took a sip of freshly squeezed lemonade. Delicious. Whoever had put the drink on The Hill's new menu was a genius. The tart sweetness was perfection on her tongue and had her dreaming of summertime. The scent of sunshine, freshly cut grass, and barbeque also helped.

She removed her laptop from her messenger bag on the iron seat next to her and adjusted the table's umbrella. Tate had warned her that early May could be a tease, but the warmth rejuvenated her summer soul. There was no way she'd sit inside The Hill today, even if the sun's glaring brightness made it difficult to read her computer screen.

Glancing around the bustling and busy patio, she spotted Tate talking with the town's upscale thrift store owner. As they chatted, one of his hands rested on the back of an empty chair at the proprietor's table while his other gestured in open, gentle movements. Tate's smile was its usual sexy mix of calm and playful. Her gaze roamed over his body. He was mouth-watering in dark jeans and a fitted navy T-shirt. The color complimented his dark auburn hair, and his clothing choices accentuated her favorite features, his ass and biceps.

Checking him out unobserved thrilled her—the man she was dating. She repeated the foreign phrase. Unlike the lemonade, it held no trace of bitterness, only sweet excitement. The long stretch of time at the hospital had done nothing to diminish her hunger for Tate. They hadn't seen each other in three days and eleven hours—yup, she was that woman now who counted the hours apart from her man. *Her man.*

Missing him physically and mentally unsettled her. She wasn't used to the feeling. Also, the fallout still worried her. Tate's life was entwined with her daughter's, and it would be awkward for everyone when things ended. Yet, she couldn't completely suppress the giddiness at being with him.

At the table next to Eden, a cute California blonde said to the brunette with her, "Finish your drink so we can snag Tate's attention before he goes inside."

Eden slid her dark sunglasses from the top of her head to her face. Pretending to look around, she focused on the two women. Were they talking about *her* Tate? They looked like college kids, barely old enough to drink.

"You've had us come here for drinks at least twice a week for nearly a month. If we keep this up, I'm going to become an alcoholic before you go on a date with him," said the brunette with a nearly full bright-blue cocktail.

Eden laughed, covering it with a cough. Guess she wasn't the only one thirsty for Tate. She bent her neck slightly, turned as if gazing at the lake, and continued eavesdropping.

"He always stays and talks for a bit when I strike up a conversation." The cute California blonde ran her long pink nails through her hair. "He's probably working up the nerve to ask me out."

"How do you know he doesn't have a girlfriend? I mean, look at him."

Blondie shook her head. "I've asked around. He doesn't. So why wouldn't he be interested in this?" She ran a hand over her perky chest and flat stomach.

Her interest annoyed Eden, yet she admired the girl's confidence, even if it eroded some of her own. She resisted the urge to suck in her belly and adjust her bra straps to make her breasts sit a little higher.

Would Tate like to date other women while with her? A burning sensation started in her chest and traveled to her stomach. It took her a moment to identify the cause. It was jealousy.

"Maybe he's gay," the friend offered.

"Sssh. He's coming this way." Blondie smiled, lust dripping from her lips as Tate came closer to their table. She pointed at their drinks. "Excuse me..."

As her poise seemed to fade with her words, Eden looked from the two women to Tate. Her heart flipped. All his focus was on her, and his smile was brighter—and hotter than the sun.

He opened his mouth as if to say something to her, but Blondie cooed, "Tate, could you come here?"

He glanced in the blonde's direction. "Can I help you?" His tone was polite indifference.

She rested her arms on the table and leaned forward in a move Eden was positive showcased her perky boobs. "I'm thirsty. Got anything to quench it?"

And a little desperate. Eden chided herself for the unkind thought.

"I'll have Marisol bring you the drink menu." He called to a petite waitress with a pixie cut, asking her to help the two women. Then without another glance in their direction, he dropped into the chair next to Eden and rested a hand on her knee.

"Is this okay?" he asked.

She nodded, resisting the urge to climb into his lap and show him how much it was okay.

"You worked such long hours these last couple of days, I thought you might not stop by, maybe sleep straight until dinner," he said.

"I was tempted but dragged myself out of bed early to work on a new research paper." She tapped on her laptop before pushing her sunglasses back on her head. "And I needed lemonade and some vitamin D."

However, with Tate sitting in front of her, his big palm resting on her knee, she was craving a different D. Her gaze fell to the zipper of his jeans. Then quickly away. Damn, her addiction to him was bad.

She looked at him, and his smirk said he knew exactly where her thoughts had traveled. "I'm glad you came here for my...lemonade."

Metal chair legs scraped on wood, and she turned in the direction of the noise. Tate's admirer and her friend were not-so-subtly listening. The weight of their gazes made Eden equal parts uncomfortable and possessive. She wanted to kiss him, not just to taste his addictive lips, but to claim him.

Possessiveness was another novel emotion in her dating life. Tate was opening sides of her that were exciting and unsettling. Yet, she was willing to explore both with him.

"I talked to Raven yesterday about us dating." She *might* have raised her voice for Blonde to hear.

"How'd it go?" He squeezed her knee and leaned closer. Eden loved how he seemed to need to touch her—to be close.

"Really well." She grinned. "I think her getting to say, 'I knew it' and, 'I told you so' made her day."

Eden closed her eyes, tipping her face toward the cloudless sky as Tate's soft chuckle soaked into her. His chair creaked as he adjusted his legs. The afternoon was damn near perfect.

His fingers traced her knee, and goosebumps shivered up her thighs. "I like this dress. Yellow's sexy on you."

She opened her eyes. "It's my favorite."

The fabric was soft and comfortable while flattering in all the right places. She'd worn it hoping he liked it. When sitting, the material ended at her knees, and Tate rubbed some of the hem between his fingers.

"I want to kiss you," he said.

Her pulse sparked. "Here?" Her gaze jumped to the table next to them. Yup, they were watching and not even being discreet. "Then others might want the same friendly service," she joked.

He laughed. "It's one I only offer to you."

That sounded like they were exclusive. Her heart flooded, and she leaned forward to kiss him—to hell with the gossipy town. Let'em talk.

"Tate? Tate Siren?" a man called.

He jerked back, looking at the short guy with a receding hairline who'd called his name. The guy stood just inside the patio area, shielding his eyes. "I thought that was you."

Tate's smile disappeared like a boulder dropped into a lake. Every muscle in his body stiffened. It brought her back to a psychology class where her professor had lectured about the 'fight or flight' response.

"Who's that?" Eden asked.

"Vince. He's from my old job." He waved to the man, but not with the ease he'd had moments ago.

"You didn't get along with him?"

"No, I do. He's a nice guy." Tate stood. His countenance seemed to sag with defeat.

Eden rubbed her forehead. "Then why do you look..." She wanted to say "cornered" but went with "...upset."

"I didn't tell anyone from my old job that I'd bought this place. I'd rather they didn't know."

"Why?"

"Shit." Tate stood when Vince walked toward them. Tate held up a hand, palm out toward her. "Stay here." He rushed away as if his demons were chasing him.

She hadn't planned on following him like a lost puppy. And while the command annoyed her, she was more confused. What happened at his old job that had him so out-of-sorts?

The two men were too far away to be heard, but Tate's body language said plenty. He smiled and laughed, even though his movements were jerky and tense. And when Vince pointed at her, Tate's eyes went wide, and she swore a tremor shook through him. He clapped the other man on the back, that fake grin still plastered on his face as he steered Vince inside.

Part of her wanted to know this story. To understand why an old colleague changed Tate into a man she hardly recognized—one with shifty eyes and false calm. However, she also understood the desire to forget parts of an unpleasant past. Hell, she'd buried and lied about most of her childhood, all in the name of protecting herself.

Through the large glass window separating the patio from inside the restaurant, she saw Tate and Vince shake hands before waving goodbye. Tate gripped the back of his neck so hard it was red when his hand dropped. He twisted to face her but seemed to look through her to some ghost of his past. Then he disappeared farther into the restaurant.

Unwilling to chase after him, she waited for him to return. The second time the server came by asking if Eden was ready to order, she closed her laptop. "I'm sorry, but I can't stay for lunch."

Tate could contact her when he was ready. She was willing to date him, but she would not chase him. She gave the server cash for her lemonade and left.

CHAPTER TWENTY-FOUR

E den rubbed her breastbone, but the stranglehold on her heart didn't loosen. She closed her eyes as if this would block out the hurt and anger. Why did the last person she wanted to talk to keep insisting they did, but the man she's been waiting to hear from had ghosted her? She took a deep breath and focused on the current phone call.

"Please tell me you didn't give my phone number to my mother," Eden begged her abuela.

"Por supuesto que no. But maybe you call her? Your madre is no longer drinking."

"I don't care. It doesn't erase what she did to me while drunk."

"No. But grief had broken her. Alcohol made her a monster. She has conquered both," Abuela said gently.

"And I'm just supposed to forget and forgive?" Eden let out a harsh breath.

"Cariño, this is about you letting go of your hurt, so you can move on."

"Oh, I've moved on."

Her abuela made a sound Eden was familiar with; it said she didn't believe her but didn't want to argue. "Maybe take her number. In case—"

Eden tilted her cell away from her ear. Someone was knocking on her front door. "Hold on sec, Abuela."

It was probably Olivia. They'd made tentative plans. Eden thought about canceling because of her sour mood. She was bitter from the combination of this conversation and two freaking days of Tate ghosting her.

She swung open the door. Olivia's gaze traveled to Eden's cell. "I'm early. Should I come back later?" she asked.

Eden shook her head and stepped aside. "Come in. It's my grandma, but she's leaving for a doctor's appointment in a few minutes. Give me a second." Humoring her abuela, Eden wrote her mom's phone number on scrap paper. Then promptly threw it in the junk drawer as they said their goodbyes. "Where are your kids?" she asked Olivia after hanging up.

She held up a baby monitor. Heavy breathing and grunts crackled from the machine. "Thankfully they haven't discovered how to crawl from their cribs yet. I'm surprised Ana hasn't. She's almost three. But she's content to play until Dasia wakes. Anyway, is it okay I didn't call first? When they crashed at the same time, I didn't want to miss the opportunity to adult with you."

"It's fine." Maybe a friendly distraction was what Eden needed. She pointed to the kitchen. "Do you want something to drink?"

"No, thanks." Olivia tilted her head. "Are you sure it's okay I came over? You look stressed."

"I'm very sure. Please, sit down." Eden settled into her favorite overstuffed armchair. "I'm finding it difficult to concentrate. I've had a crappy week at home and work."

Olivia sat on the end of the couch closest to Eden. "What happened?"

She skipped over her disappointment with Tate and the aggravation surrounding her mom's plea that they talk and voiced another worry. "It seems like every time I talk with my grandmother, she's going to one doctor's appointment or another. She tells me she's fine, but I'm worried. She keeps mixing up names and confusing dates."

"Is it possible for you to take time off during your fellowship and visit her?"

"I'm not sure, but I'm going to find out."

"I hope you're able." After a few beats of silence, Olivia asked, "Is anything—anyone—else bothering you?"

Eden shrugged. She didn't want to talk about Tate. "Did you sign the girls up for story time at the library?"

"Girl, I see what you're doing. Distracting me won't work. Tell me what else is wrong. Talking to a friend will help. What else is making your week crappy?" Olivia tucked her legs under her. Her gentle, understanding eyes crumbled a little corner of Eden's wall.

"My fellowship is almost over and I'm nearly positive the hospital will hire me, but I worry the move will be hard on my grandma." She pressed her thumb into the cuticle of her index finger. "And what if she doesn't want to leave?"

"To live with you—her granddaughter." Olivia's brows furrowed. "Aren't you two super close?"

"But that doesn't mean she'll want to leave behind her friends for me. Again." Her abuela had left behind her home country—her friends, family, and culture to raise her emotional basket case of a granddaughter. Would she truly want to move again? She had a great circle of friends and was always busy with them or in her amazing garden.

"Have you asked her?"

"Yes," Eden sighed. "And she tells me she's fine with moving, but what if she's saying that because she doesn't want me to feel guilty? What if she's doing it out of a sense of family obligation? Heck, maybe she even wants to return to Mexico."

"Or...maybe she'd rather live near the granddaughter she raised. And be part of her great-granddaughter's life."

Eden nodded. "Tate said the same, and it does bother her that she's not a bigger part of Raven's life."

Olivia clucked her tongue. "I'm sure she misses being with you too."

Eden shrugged. Tate had also said that as well. But he or Olivia didn't understand. Eden wasn't the easiest person to love. Even as a kid, she'd been closed off. Which probably bothered her exuberant abuela, but she was too kind to point out her granddaughter's shortcomings.

Still, hearing two people say with confidence the move would benefit her abuela did remove a little weight of her guilt. She rested her head on the back of her chair. "Thanks. You were right. I do feel better."

"You're welcome." Olivia grinned. "Now, keep going. Tell me what else is bothering you."

Eden admired her friend's relentless yet caring nature. She waved a hand. "Nothing earth-shattering. I'm annoyed with our landlord."

An uncomfortable tightness gripped her. She should have lied. His hot pursuit of her, followed by his ghosting, was a level of Dr. Jekyll and Mr. Hyde she had no desire to wrap her mind or heart around. She'd rather ignore him, pretend like he didn't matter.

"I saw him earlier this week on your porch without a shirt." Olivia fanned herself. "I'd be able to overlook an annoying personality if he changed a few lightbulbs at my house in only those lovely worn jeans..."

Eden laughed. "Oh, yes. I'm sure Elijah would love that."

"*Pfft*. He's never home."

"Has he been working more than usual?"

Olivia wilted. "About the same. Which is too much. But I can't complain because when we'd discussed him taking this job, I'd encouraged him to accept it, even though I know it meant moving and that his hours would be longer."

"Why did you tell him to take it?" Eden worried she was being intrusive, but Olivia seemed unbothered.

"Because they promised the crazy travel would only be for the first few years, and the pay is fantastic. Elijah swore when things slowed down, we'd use the extra income to open my bakery. Also, he and I met in Detroit and loved it there, but neither of us wanted to raise the kids in a fast-paced city. This little lakeside community sounded ideal. Everything was perfect on paper. The reality is a little more difficult. And more isolating. Most of my family lives in Dearborn—over two hours away. His family is a little closer in Lansing, but still, it's mostly just me and the girls."

Eden felt for Olivia. It also made her grateful she wasn't married. Her husband would probably end up as unhappy with her long hours as Olivia was with Elijah's.

"Anyway, enough with my pity party. I have no reason to complain. I live in a beautiful town, have amazing, happy children, and will have enough money saved in less than two years to get a shop on Main Street. Now stop distracting me with my life. I want to talk about yours." She wiggled deeper into the couch. "Specifically, the part that revolves around our hot landlord. What happened? And start from the beginning. I want to know it all, including how he ended up half-naked on your porch."

Eden smiled. Olivia was nosey, but it was in a playful way that didn't grate. "There isn't much to tell. A while back we accidentally kiss—"

Olivia's brows shot up. "Whoa, whoa, whoa. Shut-the-front-door—"

Eden snorted. "'Shut-the-front-door'?"

"Hey, I've got babies. I'm learning to curb my sailor-mouth." Olivia snapped her fingers. "Stay on course and explain to me how you accidentally kiss someone? Were you two walking and tripped, falling into each other's lips?"

Eden grinned and shook her head. "No. I'd stopped by The Hill after it was closed. We ended up dancing. Then kissing." She skipped the minor blow-out with Lilith, sticking to the pertinent details. "He wanted us to be more than friends. At first, I hesitated because of his connection with Raven."

"Why does that matter?"

"We probably won't work out, and then we'll be stuck seeing each other at any events concerning Raven. It could be awkward."

"Wow, you're a bit of a pessimist, huh?" Olivia teased.

The corner of Eden's lips pulled upward. "Now you sound like Tate. And I like to think of myself as more of a realist," she retorted playfully. "But anyway, I decided to follow my, well, not my heart..."

"But your horny hormones." Olivia wiggled her brows.

Eden laughed. "Yes, that works." Her smile fell. "But I think he changed his mind."

"Why in-the-hell would he change his mind? You're the complete package—hot and smart."

She was also a complete mess under pretty packaging. But she appreciated Olivia's loyalty. "Thanks. Maybe I should date you."

Olivia giggled, then parroted Eden's earlier words. "Oh, yes, I'm sure Elijah would love that."

Eden laughed with her. "*Pfft.* He's never home anyway."

"If I told him I'm dating you, he'd quit his job to follow us around."

They broke into fits of laughter. Eden wiped tears of mirth and stood. "I need some tea. What about you? Do you want your usual?"

Olivia nodded, and Eden went inside to brew some. She returned a few minutes later with the tray. After settling into her seat, Olivia started right in where they'd left off. "What makes you think he changed his mind?"

"Earlier in the week, I went to The Hill for lunch and to visit him. It started out nice. Until some guy from his old job showed up. Instead of introducing me, Tate took off like his ass was on fire. Then after the guy left, Tate never returned. Since then, he's ghosted me. No calls, no texts. Nothing." The hurt and humiliation returned. She didn't deserve that kind of brush-off.

Olivia's mouth pinched, and her brows pressed together. "Tate doesn't seem like the type to pull that crap. Have you tried calling or texting him?"

"Did you hear the part about him ignoring me? Besides, I don't want anything serious. Therefore, he doesn't owe me an explanation. If something about running into an old coworker changed his mind about us, that's fine." Her heart whispered she was lying again.

Olivia set her tea on the driftwood table between them. "But what if he isn't ignoring you? What if something happened to him? He could've been hit by a train or could be in the hospital with some deadly virus."

Eden snorted. "I drive past The Hill every day. I've seen his truck."

"When did this all happen—the coworker and ghosting?"

"Two days ago."

"I was there yesterday." She tapped her chin. "He seemed run down, not his normal easy-going cheerful self. But the restaurant was packed, and he must've been short on staff because he was waiting tables. I thought he was just worn out, but now that I think about it, he did seem jumpy, off. When we discussed the next pie order, he kept eyeing the entrance like he was expecting someone unpleasant to walk in and demand a table."

"Huh," Eden blew on her tea before taking a small sip. "I'd been so pissed at him, I forgot that he had seemed nervous, even panicked, when his old coworker appeared on the patio."

"How so?"

"When I first arrived, he was flirty and all smiles. Then that guy, I think his name was Vince, showed up and bam." Eden smacked her hand. "A fortress of dread seemed to slam around him."

Olivia rubbed her collarbone. "Maybe he owes the guy money, and he was there to break fingers or legs."

Eden's head jerked back. "Umm...that got dark real quick."

"Sorry." Olivia grimaced. "I'm obsessed with true-crime podcasts. The last one was about an accountant who was a loan shark on the side. Bloody stuff." She shuddered, then waved a hand. "Anyway, the point is, is this normal behavior for him? The ghosting?"

"I don't know. We've barely started seeing each other." She paused. "But I don't think so."

"See? Maybe something is wrong. And he has a reason for avoiding you."

Eden tucked in her chin and looked at Olivia. "Is that usually the case with ghosting?"

"No," Olivia admitted. "But is Tate worth at least finding out his reasons?"

"Maybe," Eden confessed. "When he's not pulling shit like this, he's amazing. Sweet and caring. He's not like any man I've ever been with. He makes me calm and at ease. Yet every time I see him my heart races with anticipation." She shrugged. "I'm sure it'll fade but had hoped to enjoy it for a little while."

"That proves it. You *should* find out what happened before writing this thing off between you two."

She made it sound so simple. Eden shook her head. "No, I shouldn't. I didn't move here for a relationship. Well, I did. The one with my daughter—not a man."

"Why can't you have both?"

"If I had to choose which to focus on, it's my daughter. She deserves it."

"Again, why do you have to choose? Raven doesn't need a martyr for a mom. And I bet you have room in your heart for both."

Eden held up her hands. "Whoa, slow it down. I agreed to date the man. I just wanted to enjoy his company...and his body, without adding pressure."

"Fine, no more talk of hearts. But what little I know about Tate, he seems like a man worth the effort. If it were me, I'd find out what's wrong," Olivia finished.

A sleepy whimper rang from the baby monitor, followed by rustling, then rattling wood. "One of them is awake. Pulling themselves up." She stood and pointed at Eden's laptop on the side table beside her chair. "Do you want to come to my place?"

To her surprise, she did, but the compulsion to finish the article she'd been working on when her abuela had called tugged at her. "Would you mind if I wrapped up a section before coming over? I'd like to get it on the page while it's still fresh."

"Sure, take your time."

And did she ever. Everything had to be read multiple times as her mind wandered back to their conversation about Tate. Doubt had trickled into her righteous anger. What if his disappearing act had nothing to do with her and something *was* wrong?

CHAPTER TWENTY-FIVE

T ate looked at his friends and family sitting around Asher and Lilith's kitchen table, then at the shitty cards in his hand. "I fold."

"Again," said Hope.

"Right?" Jackson agreed. "Our master bullshitter isn't even trying."

Heads nodded all around. They were right. He'd wanted a distraction from his troubles. Instead, those troubles distracted him from the game.

Probably because he couldn't deny the truth any longer. He'd fucked up with Eden. His knee-jerk reaction to protect her by cooling things between them was a dumb-ass idea. Three days—three fucking days since they'd talked or texted.

Even though Vince had come to The Hill by chance, he'd mentioned a fishing trip with his buddies. Tate worried Vince would mention it to Katrina since they probably still worked together. And Tate hadn't been able to think of a way to ask Vince not to say anything to Katrina without it coming off as odd. Instead, he'd been careful not to tell Vince he owned the restaurant in case it tempted Katrina to seek him out and cause trouble.

He had waited for her to come screeching into his life like a banshee nightmare. But she hadn't. There were no visits, voicemails, or messages. Maybe Vince would forget, never mention it to her. Or, even better, Katrina had lost interest.

Hell, even if she hadn't, the chances of her showing up at The Hill while Eden was there were so slim it bordered on ridiculousness. He could keep his wreckage separate from her.

What he couldn't do was stay away from her any longer.

Footsteps pounded toward the kitchen, snagging Tate's attention. He turned to see Raven running into the room, shopping bags in both her arms. She stopped next to Asher's chair. "Dad! You're playing cards without me?"

Behind her, Eden stood like a fantasy in a pink dress. It wrapped around her, fitting snuggly on her chest and waist, then flaring at the hips and stopping at her knees. The material looked soft like her skin. Damn, he wanted to touch it—touch her.

Less pleasing was the way her gaze refused to land on him. Shit, he'd really screwed up things between them. His reasons—so important then—appeared flimsy and weak. Weak as him. He had to stop letting Katrina live in his head—the rent was too high.

Someone tapped their cards on the table, and Tate followed the sound to Asher. "Yes, daughter," he said. "I'm playing cards without you. I'm trying to win back the money I lost when you and I played."

Raven cocked a hip, crossing her arms. "I want in."

"Sorry, we're playing teams," Asher said.

"Want to join us, Eden?" asked Lilith. "Then Raven could join."

"No, thanks. I'm tired and tomorrow's going to be a long workday." She pointed toward the driveway. "Now that your bags in the house, let's get your science fair project from the car."

Tate stood. "I'll help. Raven, you can take my spot."

"You done playing?" Hope asked.

"Yeah, I'm going to head home after I help Eden."

Jackson smirked. "Oh, are you suddenly tired too?"

"Yup, sure am." Tate rubbed the side of his nose with his middle finger. The other man laughed.

He followed Eden. When they reached her car, she opened the back driver's door. A massive eyeball glared at him as if judging him for his stupidity. For letting Katrina get to him. Again. And possibly for ruining things with Eden.

Leaning closer, he poked the pupil. A yellow hose was attached to the back, leading to a pink bundle he assumed was a brain. At the other end, facing the eye, was a flashlight on a stand. This project must have taken days, even weeks, to assemble.

"Wow. That's impressive. And a little creepy." He flicked the flashlight on and off, and she muttered something about his fingers working fine.

He twisted to look at her. "Huh?"

"Olivia suggested you're ghosting me because the man who visited earlier in the week wasn't from your old job, but a loan shark who's threatening to break your fingers."

Tate let out a surprised bark of laughter. "Damn, that's dark. Was that her first guess or last?"

Eden's lips twitched. "Her first was that a train ran you over." She leaned against the side of her Mustang, her levity leaking away. "She figured it had to be something important. Me too. Because you pursued me hard, Tate. Then disappeared. Why?"

Wow, Eden didn't dodge or ease into things. Good, he preferred it that way, even if he wasn't ready to talk about Katrina.

"Did it have something to do with your frenemy?" she asked.

He scratched his cheek, confused. "My what?"

"An enemy who pretends to be a friend. The man from your old job."

"No, Vince is fine, a good guy. But he's a friend of an enemy." He rubbed the back of his neck. "Enemy. That sounded really dramatic. Anyway, seeing him knocked me out of sorts. Freaked me out a little."

"Why?"

"Come over? I'll explain." If he was going to share his embarrassing past, he'd rather not have the conversation in Asher's driveway.

She stared at his house as if considering, then pointed at the eye thing. "Let's get this to Raven."

Did her non-answer mean she was done with him? He couldn't blame her. Ghosting her had been shitty. But he wasn't ready to give up on them.

He shifted, shoving his hands in his pockets. "I dated someone from my old job. She was a very difficult woman who became impossible when we broke up. I didn't tell her where I was moving. She and Vince work in the HR department together. I'd convinced myself he'd tell her where I was, and she'd show up, eager to trash my new life." He rocked on his heels. "Yours too if she found out we're together. Seeing a piece of my past step into my present knocked me off balance. I'm sorry."

Her gaze ran over him, and the quiet filled the evening air between them. Her stare was so intense it felt like she was looking into his mind and seeing just how badly he'd handled it. Did she see how his insomnia had returned with a vengeance? Or that he'd changed the locks at his house and closed the windows at night? The cool lake breeze invited nightmares of an unwelcome blonde visitor. He'd even considered putting the restaurant in Lilith's name. Once he'd calmed down, humiliation at his actions filled him—though he still kept the windows and doors locked.

"I'll come over."

The weight of gloom eased off him. "Yeah?"

"For a little bit. I agree we should talk."

She rubbed her arms. He noticed the goosebumps and pointed to his house. "Get inside and get warm. I'll give this to Raven." He took the eye project from Eden. "And I'll move your car to my driveway so you're not blocking Jackson's truck."

"Thanks." They exchanged keys.

Before she let go of his hand, he squeezed it. "I missed you."

She leaned into him, resting against his chest. A gust of cool lake wind wrapped around them, and Eden shivered in his arms. He kisses her lightly on her head. "I'll meet you inside."

He didn't start toward Lilith and Asher's house until his front door closed with Eden inside. Alone in the approaching darkness of night, his happiness crashed against his agitation. She was giving him another chance, but his insides knotted at the questions that might be waiting for him. Would she demand he tell the whole sorry situation with Katrina? It might scare Eden off. Or she might view him differently, see him as less of a man, or fear he was capable of what his ex had accused him of being—cruel and unlovable.

Sighing, he shifted Raven's project. He wouldn't delay talking with Eden. He'd answer whatever question she asked if it meant she'd give him another chance.

CHAPTER TWENT-SIX

e locked his front door and was surprised to see the living room dark and empty. He checked the kitchen. The light over the sink was on, but Eden wasn't there either. He called her name.

"I'm in your bedroom," she replied.

He headed that way. Sleepless nights and the upcoming conversation had exhaustion settling into his bones. But he'd do whatever it took for her to give him another try.

The dim lamp on his bedside nightstand illuminated Eden under his green comforter. "Are you tired?" he asked.

"No, Tate. I'm not tired." She dragged down the blanket, revealing her full breasts and peaked nipples.

He sucked in a breath. *Suddenly I'm not tired either.*

Pulling off his shirt and tossing it aside, he crawled up the bed. He stretched over her body, nuzzling into her neck. Her scent of coconut and vanilla was addicting, and he wanted the scent all over his skin. He pushed the blanket past her waist and was rewarded with a completely nude Eden.

"You're gorgeous. Every inch."

"Speaking of inches…" She pressed her palm against his rock-hard dick, then unfastened his belt. "Please, no playing tonight. I need you inside me now."

She'd get no argument from him. Twisting, he opened his nightstand drawer and grabbed a condom. Her hand slipped inside his boxer briefs, stroking him. He fell onto his back, arching into her perfect pressure.

Eden's throaty laugh filled his room, turning him on more. She let go of him and picked up the foil packet he'd dropped. "Did you get sidetracked?"

He skimmed a hand down her stomach and then between her legs as she opened it. "Your touch is wonderfully distracting."

He pressed his palm against her clit. Sliding his middle finger inside her, he moved in the rhythm that made her moan and writhe. The unopened condom packet fell from her fingers.

"Eden, honey, are you losing focus?" he said against her neck.

"What did I say about teasing and playing tonight?" she panted.

"Does this feel like a game?"

Her back bowed, and he took her breast into his hungry mouth. She moaned his name, which spurred him on, and he pressed his fingers deeper inside her velvety softness, maximizing her pleasure. He stroked and circled until her body shook, and his name became a chant on her lips. Then she shattered, gripping his biceps as if needing something to keep her tethered to earth.

She squirmed away, gasping. "It's t-too much."

He kissed her gently, skimming his lips along her collarbone to her mouth. Pulling back, he expected to see drooping, relaxed lashes. Instead, naked lust stared at him. She nudged his shoulder, and he dropped onto his back. Straddling him, she ripped open the condom. As she rolled it on him, he grew harder in her hand.

Coming up on her knees, she took him into her in a single, fast thrust. Sheathed in her heat, he groaned, "You're perfect."

"Far from it." She circled her hips. "But our *fit* is perfect."

That was the truth. His body agreed as nearly every nerve raced, chasing bliss. He gripped her waist, lifting her, then taking her deep. She laid flat against him, her breasts pressing into his chest. Between kisses and whispers, he slipped toward ecstasy.

"Are you close?" He was on the precipice but didn't want to go over without her.

"Almost," she whimpered.

Cradling her head, he flipped her onto her back. He thrust, deep and hard, pressing into her body, using his pelvic bone to massage her clit. Her short nails dug into his ass. "Yes. Right there. Don't stop." Within seconds, she was whimpering his name and coming again, this time taking him with her.

He collapsed onto his side, resting a hand on her left breast. Her heart pounded in his palm, slowing as the silent minutes ticked by. When his pulse stopped, he kissed her lips lightly. "I'll be right back."

After disposing of the condom, he slid into bed next to her. She rested her head on his shoulder, looping a leg across his waist. He waited for her questions. She'd demand answers for why he'd ghosted her. And she deserved them.

Instead, she asked if he'd crack a window. "The best part of Michigan is the summer, night noises," she told him.

He considered refusing, but he was tired of his worries ruling him—still, 'better safe than sorry' was a good motto—and he clicked the side tabs so the window couldn't be forced up without making a lot of noise.

With her nestled into his chest, his eyes drifted closed. An unpleasant idea hit him on the cusp of sleep, forcing his eyes open. Maybe she hadn't asked more because she didn't care—didn't care about him. He was just someone to have fun with and fuck. They'd talked of dating but not of being exclusive. He'd always been a monogamous dater, but that didn't mean she was too.

He kissed her neck. "Are you awake?"

"Not really." Her voice was laced with sleep.

Never mind. He'd drop it and go with the flow. Hell, he should be grateful he didn't have to explain his past with Katrina.

Eden wiggled against him. "Any reason you're asking?"

Keep it simple. Keep it in the present. "Are we dating other people?"

"I hardly have time to see you, and when I do, you keep me plenty satisfied." She rolled over and kissed his chin. "Why? Do you not want to be exclusive?"

"I don't. I'm not interested in seeing other people."

"Okay. Neither am I." A drowsy smile tugged on her lips. "Anything else?"

He shook his head, and her eyelids shut. This time they stayed closed. The next minute, her breath evened out into sleep.

But a tightness in his chest wouldn't let him follow. Eden was back in his bed, and he'd dodged the dreaded talk. But why? Why didn't she ask? Maybe digging deeper didn't matter because she preferred to keep things shallow between them.

Had he gotten her back only to learn he'd never really had her?

CHAPTER TWENTY-SEVEN

Bright lights glared behind Eden's eyelids, and they snapped open. Credits scrolled on the ginormous theater screen. The aroma of popcorn and grease filled her nose as people around her stood and stretched. Damn. She'd drifted off.

"Mom," Raven huffed. "You fell asleep again."

Eden rubbed her eyes. "What did I miss?"

"Did you even make it through the opening credits?"

She shifted in her seat, scratching her temple. "Maybe."

"You're worse than Grandpa Crowley. Whenever we watch TV together, he's always 'resting his eyes.'" Raven made air quotes.

"I'm sorry. This fellowship is kicking my butt." Eden laughed, but guilt tightened in her chest at the slight lie.

May had flown by, and it was already June. Nearly a month had passed since she and Tate began officially dating, and her addiction to him wasn't lessening. If she wasn't working or with Raven, Eden was with Tate. Even on the days they were busy, one of them usually ended up at the other's house at night. And not just for sex. Half those evenings were spent doing couples stuff, like cuddling, watching TV or reading together.

She rubbed her forehead. Tate was becoming important to her, but she *had* to keep her priorities straight, her fellowship and Raven.

"Next time we'll pick a place that doesn't basically give me a bed." She patted the reclining seat. "These are so much more comfortable than when I was your age. These sofa seats didn't show up until I was into my teen years."

She offered her hand to Raven, who took it and pulled herself up. "Were there even movie theaters when you were a kid?"

Eden tugged playfully on one of Raven's long locks. "Ha. Ha. Funny girl."

On the way down the stairs and toward the exit, she asked, "Will you keep working this much when your fellowship is over?"

"No. It'll still be a lot, but not this intense." She held up both hands, crossing her fingers. "Maybe I'll get enough sleep that I won't doze through half the movies we see."

"More like all of them," Raven grumbled, but thankfully, she was smiling.

Out in the main lobby, Eden bumped her daughter's hip. "Where do you want to go for dinner?"

Raven glanced at her cell. "Could we get a snack instead? Lilith's making my favorite dinner. I want to be hungry for it."

The mention of Lilith jiggled loose a reminder of something Eden had meant to bring up. She smoothed her clammy hands down her jeans. "If you'd like to call Lilith mom too, but are worried I'd be upset, I want you to know I'm fine with it."

The many parenting books she'd read were mixed on this topic, so she had to go with her gut. And her gut was pretty conclusive. Asher's fiancé was as much of a mom to Raven as Eden. Maybe even more—hell, that truth hurt.

They stepped through the sliding glass doors into the parking lot, and she squinted against the bright, hot afternoon sun. Raven slid her arm through Eden's as they walked toward her car. "No. I love Lilith, but you're my mom." Her words squeezed Eden's chest, and tears gathered along her bottom lashes. She might not deserve the title, but she loved the absolution in her daughter's voice. "Also, switching from Ms. Brooks to Lilith was weird enough when she went from neighbor to Dad's girlfriend. Hmm, maybe Lilith Mom."

Eden ran a palm over Raven's hair, tucking a piece behind her ear. "That works too."

She unlocked the Mustang, trying to ignore the restless worry crawling up her spine. This conversation—life in general—was going too smoothly. That could only mean one thing. Something was bound to break, to shatter the peace. Before getting into the car, she glanced toward the robin's-egg blue sky, looking for clouds. Sooner or later, they'd arrive.

Eden started the car, the engine rumbling to life.

Raven adjusted the A/C. "Besides my great-grandma, do we have more family in New Mexico?"

Ah, there were those grey clouds, her awaiting storm. This question was the perfect chance to clear up the lie about her mother. But revealing the truth might ruin all the progress they've made. Raven would demand to know why her grandmother was kept from her.

Eden's heart thudded. Sweat prickled her skin, and she swore the scar under her tattoo tingled. If she told Raven why, would she think Eden was capable of the things her mother had done in a rage? And could she blame her? It was Eden's worry—the reason she kept her emotions under lock and key.

And she wasn't foolish. Her lie was big. Raven might be angry with the deceit and break off their tenuous relationship. And for what? A grandmother who didn't deserve her. The risk wasn't worth the reward. Yes, lying was wrong, but she wasn't doing it to hurt her daughter. She was doing it to protect her.

Eden gave a mental head shake. No, she wouldn't reveal the truth, but she could offer a different piece of it. "You have great-grandparents on your grandmother's side in New Mexico, but I never saw them as a kid. Nor did I visit as an adult."

"Why?"

"They didn't want their daughter to marry a Mexican," Eden said bluntly.

"That's dumb."

"I agree. He was such a great dad, treated me and mom with gentle kindness."

"You were little when he died. Do you remember him?"

"Not enough. But somethings. Like, he loved to laugh and give hugs. He read to me all the time. And he'd take me to the science museum nearly every time I asked—which was a lot."

Raven's eyes swelled with tears. "He sounds like my dad," she sniffled.

"He was a great dad, just like yours. I miss him." Eden reached across the console, choking on her loss, and took Raven's hand. "But my *abuela* is amazing. I loved living with her."

"What about your mom?"

Eden's pulse jumped as if shocked. Was Raven asking what happened to her grandmother—how she died? She couldn't look into her daughter's eyes and tell a bald-faced lie.

She clicked on her seatbelt and pointed for Raven to do the same. "What about her?"

"Do you miss her?"

Eden sagged into her seat as the release of tension made her stomach drop. "Not much."

Raven's eyes widened. Eden had been too honest. She rushed to clarify. "She was like her parents..."

"A racist who hated Mexicans?" Raven huffed. "Then why did she marry one?"

Eden laughed, though it wasn't funny. "No, thankfully that awful trait didn't get passed down to your grandmother."

A memory of the last time she'd seen her grandparents crowded Eden. She'd been around six or seven. They'd called her a baby beaner. When her mom raged at them, they'd tried to play it off as a joke or cute nickname. But mom had told them to leave and not to return until they could respect her husband and child. Eden never saw them again.

"Then what?" Raven asked, interrupting the bitter past.

"Like them, she could be mean. Even cruel."

"Wow. She must have been a real bitch for you to not miss her much."

A surprised choke-laugh escaped Eden. "Raven! You're eleven, you shouldn't swear."

"Dad says people can say really mean things without swearing. That it's more important on how I use my words than what words I use. Like, I could call someone an asshole and it would hurt less than telling them they're worthless."

"He has a point," Eden admitted, even if hearing her daughter swear was disconcerting.

Raven grinned. "But he also told me to choose wisely when I swear because if I get in trouble at school or at a friend's house for it, I'm grounded."

"Then I shouldn't tell him I was terribly offended that you swore," Eden teased.

Raven's eyes widened. "Were you?"

Eden shook her head. "No. My mom was rather bitchy."

"Well, I can tell you as your daughter, you're nothing like her."

Eden sucked in a breath, but her chest expanded, blooming with wildflowers of happiness. Raven had inadvertently voiced and denied Eden's greatest fear. She wasn't sure the statement was true, especially with the taste of her lies still bitter on her tongue, but it was a balm to Eden's bruised heart.

"Thanks, but it's easy when I have a daughter like you." She reached over with her free hand and patted Raven's knee before twisting the key in the ignition.

Raven twisted in her seat, facing Eden. "Thanks, Mom."

She smiled. "That's an easy truth to tell." Her conscience twanged, wishing everything was that easy and simple between them. "Since lunch isn't an option, do you want ice cream?"

"I never refuse ice cream," Raven said so seriously Eden laughed.

She merged with traffic, more than ready to leave behind their talk. Raven didn't need to know her grandmother was alive and well in New Mexico. She, and the hurt doled out by her, wasn't worth remembering.

Eden said a quick and silent prayer that her mother would stay buried in the past.

CHAPTER TWENTY-EIGHT

Midday sun glistened off the water as Tate stepped around the purple bushes lining the perimeter of his property. The soft flowers brushed his legs, emitting a woodsy herbal fragrance that smelled of summer's arrival.

He held up his large bowl. "I brought the watermelon."

"Perfect." Asher flipped a burger, and the hiss from the fire sent the tantalizing smell in Tate's direction. "Are you hungry?"

"Always."

Lilith and their dad were clipping a red-and-white-checkered tablecloth to the picnic table. She straightened, putting her hands on her hips. "Where's the homemade lemonade you promised? You know it's my favorite."

It was their mom's recipe and was amazing—a barbeque must. Still, she was his sister, so he had to give her a hard time. He paused, looking back at his house. "Oh, shit..."

"You better be joking. Or turn around and start squeezing some lemons."

He grinned. "Chill. I made it. Eden's bringing it. She just woke up from a nap and wanted to take a quick shower before coming over. She'll bring your precious lemonade."

"You and Eden." Dad scoffed, shaking his head and sitting on the long bench.

Tate clenched his jaw, then forced himself to unhinge it. "Don't start."

Lilith's gaze swung between them. "What's going on?"

"Dad doesn't approve of me dating Eden." Tate set the bowl of watermelon on the table. "He thinks your fiancé has dibs."

Asher turned from the grill. "Me? Why?"

"Because you dated her first." Dad took a long swallow of beer, then tapped the can on the table. "Don't you have—what do you young people call it—a bro-code?"

Tate busted out laughing, followed by Lilith and Asher. "Shut up," Dad muttered, but he was smiling.

"You make us sound like a couple frat boys." Tate grabbed a drink from the cooler.

Lilith giggled. "Yeah, Dad, Tate's college days are long, long behind him."

Tate shoved Lilith playfully. "They aren't *that* far in my past. And remember, no matter how old I get, you'll always be older, you old woman."

"And she'll always be hot," Asher said, earning a loud kiss on his cheek from Lilith. "And as far as Eden goes, we're so far in each other's past, her with Tate is a non-issue."

His dad looked toward Raven. She and Chloe were chatting on the dock with their feet dipped in the lake. "But you have a kid together."

He shrugged. "That's all we have. And don't get me wrong, Raven is my everything, but Eden isn't—nor am I to her. Even back then. We weren't dating long when she got pregnant." His gaze drifted to Raven. "We love our daughter, but we've never loved each other."

"Was I only supposed to bring lemonade?" Eden called, stepping from Tate's yard.

All four of them froze like criminals caught in a cop's spotlight. "Am I interrupting?" she asked.

Tate came toward her, taking the pitcher. "More like rescuing."

She smiled. "I'm always happy to be your knight in shining—" She glanced down, "in a bathing suit and sundress."

He bent and kissed her ear "Are you wearing the red one?" he whispered.

She'd worn the bikini the last time they'd taken a sunset swim at her place. The simple triangles had barely covered her beautiful breasts, and the ties at her hips teased and tantalized, begging him to untie them with his teeth, which he did under the dark, moonless sky on her dock.

"Given this is a family gathering, I went with a one-piece." She handed him the lemonade. "But when I packed my overnight bag, I did throw in that *toy* you love."

He groaned. "Great, now I'm going to be thinking about it throughout dinner."

She leaned closer. "Anticipation makes everything taste better."

"Mom!" Raven called from the dock, waving.

Eden waved back, and Asher called to them, telling them it was time to eat. Tate nudged Eden's shoulder as they walked toward the picnic table. "Perfect timing. How fast can you eat?"

"An-tici-pation," she whispered, her husky voice wrapped around his damn dick.

While setting the lemonade on the table, he shot his dad a warning look. "Do you remember Eden?"

"I'm old, not senile, son."

Tate wasn't sure if his dad was referring to the fact they'd just been talking about her or that he had met Eden plenty of times during family gatherings. He didn't know or care. All that mattered was he kept his tone polite.

Eden smiled. "How are you Mr. Siren?"

"Please, call me, Harrison. It's nice to see you again," he said, reaching for a burger.

Tate let out a breath but not all his tension. His dad loved to press on people's sore spots. But it seemed he was willing to play nice. Plates were made, emptied, and filled again, and through it all, conversation flowed without strain.

Way too much food later, Tate pushed away his plate. "I can't believe I ate that many burgers and corn."

"And half the watermelon," Lilith added.

"You ate the other half," Tate volleyed back.

She rubbed her stomach. "I couldn't help it. It was so good."

"I agree." Chloe popped the last slice in her mouth.

"We could go for a swim. Work off some calories," Eden suggested.

The shade from the massive willow at the edge of the deck had shifted, and it was hot in the sun's rays, but Tate wasn't sure he could move. "Will you roll me to the dock and push me in?"

"I'm afraid you'll sink to the bottom," she teased.

"I might. I practically have a whole cow in my gut."

"Well, I think swimming's a great idea." Raven said.

Chloe stood. "I agree."

"We'll meet you in the water," Raven told her mom, and the two girls ran toward the lake.

Tate chuckled. "It is warm, but damn, they're running like their asses are on fire."

"The heat has nothing to do with it," Lilith sighed. "They're trying to get out of their after-dinner chore. We cooked, so they're supposed to clean it up." She called to the girls, and they slumped back.

Tate chuckled, stretching in his seat. "Reminds me of when we were kids."

Dad snorted. "You two were the worst about it. If you weren't fighting about who's turn it was to wash the dishes, you were accidentally breaking them." He glanced at Eden and Asher. "Never let these two butterfingers touch your favorite cup."

"Ugh, Dad, how many times do I have to apologize?" Lilith's gaze went around the table. "I was twelve when I broke his favorite coffee mug. He's still upset."

Tate pointed at Lilith. "Was that when you cut your palm and had to get stitches?"

She held up her hand, revealing a small scar. "Yup."

Tate took a sip of his lemonade. The tart flavor tasted of childhood memories. Eden's cool fingertips ran along the straight scar next to his eyebrow. "How'd you get this?" she asked. "I hope it wasn't when you were washing dishes."

Everything sweet became bitter in an instant as her joke landed like a boulder in his gut. He didn't want to talk about that nightmare. It reminded him of the unwelcome text he'd gotten late last night—the first one since Vince's visit. It had been two sentences.

Unknown number: Should I come to you?

He took a deep breath, forcing air past the invisible hands wrapping around his throat. "It's a dumb story."

"Did you fall from a jungle-gym as a kid? Or was it some crazy dare as a teenager?"

He brushed away her hand. "Let's go with either of those."

"No, you didn't get it while living at home." His dad tilted his head. "How did you get it?"

Christ. They were all looking at him. His dinner roiled and rebelled in his stomach. "It's a long story."

He glanced at Lilith and prayed she'd tell it because he didn't remember what he'd told her. She'd stopped by for a surprise visit right after he'd returned from the hospital. He'd been rattled and on painkillers and had made some shit up. If he got it wrong, she'd be suspicious.

Lilith giggled and set her lemonade on the table. "Please, can I tell them?"

He slumped, pretending his reaction was from embarrassment, not relief. He rubbed his forehead. "If you must."

"It happened when he was living in Royal Oak," Lilith began. "He opened a cupboard for a mug, and dropped it—"

"Some things never change," their dad said, making everyone laugh.

"Anyway, after grabbing it, he came up fast and hit his face on the open door. It was so deep he had to get ten stitches."

Dad chuckled, "Wow, son. You make me proud."

He glanced at Eden. She was studying him. Sweat prickled under his arm and along his spine. She was a surgeon and probably saw the inconsistencies in his bullshit story.

She opened her mouth. "But..."

Shit. Here it comes.

"Forget it." She pressed her lips closed and looked away.

He forced a false chuckle through his lips. It sounded empty. "In my defense, I hadn't had coffee."

"I get it," Asher said. "I have a coffeemaker that grinds and makes each cup individually. On more than one occasion, I've put my mug on the tray upside down and didn't notice until coffee was all over the counter."

Chloe had returned from the kitchen and was gathering the last of the dishes. She grinned at her mom. The expression on her angelic face could only be described as troublemaking. "Mom, remember when—"

Lilith covered her daughter's mouth. "You promised you wouldn't tell."

Tate did his best to smile. "Oh, do tell."

Raven took over, and Chloe giggled through Lilith's fingers. "Dad usually drives us to school, but he had to leave early for work..."

"Traitors," Lilith muttered, smiling.

"We woke up Mom, but she fell back asleep. And when we woke her again and told her we were going to be late, she jumped out of bed, grabbed the keys, and went to the front door. She was in her underwear." Chloe's eyes widened. "Only her underwear."

They all burst out laughing. "On the days I have to go to work early, I make sure she wears pajamas," Asher said.

From there, the conversation moved on to other sleep-deprived disasters, Tate's scars all forgotten but by him. He was restless, and agitation crawled through him. The combination made his skin too tight.

Eden squeezed his hand. "I'm still so full. I need to burn off this food. Are you ready to swim yet? Girls are you done with the dinner clean up and want to go with us?"

"Yea, we're done," Raven said. "But Chloe started a movie. We'll go later."

Eden looked at Tate, her eyes asking if he was interested. Hell, yes. It was exactly what he needed.

"Yes." He kissed her quickly and hard. "Let's go."

When his bare feet hit the warm aluminum dock, he ran to the end and dove into the shockingly cold and silent water. It loosened some of his tension, but his body screamed to move when he broke the surface.

"Race you to the public park?" Eden asked.

Was it luck that she wanted the same as him, or had she sensed his mood? He'd ask later. Right now, he just needed to push himself.

He nodded, and they took off. She was a good swimmer, and keeping pace with her was perfect. They kept within the safe strip between the shore and the boats. After about twenty minutes, they reached the public beach's floating dock. Since it was a Sunday and most of the weekend renters had gone home, they had the place to themselves.

He grabbed a rung of the ladder but didn't get out of the water. Eden did the same, holding on to the other side. His heart pounded at the exertion, but his mind was calm again. Water dripped from Eden's long lashes, nose, and partly open, full lips. She was so damn beautiful.

He smirked. "You're a wet dream. Literally."

"Ah, my man has a way with words."

My man. He really liked that phrase on her pretty mouth.

She wrapped her legs loosely around him. "Do you feel better?"

So, the swim had been for him. He kissed her. "I do. My dad's a decent man. He loves us, but he has way too many opinions. And thinks he has all the answers to *my* life. It grates on my nerves."

Tate's excuse was bullshit. Yeah, his dad could be difficult, but he'd been fine once Eden had arrived. But it was better to complain about his overbearing father than remind Eden of his bullshit scar story.

"Parents definitely don't know everything. Some don't seem to know anything."

Tate heard sadness behind her words. "What about yours? Where do they fall?" he asked. "Wise or fools?"

"My dad was great. My mom wasn't," she said in a clipped, cool tone. "They're gone now."

Sorrow filled Tate. His relationship with his parents wasn't smooth or easy. Lilith was close to their mom, but he wasn't as much, maybe because of the distance. He'd been practically a toddler when she moved to Florida. And their dad loved them, but it came with so many opinions and expectations. Yet, losing either of them would gut him.

"I'm sorry," he said. "When?"

"A long time ago. When I was a kid. A few years younger than Raven."

He wanted to hold her closer, but she let go of the ladder, pushed away from him and floated onto her back. "It's fine. My grandmother raised me. She's a wonderful woman."

Still, his heart ached for Eden. Losing her parents at such a young age must have been difficult.

He considered asking how but worried that might come off as nosey instead of concerned. Before he could decide, Eden righted herself and said, "Don't look so sad. Really, it's fine. I remember the good things and let the rest sink into the past."

"But are you worried?" He sank deeper into the water, coming toward her.

"About?"

"What if the past is waiting in the deep depths of you...and sneaks up from those murky waters when you aren't paying attention?"

He'd meant it as a joke to lighten her solemn mood. But the worry that flashed through her eyes gave him pause. What was she burying? He wanted to push, but her closed-off frown said to drop it. And since he was avoiding his past, he'd give her the same reprieve.

He grinned, coming closer.

"What are you up to?" A ghost of a smile flickered at the corner of her mouth.

"Nothing. Just warning you to look out for what sneaks up from the murky waters of our past—or lakes." He ran a finger, featherlight, along her thigh.

Her eyes flew wide, and she kicked away, screaming, "What the hell is that?!"

He held up his hands, laughing. "Sorry, it was me."

She stopped panic-swimming and glided toward him. "Really?"

Nodding, he apologized again and opened his arms.

She came closer. "Do you want to know my answer?" Her eyes narrowed, and her lips twitched.

"To what?"

"What I do when the past—or lake creatures—sneak up on me?"

"Sure." He lifted his chin in a quick nod. "What would you do?"

"I'd drown it." She sprang on him, dunking him.

Water went up his nose, and a second later, he broke above the surface, spitting out the lake and laughing. "I deserved that."

"Yes, you did." She swam a lazy circle around him, looking pleased with herself.

He had to admit she had a point. The past was the past. It didn't have a place in the present or future.

However, worry whispered that the worst part of his past refused to remain there and would keep reaching out to him, downing his hopes and happiness.

CHAPTER TWENTY-NINE

Tate's head rested on Eden's lap. She ran her fingers through his silky-smooth hair, loving how his nearness settled her soul. He laughed at something on TV, and her gaze snagged on the scar that slashed through his laugh lines. The bullshit story from this afternoon came back to her. Her gaze shifted to the window and the lake beyond it. He hadn't gotten it from his cupboard door. The angle was off and was too long.

"Do you want me to find something else?" Tate asked.

She looked down. He was watching her instead of the show. "No, this is fine." It didn't matter what was on TV. She was too distracted by the questions pressing on her tongue, pushing to escape.

He shifted onto his back and looked at her. "What's wrong?"

She squinted. "What makes you think something is wrong?"

"You're staring at me instead of the TV."

"Maybe I think you're more intriguing than the show."

"Understandable." He grinned, but after a pause, it slipped, "But I think it's something else."

She glanced unseeing at the TV. "Just thinking about you."

"Anything specific?"

"Um. No."

He made a sound that said he didn't believe her. "Tell me, Eden. I want to know what you're thinking."

She doubted that, but since he'd opened the invitation on the subject, she asked, "How did you *really* get the scar?" she asked.

He sat up, resting his feet on the coffee table with his gaze fixed on the TV. "What gave it away? That my story wasn't true?"

"The size and position of the scar doesn't match with the injury you described." The flash and flicker of the movie played across his face. He still wouldn't look at her. She rested a hand on his thigh. "It's none of my business. You don't have to tell me. I get keeping skeletons buried."

He ran a hand down his face, pulling roughly on his chin before tapping on his chest a few times with his palm. "My ex did it."

Eden gasped as her stomach clenched. "How—"

"Like an assassin. That woman was wicked quick." He joked, but it sounded hollow.

He was deflecting. Taking his hand, she squeezed it, trying to tell him without words that he didn't have to talk about it.

"The whole incident was dumb as shit. We were cooking when the argument started. I can't even remember what it was about. When we sat to eat, I told her to let it go. She wouldn't and worked herself up more. I stopped arguing with her." He let go of Eden's hand, rubbing his palms down his thighs. "Turns out she doesn't like the silent treatment. She slammed her steak knife into the side of my head—blade side."

"That's....wow..." Words failed Eden as anger pounded through her.

Maybe even fear. Fear that a little Katrina could be in her. Her childhood years were spent with a mother filled with drinking and rage that ended in bruises and broken bones. And Eden recalled the explosive emotions of her adolescence and the struggle of learning to bury them.

Tate let out a heavy sigh. "Thankfully her aim was off. Another inch, I might be sporting a scar and glass eye." He ran a hand through his hair, gripping the back of his neck. "Before that night, I told myself her rages weren't a big deal because her shoves and slaps didn't hurt. And she convinced me her outbursts were my fault because I was being a typical, dense guy, closed off and unemotional."

"You?" Eden scoffed. "I know a thing or two about being withdrawn and cold. You are most definitely neither. Being around you is like being outside on a summer day. Warm. Perfect."

His eyes softened, but doubt drowned in them. "Did you think that when I overreacted the night we first kissed? Or ghosted you when Vince stopped at the restaurant?"

"Well, no," she admitted. "But after learning about your ex, your actions make sense."

He shrugged, pulling one of his legs under him, he faced her. "And I don't think you're either of those things. More like, cautious and hot—sexy."

She believed him about as much as he seemed to believe her. Instead of debating the point, she asked, "You and Lilith seem close. Does she know the truth?"

"No. She thinks the story told today was what really happened. I didn't tell her because she'd have gone after my ex and ended up in jail." He grinned, then it fell away. "And I was worried about the consequences. Lil would've insisted I have Katrina arrested for assault. And that would have been risky for me. More than once my ex had threatened if I called the cops on her, she'd tell them I was doing the hitting, and any marks I had were from her defending herself. I couldn't take the chance of having the stain of domestic abuse on my record."

"How is that possible? If you were the one calling the police?" Eden asked as her simmering anger boiled. Katrina had not only hurt this kind and beautiful man's flesh but went after his mind.

"Depends on what type of officer showed up at my door." His jaw flexed, and he let out a heavy exhale. "During one particularly loud argument, my neighbors called the police. *I* was nearly arrested. It wasn't until Kat admitted she'd thrown all the shit shattered around my place and that I hadn't touch her, that they removed the cuffs from my wrists." Tate shook his head. "They never asked if I was okay. And one of the cops told me *I* needed to get better control of my woman."

Eden covered her mouth. She could see it all as clear as crystal, breaking her a little. He'd been cornered and trapped with that awful woman. No help. Completely alone.

"Anyway, after that incident, we broke up. Or, I should say, *I* broke up. She insists we're still together." He straightened his arms, gripping his knees. "When I returned from Urgent Care, I called my boss and requested an immediate vacation. He wasn't thrilled and was even less thrilled when I put in my notice that I was leaving. But I'd need a change—in my personal life and career. Then I ended things with Kat over the phone. I couldn't risk doing it in person, not with her threat of using the police against me."

Eden's muscles quivered to inflict the same sort of pain on his ex, but her touch was tender as she rubbed his bicep. "That was smart."

"Maybe, but I'd always considered any guy who broke up with a woman over text or phone a spineless asshole."

"That's only true when their girlfriend isn't mentally unbalanced."

He tilted his head from side to side. "Anyway, all of this was a push to do something I'd been considering for a while—leaving my old job. I was good at it and loved the money but was bored. I hated spending most of my day behind a desk. Lilith had mentioned the owners of The Hill were looking to sell. She got me their number, and we came to an agreement."

"Best decision you made." It had led him on the path to her.

He snorted. "Tell that to my dad. Anyway, I agreed to stay at my old job long enough to hire and train my replacement. That month was awful. Kat kept her distance during working hours, but leaving the office in the evenings were uncomfortable..."

Eden squeezed his hand and rested her head on his shoulder. "What did she do?"

"She'd wait at my car. Sometimes to talk or rage at me. Other times to seduce or threaten. It got so bad. I started taking an Uber to and from work just to avoid her. My last day was a fucking nightmare. She'd come to my condo late that night. I'd changed the locks, which must have pissed her off. She banged on my door, screaming to let her in. Since she wasn't inside my place and was yelling loud enough to wake people two cities over, I called the police. It turned out better than the other time."

"What happened?"

"They told her if she didn't leave they'd arrest her. After she left the officers suggested I get a restraining order. They gave me their names and badge numbers, offering to back my story, if I needed it."

"Did it help?" Eden asked.

"She calls and texts me, but I haven't seen her since that night." His sudden pinched expression told Eden he didn't believe it was over. "That was back when I was living in Royal Oak. Almost six months ago."

"And you never told anyone close what had happened, during and after?" Eden wasn't sure why that surprised her. She rarely mentioned the awful parts of her childhood.

"Why would I? It was a rocky relationship—nothing more."

It was definitely more. It was domestic abuse.

"And there was no way I could have brought it up to friends at work. They thought she was great. It had me second guessing myself. I kept thinking I needed to—what was the word my dad always used?" Tate rolled his eyes and snapped his fingers. "Oh, I've got it. 'I needed to man-up.'"

"I hate that stupid phrase," Eden groaned.

"Same. If I ever have kids, it'll be verboten in my house." He grinned, and this time it looked genuine. "My dad used it a lot with me. Lil and I were the only kids in our neighborhood, so we were each other's playmates. Sometimes we played baseball or built mud-castles, other times it was house and Barbies. The last two drove my dad nuts. He'd tell me to stop being a girl. But playing pretend with a train that had a face on it wasn't much different to me than playing pretend with Ken. And I didn't see what the big deal was, my sister was a girl, and I thought she was great."

"Now I'm picturing you in a tutu and princess crown." Eden pinched his cheek. "I bet you were adorable."

"No, sorry, I stayed away from dresses and makeup." He laughed, scratching his cheek. "Okay, maybe once. But it was Lil's idea."

Eden kissed him through her giggles. She would've loved to see Tate as a kid. He had to have been as adorable as he was handsome now.

"Um, if you tell anyone about me being a pretty princess, I'll be forced to make up a story about you."

She ran a hand through his hair, tugging playfully. "What will the story be?"

"Humm." He tapped his chin. "I'll tell people you turned your spare bedroom into a sex dungeon."

"Then I'll tell people you're my favorite pet," she shot back.

His full-body laugh filled the living room. She adored the sound. "Okay, scratch that story." He grabbed his forgotten beer from the side table and took a sip.

"No, no. I'm warming to it."

"Well, if it turns true, let me know if you need help testing out your equipment."

"Thanks, I appreciate it. Playing with myself is only so much fun."

Tate was mid-sip and choked on his beer. "Christ, woman."

She winked. "You know you like it."

"Especially when I get to watch." His gaze traveled over her body, heating. "The image nearly distracted me from coming up with a better payback story if you leaked my tutu secret."

"Come up with anything new?"

He tapped his chin. "Oh, I'll show up at your work and tell everyone I'm your secret husband—"

"Why would that bother me?" Instead, it sent a warm thrill through her. Refusing to look too closely at the emotion, she climbed onto his lap and returned his beer to the table.

He leaned forward, kissing her long and slow. Leaning back, he grinned. "You didn't let me finish. I'll show up in jeans and a T-shirt but with my underwear on the outside. Maybe even a cape."

Her gaze dipped to the zipper of his jeans. "You don't wear underwear."

"Then I'll wear yours. Maybe one of your bras too."

She giggled, loving his playful side. "And how are you going to get your hands on them?"

"How do you know I haven't already? I could've stolen them the last time I was over."

"I have ten, and all were accounted for last time I did laundry."

Tate chuckled. "Why am I not surprised you know exactly how many under-garments you own? I bet you have a set laundry day."

"No." She ran a finger back and forth along the collar of his shirt. "Okay, fine. I kind of do. It's always the first day I have off." Sliding her hand under his shirt, she cooed, "All this talk of clothes has me wishing…"

He ran his lips up her neck to her ear, then whispered, "What does it have you wishing?"

"That you'd get out of them."

"A woman after my heart." He removed his T-Shirt, then took off hers.

"I want more than your shirt off." She shifted and gripped his erection through his jeans.

She wanted all of him. His heart and body.

That wasn't possible because she'd never give all of herself to him—to anyone. She slid from the couch onto her knees, focusing on what she could give.

CHAPTER THIRTY

Walking through the low iron gate of an outdoor garden at CS Mott Children's Hospital, ambivalence gripped and bit at Tate. He tried to shake the emotion, but it held tight. He'd come close to canceling his lunch date with Eden. Last night's confession left him raw and exposed. He wasn't sure if he was ready to see her. Sure, the sex that followed had been fucking fantastic, but that only confirmed they had great chemistry—which he'd known since their first kiss.

She was gone when he'd awakened, so he hadn't been able to get a read on her. Did she think him weak? Or worse, that he was a problematic man to date.

He spotted her sitting at a picnic table under a maple tree, peering at her phone. As if sensing him, she looked up and waved, wearing a smile warm as the sun.

"Thank you for coming here." She kissed him lightly on the cheek as he set their food on the table. "Today has been crazy. Leaving the hospital for lunch would've been impossible."

Sitting on the long bench beside her, he pulled their wrapped sandwiches from the Zingerman's paper bag. "It's not a big deal. I had a couple of stops to make in the area. When I leave here, I'm visiting a nearby craft distillery then heading to another one in Detroit."

"Well, it makes a difference to me. It's going to be a really long day." Lowering her voice, she said, "And getting to see you makes it better."

Wow. Was Eden admitting that she missed him? He leaned closer to kiss her but halted. They were at her work.

She glanced around, then bridged the gap between them, pressing her mouth to his. Her touch was a mix of chaste and hot, moving toward scorching.

"Glad to see you're enjoying your lunch," came a woman's voice from the park's entrance.

Eden pulled away, her cheeks an attractive shade of pink. She straightened her shirt collar even though it wasn't crooked. "Hello, Amy. I'm surprised to see you here. You always eat at your desk."

"The weather is way too nice to be inside." Amy rocked on her heels, glancing toward the hospital as if deciding to stay or go.

"Sit with us," Eden said. "This is my—um, boyfriend, Tate. Tate, this is my scribe, Amy."

Boyfriend. The title knocked him off-guard in the best way possible. The punch was one he happily rolled with and offered his hand to Amy.

She shook it, looking at Eden. "Boyfriend, huh? I thought Tate was *just* a friend?"

Eden cleared her throat. "Things changed."

"Apparently." Amy's eyes flashed with mischief. "So, I guess you won't be setting *me* up with him?"

"Nope." Eden's pink cheeks turned a gorgeous red, and her lips twitched. "And don't you remember our talk about filters?"

Amy grinned, sitting across from them. "Yes. And don't you remember mine is broken?"

"How could I forget?" Eden muttered, humor infusing her voice.

Amy removed a spoon from her lunchbox and pointed the utensil at Tate. "A while back, Eden mentioned you. I was intrigued and wanted her to set me up with you. She's been dodgy about it." Her gaze traveled over him. "Now I see why."

Tate glanced at Eden. "A while back, huh? Was it the day I moved to our little lake house community? No, I bet it was the first time we met, at the Halloween party. Have you harbored a secret crush all along?" he teased.

She tilted her head. "You were there?" Her grin at the obvious lie made him laugh.

Amy tapped the tablet she'd set on the picnic table. "Well, whenever it happened, it was my loss, but the hospital's gain. You must be the reason our doctor here is being less scary." Tate's laughter grew as Eden shushed Amy. "What? It's true."

Eden crossed her arms under her perfect breasts. "Fine, humor me and boost Tate's ego—"

"Hey, I need it after you claim not to remember meeting me at Halloween," he joked.

She grinned, rubbing his thigh. "How have I become less scary? And really, I only want to know so I can rectify this mistake."

"This morning, you received a text right before meeting with the interns." Amy pointed at Tate. "Was it from him?"

"Probably," Eden admitted.

"Well, your face lit up, and then you *smiled* at one of the interns." Amy turned to Tate. "Those are only reserved for patients."

"That was not me being nice." Eden bit into her sandwich, swallowing, she smirked. "I did it to unsettle him. To get him to stop talking. And it worked. He was quiet for the rest of the day."

Amy cackled. "This is why when the university hires you—"

Eden held up a hand. "*If* they hire me."

"*When* they hire you," Amy continued. "You'll be running the pediatric floor within the week."

"Let me get hired first," Eden winked, "Then I'll aim for hospital domination."

"Okay, fair," Amy agreed.

The three of them finished their food, and as Amy gathered her lunch containers, she asked Tate, "I practically live here, and I'm positive Dr. Perez does. How'd she land you—and more importantly—do you have a single brother?"

"Nope, just two sisters."

"Wait." Eden touched Tate's arm. "You have another sister?"

"Yeah. I have a half-sister, Miley. She lives in Florida with my mom and stepdad, Ted. She's finishing her bachelors and has applied to law school at UMich," he said proudly.

"Well, that's a bummer," Amy replied.

That was a little rude. He quirked a brow. "Excuse me?"

Her eyes widened. "Oh no, congrats on your sister graduating and taking on law school. I meant, it's a bummer that you don't have any single brothers." Eden shook her head, and Tate snorted. "So, how'd you two meet?"

He glanced at Eden, unsure how much to reveal about their connection. She and her scribe seemed to get along well, but Eden wasn't the type to share her history. They'd been dating for around a month, and he knew next to nothing about her past.

"That's how we met. Through his sister." Eden raised a hand, tilting it up and down. "Sort of. My daughter's father is engaged to Tate's sister."

As if mentioning him had summoned Asher, Eden's phone rang, and his face appeared on the screen. She swiped the call to voicemail. "He's probably reminding me that Raven has a game tomorrow. I'll call him back later."

"Damn, you attract all the hot men." Amy's cheeks flushed red, reaching her ears. "That might have been out of line. Sorry."

"Maybe, but it's also true. Tate is hot. I've traded up," Eden replied.

Her words warmed him. He wasn't in competition with Asher or any man, but it was damn sweet that she seemed to admire him as much as he did her.

"That, you have." Amy glanced at her watch. "I better get back. It was great meeting you, Tate."

He nodded goodbye, and when she was out of hearing, he asked, "Traded up, huh?"

"Definitely." She smiled. "Asher's a great guy, but not the guy for me."

It was on the tip of Tate's tongue to ask if he was the man for her. But given her initial hesitation to date him and the way she didn't seem to like looking closely at relationships, he kept his mouth shut.

"I'm so glad he didn't take me up on my suggestion to play house." She crumbled her sandwich wrapper into a ball. "I want Raven to see genuine love, like what Asher and Lilith have, and not the false farce that he and I would have been."

Recalling how he'd acted when learning about that suggestion curdled some of the lunch in Tate's stomach. "Lilith's story shouldn't have blindsided me. I let my past cloud who I know you are."

"What do you mean?"

He gathered the rest of their garbage and glanced around for a trash can. It was better than looking her in the eye as he admitted his stupidity. "My ex liked to play games to make me jealous. I'm not that guy. Usually. And it bugged her, so she'd push and push situations with men to get a reaction out of me. You seeming to pine after Asher while kissing me hit close to my past. It knocked a nerve, and I overreacted."

Eden took his hand. "I get it, and I promise not to play games with you."

A breeze of relief blew through him. He hoped she was telling the truth. He was bone-weary of drama and forced crises.

But he didn't want to talk or think about Katrina anymore. She'd taken up enough of his past. He didn't want her near his future. Running his finger along Eden's knuckles, he asked, "So, I'm your boyfriend?"

Her gaze dropped from his. Then she brought it back. "That slipped out. I didn't know what to call you. I should've just said your name. Or Tate, the man I'm seeing."

Wow, a babbling Eden. It was cute.

She must have seen his amusement because she swatted him playfully. "I'm going to stop talking."

"I want to be your boyfriend—I want you to be my girlfriend. I mentioned it because you were so reluctant to date me." He ran his thumb over her mouth. "And honestly, I don't care what you call me...as long as you call me."

She groaned. "That was incredibly corny." She kissed him. "And sweet."

Her phone rang, breaking them apart. She checked it. "That's Asher again. I should call him, then get back to work."

"Okay."

She kissed him once more before making her way inside. Tate watched her, his heart full and warm.

Damn, he liked his smart and sexy girlfriend. Hell, he more than liked her; he was tipping over the edge, close to falling in love with her.

He hoped the fall wouldn't leave him broken.

CHAPTER THIRTY-ONE

Tate heaved a satisfied sigh as his office door clicked shut behind him. He'd finished the drudgery of pencil-pushing right as Eden texted him to say she was stopping by with Olivia. Stepping into the main dining area of The Hill, the bright June sunlight streamed in from the windows along the outdoor seating and drew his attention to the patio. Every table was full. He hoped these perfect summer days would last well into September. They were great for business.

He spotted one of his favorite servers covering the area. "Hey! Marisol."

She turned, holding a tray with an impressive pile of plates on it. "Yeah?"

He opened the door to the patio for her, and they went inside. "Once table twenty-one or two clears out, will you keep it empty?" Eden's week hadn't gotten any easier after their quick lunch at her work, so the least he could do was make sure she had the best table in his place for her first day off to relax.

"Sure, boss."

"Boss, huh?" Came a voice he'd hoped never to hear again.

Katrina. Tate froze as his stomach roiled. He twisted around slowly, every limb coated in misery.

Her curly blonde hair framed a heart-shaped face, and her big green eyes were the picture of innocence, but her cupid lips were pulled into a false smile that oozed trouble. Tate's gaze flickered to the guy sitting across from her. He had a buzzcut and the build of a man who spent a lot of hours in the gym. His deep frown said he wasn't pleased that Katrina had called Tate.

That made two of them. However, he was happy to see the guy. She hadn't come alone, which was a good sign. Maybe she wanted to show him she'd moved on. Good—though he pitied the man.

Tate debated turning in the opposite direction, walking away, and pretending he hadn't heard or seen her. As if sensing his escape, Katrina called out, "Tate Siren. It's been too long."

Not nearly long enough. Eternity would be too soon. Walking to her booth felt like heading to the gallows. "Hi, Katrina. What brings you here?" He kept his voice bland and emotionless, despite his insides roiling with dark dread.

She tilted her head. "Why so formal? Am I no longer Kat? Your Kitten?"

The guy with her sat up straight, his lips forming a snarl. Tate wanted to tell him Katrina wasn't anything to him. But he wouldn't give her a reason to escalate this shit show.

"Vince told me you went into the restaurant business." *Fucking Vince*. Katrina kept talking as if they were having a friendly chat and she was welcome in his life. She rested her pointed chin on her hand. "He told me the food was great here. And since John and I were passing through, I suggested we stop in for a bite. I had to try *your* place."

Tate hadn't told Vince he owned The Hill. He'd kept things vague in case anything got back to Katrina. It seemed she'd done her research. What he didn't know was what she planned to do with the information.

John's tense posture loosened, and he settled into the booth. "Ah, so you two just used to work together?"

"Yup." Tate knocked his knuckles on the table. "I hope you both enjoy your dinner." He turned to leave.

"Well, we dated too..." Katrina said.

Shit. Old, familiar heavy dread pressed tighter into him. *Here we go.*

"I didn't mention it, in case you refused to come here," she cooed to John, rubbing his hand. "And I wanted to see if this place is as good as Vince claimed."

He studied Tate, running a hand over his short brown hair, flexing. "I never figured you'd be into gingers," he grunted.

"I was most definitely into him," she replied.

Fucking hell. Katrina was playing her favorite game. The one where she was the prize they fought over. And the way John went tight around the eyes and his nostrils flared said he was willing to play. But Tate wasn't and he wouldn't participate in her broken love or her drama.

"'Was', being the key word," Tate said. "It was a while ago. You've obviously moved on."

"Tate, did you snag us a table on the patio?" Eden asked from the restaurant's entrance.

No. No. No. She walked toward him with Olivia. "Yup. Marisol will help you." He kept his voice neutral, almost clipped, though his heart banged against his chest.

Tate swallowed a curse as Olivia headed outside, but Eden kept coming toward him. "What's wrong?" she asked.

He wanted to reach for her, touch her, remind himself dating wasn't this mess sitting at his booth. But even more, he needed her away from Katrina. She'd do her damnedest to pull Eden into their disaster.

"I'm fine. We'll talk later, okay?"

He could see the question in Eden's eyes, but she nodded. "Um, alright."

"Seems I might not be the only one who's moved on." Katrina's glare bounced from Eden to Tate. "Is this the spic Vince saw you with? Are you two dating?"

Through his fog of anger, he heard John mutter, "What the fuck, Katrina?"

Screw the consequences. "Get out," Tate said through the pounding in his ears, then shouted to the kitchen, "Andy, cancel the order for table ten."

"What did you call me?" Eden demanded.

Katrina ignored the question. "Are you dating Tate?"

"Eden, please go sit with Olivia."

She stepped closer to Katrina's booth. "Yeah. I'm the spic dating him. Are you the piece-of-shit-crazy-ex?"

Katrina's eyes widened. "What lies has he told you?"

"Get out," Tate repeated. "Don't come back. You shouldn't be here. Have you forgotten about the restraining order?"

"What restraining order?" John sputtered.

Tate faced the other man. "The one I have against her. Do yourself a favor, dump her before you realize why you will need one."

"Don't listen to him," Katrina screeched. It bounced through the now silent restaurant. The only sounds were the clanking of pans from the kitchen. "He got it out of spite. He did it to get back at me when I dumped him."

She was full of shit on both counts, but he wouldn't waste his energy setting her right. "If I see you here. Or near her"—He pointed at Eden—"I will call the police. Again. This time I'll press charges. Let's see how much the firm will like you having an arrest record."

"You're an asshole," Katrina snarled, standing. "Let's go, John. I've lost my appetite. I don't want to eat at this dump."

Tate moved aside, but Eden held her ground. When Katrina was in front of her, Eden leaned in and whispered something. Katrina went white and hurried from the restaurant with John trailing behind, looking shell-shocked.

"What did you say to her? Tate asked.

"Nothing important. I better get to my table before Olivia thinks I ditched her." Eden kissed him, lingering until wolf whistles erupted from around the restaurant.

He glanced around and saw nearly every set of eyes was on him and Eden. All the attention was like ants crawling over his skin.

He smiled half-heartedly and said to the room, "Did you all enjoy the show?

A regular shouted, "Yeah, but next time could we have popcorn?"

Laughter filled the room, breaking the last of the lingering tension. Hopefully, there would be no "next time."

CHAPTER THIRTY-TWO

Eden stepped from inside Tate's living room to his balcony. The evening breeze fluttered the napkins in her hand she'd grabbed for everyone sitting around his table outside. She shivered. The heat and humidity that clung to most of June dropped away in its final week. Her body was used to hot—not warm—during the summer months.

"Mom," Raven pointed toward the lake. "Want to go on the paddle boat with me and Chloe?"

Eden hated refusing her daughter, but the sun was close to setting. It'd be cooler on the water. "Let me see if I brought a jacket or sweater." She handed each of the girls a napkin, then Tate, Lilith, and Asher.

Raven wiped strawberry shortcake from her mouth. "Really? I'm warm."

"That's your Michigander skin." Eden sat between Raven and Tate. "Once the temperature drops below seventy-five degrees, I feel like hypothermia is setting in."

Raven grinned. "Okay, you should stay here. Wimp."

Eden laughed, tugging on her daughter's ponytail.

"You are better off," Asher said, pointing at the girls with his drink. "I've seen you two out there on that boat. Trying to push each other into the lake."

Chloe grinned. "I got her in first, last time."

"Yeah, but I snatched your ankle and pulled you in with me."

They laughed as Eden shuddered. "Sorry, honey. I'm definitely going to pass."

"You two are in charge of loading the dishwasher when you get back," Lilith said.

"And be back before the sunset," Asher finished.

Eden rubbed her hands over her bare arms as their retreating forms disappeared around the corner. A minute later, they reappeared on the path leading to the dock.

Lilith tapped the iron table with her fork, snagging everyone's attention. "So, Tate, I heard there was an incident at your restaurant the other day."

He groaned, and Eden heard his exhaustion and reluctance. He looked toward the girls. "Think they'd let me go with them?"

Lilith squeezed his hand. "Tate..."

"Lilith." He widened his eyes and shook his head, pulling his hand from hers. Then he sighed, taking a sip of his drink. "There isn't much to tell. Katrina stopped in. She was in a mood and wanted to start shit. I asked her to leave. She did. End of story."

"I don't think that's the full story. Wyatt's wife was there. She overheard you saying you have a restraining order against Katrina."

"Freaking small towns," Tate muttered, his lips pressed together as if the conversation tasted bitter.

Lilith tilted her head. "Why didn't you tell me things were that bad between you two?"

Eden, of all people, understood that need, but she felt for Lilith. Her hurt and confusion were apparent in her voice and every gesture.

Tate must have seen it too as his next words were softer, though spilling with lies. "Lil, my thing with Katrina was nothing."

"A restraining order doesn't sound like nothing." Lilith's gaze dropped to her glass, and she circled it with her fingertips. "I thought we were close."

"You weren't exactly an open book about your marriage," he said without malice. From what Eden knew of Tate, he was too kind to lay the guilt on his sister.

"The less you knew, the better." She grinned. "I didn't want you in jail for killing Marshall."

Tate snorted. "That's the same reason I didn't tell you about Katrina." He stood, clearly ready to end the topic. "Anyone want a refill on their drink?"

Asher and Lilith nodded. Eden shook her head. She'd brought her favorite tea to his house, but it had more caffeine than coffee. "I have to work tomorrow, so I should stop. I need to be able to sleep tonight." Sometimes she wished her job was the regular Monday to Friday, nine to five, kind. Starting her work week on a Sunday was a bummer. She missed a whole free day with Raven.

Tate disappeared inside, and Lilith tapped Eden's hand resting on the table. "I also heard there was a whispered exchange between you and Katrina. One that had her running from the restaurant."

Eden waved a hand. "That wasn't me. She was already leaving."

"But you said something to her, didn't you?"

Eden shrugged, her heart skipping a beat. Rage had swallowed her at meeting Tate's ex. It wasn't jealousy or even the petty slur—those spoke of Katrina's shortcomings, not Eden's. No, it was the cruelty thrown at Tate and even the man with Katrina. It had dragged Eden back to her childhood. Her mom hadn't been as calculating, but her drunken rages had cut the same as Katrina's cruelty, damaging those on the receiving end.

"What did you say?" Lilith asked.

"It was childish. I'd rather not repeat it."

"I'm feeling vindictive right now and need a little childish wrath."

Eden understood the urge. She leaned closer to Lilith. "I told her if she came near me or Tate, I'd cut her through muscle and bone. And that it wasn't an empty threat. I was a surgeon and knew where to slice to make someone hemorrhage slowly and painfully."

Lilith grinned and patted Eden's hand. "I like you. I like you a lot."

The camaraderie was really nice, but the threat and Katrina's reaction covered Eden with slimy guilt, mainly because it had felt so damn good. Had her mother experienced the same rush when she'd frightened and cowered Eden?

"Why do you like her? Not that there aren't many reasons," Tate said, balancing a tray of drinks in one hand and closing the glass sliding door with the other. He kissed Eden's temple before setting a mug in front of her. "I stopped at a popular tea shop in Detroit. I found one similar to the one you love in decaf."

Her heart melted, falling through her rib cage and landing in Tate's hands. Lemon and honey wafted from her tea. He'd even added the extras she loved. She picked up the mug, held it under her nose and inhaled.

She'd been thrilled to discover that her career didn't threaten Tate. This was an issue the few times she'd dated. And he didn't guilt her about the long hours. Then, on top of everything, he was also thoughtful, always considering her needs. How did a woman like her end up with a guy like him? She didn't deserve him. How could they possibly last?

Yet her heart dared to beat for the possibility of a future with him. Everything she'd been too afraid to dream of might be right here, in this little community tucked between Michigan's thousands and thousands of lakes. Was a home and love within her grasp?

CHAPTER THIRTY-THREE

The muffled thump of Tate closing his book pulled Eden's attention from her laptop. After a five-day work stretch, it was her first day off, so they'd already had sex. Twice. But when he set the hardcover on the nightstand and arched against the mattress, his naked torso flexing as he stretched had all her attention.

"Almost done?" he asked.

"For now." She slid a hand down his stomach, cupping him gently. "Because I'd rather work on you."

He rolled onto his side, kissing along her neck. His sensual trail of kisses moved along her shoulder. He stopped at the tattoo covering the burn scar from her childhood. "How did you get this?"

Her heart split. The desire to share all of herself with the man she was falling for was strong, but she'd held tight to her secrets for so long that she couldn't seem to let them go.

"I went to a tattoo parlor," she hedged.

He snorted. "Uh, thanks. I meant what's under it."

"A childhood accident." *That was no accident.* The admission was small yet cut through her. She pushed away the painful memory before it could consume her.

Outside the open window, the katydids and crickets sang their songs of summer. The calm night chorus filled the heavy silence of all she couldn't share.

"That's it. That's the story." He laughed, though it sounded more hurt than humorous. "Good thing you went into medicine instead of storytelling."

"I'm sorry, Tate, I really am, but I'd rather not get into it. That past is a place I'd rather not visit."

"I won't push, make you talk about something you don't want to." He ran a finger along the burn's puckered edges. "Just know you can trust me with more than your pleasure. I will hold you in your pain too. Be there for you."

She heard what he wasn't saying—he'd shared his secrets, and it hadn't ruined things between them. But he'd never seen her drowning in her emotions, falling apart. And she'd never show him. That version of herself was for her alone to hold.

Eden straddled Tate, and his hand fell from her shoulder. "Thanks, but I'm fine." She kissed him hard, nipping at his bottom lip. "We all deal with pain in different ways. I cut it out of my life."

"But what if you removed more than you intended?"

She pressed her hand against his chest, over his heart. "Stop with the analogies and curvy corners of speaking. Say what you mean."

"What if you remove the vulnerability that lets you love?"

She scoffed, annoyed at his insinuation. "I love my daughter and abuela."

He ran his fingertips along her spine. "Besides family. Have you ever been in love?"

Her fragile heart raced in fear and exhilaration because she was falling in love for the first time. With him. But instead of speaking the truth, she leaned on the past. "I've barely dated, focusing on my career, not love."

"And you honestly believe that's why you've never been in love—your career?"

"Fine. Maybe there's more to it. I've never looked too closely. Hell, my old therapist would probably agree with you. But romance was never my focus." She tipped to her right, intending to get off him. His questions and hints made her feel like a broken toy. One he might soon toss aside.

Tate gripped her waist. "What was your focus?" His gaze flickered to her scarred shoulder, then to her eyes.

She stiffened. "I saw my psychiatrist when I was living in California. I wanted help with my fears of becoming a mother. Besides, what makes you think I'm burying anything heavy? Maybe it's growing pains."

"Both your parents died, and you won't talk about it."

"Oh, that," she whispered. An ache tightened in her throat as she swallowed her lie. "Like I said, my focus in therapy was on how to build a better relationship with Raven."

And how to overcome my fear of being alone with my child–the dreadful worry that I might hurt her.

Letting go of Eden's wrist, he slid his fingers through hers. "Why am I not surprised that you were in charge—directed—your therapy session?"

She grasped at the topic change. Or, more accurately, she pinched it—as in Tate's nipple. She twisted it playfully. "Are you calling me bossy?"

He sighed, and she feared he'd keep pushing. She didn't want to fight with him, afraid of where it would end. That *they* would end.

Instead, he wrapped her hair around his fist. "That's what I like about you." He pulled. The sensation started at her scalp and traveled between her legs. "I love when you try to take control."

This was a distraction she'd happily ride.

"*Try?*" She rolled her hips, and he sucked in a breath, loosening his hold.

She slid her hands through his and pinned them at the sides of his head. Thrusting again, and very happy that he slept naked, as the thin sheet between them shifted lower on his hips.

"Who's in control?" she purred.

His eyes were molten glass as his hips moved in rhythm with hers. "You are," he groaned.

She removed her tank top, and he gripped her waist, lifting her. With a yelp, she grabbed the headboard as he placed her on his face. She moaned her approval.

"Who's in control now?" he asked.

"From this position, I'd say, it's still me."

"We'll see." Keeping a tight hold of her hips, he teased her with light licks in all the places she needed, but without the required pressure. "More, Tate," she demanded.

He laughed, and it vibrated with sensual sin. "Are you in control? Or maybe losing it?"

She panted, refusing to answer him, even as her body plead for more. He brought her to the very edge of her orgasm, and then switched to feather-light strokes of his tongue. She couldn't come, but the pleasure of his slow touch had her close to losing her mind. "Tate, please," she begged.

"Who's in control?"

"You are."

"Of what?" He twirled his tongue around her clit.

She whimpered and tried to press into him. His grip on her waist made it impossible. "My orgasms. My bliss."

"That's right," he nearly growled, then gave her exactly what she needed, devouring her.

She came apart in a matter of seconds. While she lifted and rolled onto her back, she heard the nightstand drawer opening over her racing pulse.

"Hurry," she demanded, licking her lips as he rolled on a condom. "I need you inside me now."

He cocked a brow. "Oh, now that you've come, you're making a grab for control?"

She smirked, and he flipped her onto her stomach, lifting her on all fours, and slid inside her. They moaned in unison. The deep penetration touched her previous climax while building on another one. His fingers dug into her hips as he pumped into her, and when one of those hands snaked around and in between her legs, she saw stars. Her arms gave way, but he held her up with one hand while his other pressed and rubbed right where she needed him.

She gasped out his name as another orgasm exploded through her. His thrusts became faster and rougher as his climax followed behind hers.

He slumped against her back, and they sank flat onto the mattress. His hot breaths on her neck comforted her, and she missed his bulk when he rolled off her. "I'll be right back."

His gorgeous frame retreated to the bathroom. After tossing the condom, he returned, and she managed to drag her limp body to his, resting her head on his chest. His steady heartbeat was becoming her home.

"You sure know how to distract a man," he mumbled, kissing her temple.

Her pulse jumped. She considered lying, but the ones she'd already spoken hung heavy between them. "I'm sorry. It's not you, but me—I know that line is trite, but it is true. I've kept things bottled up for so long, the cork is stuck."

"I get it. I was the same when I was with Katrina. And after." He hugged her closer. "I'll be here when you're ready."

Would she ever be ready?

She propped herself onto her elbow and looked at him. His eyes were closed, and his mouth was relaxed. She traced a finger along his lips, and a sleepy smile formed. Maybe she could talk with him and share more of herself. Given what he'd been through with his ex, he might even understand her demons. Or he might leave because he didn't want to deal with another emotional wreck of a woman. Her heart clenched.

"Tate?"

"Hmm?"

"Did you breakup with your ex because she was high-strung and temperamental?"

He cracked an eye open and grinned. "I left her because she stabbed me in the face."

Eden smiled at his brutal humor, brushing a lock of fallen hair from his forehead. "Did she snap or was she always..." Eden searched for the right word. "Emotionally difficult."

"Oh, she was waving a shit-ton of red flags before things ever got physical. I just kept explaining them away, making excuses for her. Now I know—don't date people who freak-the-shit-out when things don't go their way." He ran a hand down Eden's spine. "Besides being wicked-smart, driven, and sexy, your level nature is one of my favorite things about you."

She winced as a heaviness filled her chest. His favorite thing about her was a farce. Her explosive emotions were kept on a tight leash, but some days it snapped. And what if he was around when it happened? He'd leave her. That's what would happen.

He kissed her. "What made you ask?"

"I'm too tired to remember." She lied, settling back against his chest. There would be no midnight confessions. She'd hold her sins close and make sure they never escaped and hurt Tate.

CHAPTER THIRTY-FOUR

Eden counted to ten over and over. And over. Since pulling out of the hospital parking lot, her frustration and rage remained in check. Barely. Her emotions rattled and roared in their cage, pounding to be let out. She smacked her palm on the steering wheel and cursed. As if dealing with Leeday's arrogance wasn't enough, now this shit.

Turning onto the private road toward her home, she glanced at The Hill. It was late and a Wednesday, so it was already closed. The restaurant was dark, but under the parking lot's lights, Tate strode toward his Bronco. He glanced toward her car, then smiled and waved.

She jerked the wheel in his direction. Gravel popped and snapped as she pulled next to him, slamming on her brakes. She yanked open her door, barreled out, and skidded to a stop. She inhaled, counting to four. Then exhaled to the count of seven and shoved her temper back behind its bars. He couldn't control his crazy fucking ex.

Tate spun his keys around his index finger once, then closed his palm around them. "Bad day?"

She nodded.

"Can I hold you?" he asked.

She nodded again. His strong arms went around her, and she could breathe again. She loved his scent of cedarwood and man. It soothed her toxic worry.

He ran a hand down her spine. "What happened?"

"The attending physician who supervises my work and makes the final decision on who to hire—me or Leeday—forwarded an email from some anonymous asshole. It was a scathing complaint about me. They claimed they were visiting the family of one of my patients. The jerk basically said I was condescending to the parents and rough with the child. They flat-out said I should be fired."

"Damn," Tate said. "How serious is this kind of complaint? I mean, it is anonymous."

"It is big deal." She sighed, resting her cheek against his chest. "But it's my first, so I should be able to weather it—if I don't get more."

"I'm sure you won't. It was probably some distraught person lashing out."

She hated how anxiety clawed at him when his ex was mentioned, but this was Eden's job—her life. Pulling back, she rested a hand on his chest. "Tate, I think it was Katrina. And what if once wasn't enough for her?"

The sudden acceleration of his heart thumped against her palm. He gripped her shoulders and stepped back, looking into her eyes. His were a glacier of anger. "Are you sure?"

"In the email, it says this person followed me out of the room and overheard me bullying a nurse, claiming I'd threatened to cut her. That I'd make her hemorrhage slowly and painfully." She cleared her throat, heat infusing her cheek. "I said something very similar to Katrina that night at the restaurant. I think she wanted to make sure I knew the email was from her without having actual tangible proof."

"Fuck," he muttered, rubbing his jaw.

The anguish in his gaze made her wish she hadn't opened her damn mouth—about the email and her childish threat. She should have done what she usually did and kept her problems to herself.

He gave a strangled groan, his hands clenching into fists. "I knew dating you was a mistake."

Eden reared away as if slapped. "Wha—"

"No. I didn't mean it like that." He reached for her but stopped before touching her. "Since I split with her, she's been texting and emailing me. I've ignored them, hoping she'd lose interest and move on. But I was afraid something like this would happen. I'm sorry."

"Tate." She cupped his face, making sure he was looking at her. "This isn't your fault."

"Yes, it is." He slid his hands over hers, removing them but not letting go. "I should have stayed away. Or at least told you sooner. Let you decide if the risk and possible hassle was worth it."

"It wouldn't have made a difference." Eden wasn't sure if she was lying, and going by his expression, he doubted her too.

She switched tracks and went with the absolute truth. "I had no expectations when I'd moved here. Only a hope of repairing my relationship with Raven. Instead, I found more than I deserve. With you."

He hugged her and whispered into her hair. "*I* don't deserve you."

His words were absurd, but she loved them anyway. They stayed like that for a while, her taking comfort in his arms, hoping her embrace offered the same to him.

Sometime later, he asked, "Do you have the email?"

"Yes."

"Would you send it to me?"

"Why? It's not obvious that it's from her. She wasn't kind enough to have Katrina@crazycunt.com as the address."

Laughter boomed from him. She loved the sound and how it smothered most of her ire. "Well, that's too bad," he said. "But send it to me anyway."

"Tate…"

"Please, send it." His voice was gentle but firm.

She wanted to refuse, to ask him to let it go and stay far away from his unhinged ex, but she kept quiet. Sure, she was worried, even a little scared. Katrina was smart, vindictive, and unwilling to let go of Tate. However, Eden would want the email if she were in his position.

"I'll send it to you."

He kissed her temple. "Thank you."

"Do you have to go home? Or can you come to my place?" she asked.

"As I've said before, I'll go where ever you want me."

"I want you with me." Her heart fluttered, quick and startled, at the errant thought. *Always.*

Was it true?

CHAPTER THIRTY-FIVE

Tate turned off his SUV, watching people come and go from the small coffee shop attached to the mall. He grabbed his phone from the passenger seat and re-read the text messages, unsure of what he hoped to find.

Katrina: I'm sorry I had an attitude at your restaurant

Katrina: And that I brought John

Katrina: I don't love him

Katrina: I love you

Katrina: I miss you

Tate: We need to talk. In person.

Katrina: I'll come to you

Katrina: What's your address

Tate: I'll be in Royal Oak on Sunday. Let's meet at Sweet Sip at 11 am.

Katrina: ok

He took a deep breath, not ready to find out but eager to start and end the confrontation. Once inside the coffee shop, he spotted Katrina tucked into a corner next to a large window. She'd always loved the sun. And, right now, the way it shone off her blonde hair gave her an angelic aura.

However, he saw the shadows and ugly underneath. Her gaze found him, and she smiled, coming toward him with open arms. Was she seriously going to pretend everything was fine?

He held up a hand. "No. Go back to the table. I'll meet you there after I get a drink."

Rage flashed on her face. Then her gaze jumped around the small café. They'd already caught the attention of a few people. She peered at the ground and hunched her shoulders as if his words hurt. "Okay," she whispered.

It seemed her performance as the wounded ex-girlfriend had begun. Christ, he was already exhausted. How had they lasted almost a year?

He stepped up to the counter and ordered a coffee. Not that he wanted the damn thing. He just wasn't ready to sit with her. After the barista handed him his mug, he trudged to her table. Thankfully, this time she stayed seated and didn't try to touch him.

He took the chair across from her, set his mug on the table, pushing it aside. "I want you to send another email to the hospital and retract your complaint about Eden."

"I don't know what you're talking about." Her eyes went big and innocent, but her sharp smile gave her away. It told the truth she wanted known.

He didn't bother replying. Just waited. He'd been over her games before they'd broken up. He wouldn't pretend to entertain them now to make things go smoothly.

For two days, he'd torn through his mind, coming up with and discarding ways to fix things for Eden that didn't involve meeting with Katrina. This was the only way. It was a little brutal, but it would work.

"Does it bother you?" she asked.

He continued to stare at her, refusing to play. It didn't deter her. "Doesn't it bother you? You're the owner of a shitty dive bar and she's a surgeon at one of the top hospitals in the country. Prestigious job, huge paycheck..." Katrina took a delicate sip of her coffee. "Does she own you inside and outside of the bedroom?"

Ah, so this was the card she'd use. He held in a laugh at her sorry-ass attempt at creating discord. He'd have stayed at his old job if all he cared about were money and status. And he was proud of Eden, not emasculated by her drive and commitment to her career.

Ignoring the jibe, he circled back to Katrina's denial and what she'd revealed. "If you weren't the one who sent the email, how do you know what hospital she works at?"

Katrina's smirk fell. "I...um... don't know. I'm guessing."

Removing a sheet of paper from his back pocket, he unfolded it and slid it to her. "I have a friend who's great with computers." *Thank you, Marisol.* His favorite waitress was getting a raise. "She traced the email. It was created the day of the complaint and from the personal computer of Katrina Orleans."

She stared at the printout, then away. Heavy silence fell between them.

He didn't mind filling the void. "I have plenty of witnesses that you were at my restaurant disregarding the restraining order. Harassing me."

"I wasn't har—"

"Did you know you could go to jail for months for ignoring a restraining order? Did you know your violating it now?"

Fear sparked in Katrina's eyes as she took in all the people watching them. "But you agreed to meet with me."

"Doesn't matter. It's not against me, so I'm not violating it. But you are." He was tempted to ask if she liked being on the receiving end of twisting the law to force another to do as she wished. Instead, he held up the sheet of paper. "I will take this, along with the hundreds of emails and texts you've sent me, to the police. I'll push and push until something is done...until your harassment is on permanent record. I'll tell anyone who's willing to listen at my old job, *your* job, that you're the main reason I left. That—"

"You didn't leave because of me. I love you." She slid a hand over his.

Her level of delusion was astounding. He pulled away and pointed to the scar less than an inch from his eye. "Love doesn't leave these kinds of marks." She opened her mouth, but he wasn't in the mood to hear the excuses that'd fall out. "A few days ago, I spoke to Autumn. Do you remember her?"

Katrina's gaze darted to the right. "No."

"You don't remember the person whose car you keyed and tires you flattened?"

"I've already told you, that wasn't me."

Tate ignored her lie. "Back then Autumn had been afraid to talk about it. Scared what you'd do." He picked up his mug, then returned it to the table. His roiling stomach rebelled at taking a sip. "As you probably know, Autumn left. You were the main reason for her too. She told me this when I found her on social media. She also told me she'd be happy to make a call to your boss, to explain why she felt the need to find a different job—if I wanted."

Katrina placed a hand over her heart. "Why would you do that? I could lose my job."

He shrugged and dropped the sheet of paper on the table. "You didn't seem to care about Eden's career when you fired off this email."

Katrina pressed her lips into a thin line and hissed, "The bitch threatened me. Did she tell you that?"

"Yes, *Eden* told me. How does it feel to be on the receiving end of threats?"

She crossed her legs, bouncing them enough that the table shook. "I'm sure you blew our fights out of proportion," she scoffed, then said louder. "Did you tell her about the time you pushed me, and I fell, bruising my arm?"

People at nearby tables eyed them. He inhaled, pinching the bridge of his nose. "Are you referring to when you threw a cup of hot tea at me, and *you* slipped and fell in it when you ran at me? Is that the time you're talking about?"

He hadn't bothered keeping his voice low, and someone nearby chuckled. If she wanted to give everyone a show, they sure as hell wouldn't be getting her version. And going by the rage splotches on her cheeks, she didn't like how this story played out.

"Stop texting and calling me. No more emails. Don't bother my girlfriend." He jabbed a finger at the printed email between them. "Fix this today. Or tomorrow I'll not only call Autumn and ask her to contact your boss, I'll go to the police about you violating the restraining order and harassing Eden. Forget about her. Forget about me."

She grabbed his hand. "I can't. I love you."

"No you don't." He slid his hand from hers. "You have no idea what love is."

"Don't tell me how I feel." She leaned forward and gripped his bicep, digging in her nails. He winced, and she released him, patting the red marks on his arm. "We had issues, but we can work through them."

He shook his head. "I'm with Eden. I'm happy."

Katrina's lip curled. "It won't last. She'll leave you, and you'll come crawling back to me."

"No. Never."

He and Eden might not last. She was holding back, and he wasn't sure why. But one thing was certain. He was never going back to hell. To Katrina.

He stood. "No matter what happens with Eden, you and I are done."

As he pushed open the café door, he heard the excited whispers of the people at the surrounding tables. He was glad for the witnesses. The public ending would make things more real for Katrina. Walking away from his past had never felt so damn good. This chapter of his life was over.

Fuck, the whole story was done. He'd start a new one with Eden—if she was willing.

CHAPTER THIRTY-SIX

Eden glanced out the window of the Whitney, hoping to catch sight of Tate's SUV, but the restaurant's balcony and lush garden blocked most of Woodward Avenue. He wasn't late, but she wished he'd hurry. Her good news was screaming and jumping to be shared.

"I don't know what to order," Raven said.

Eden scanned the menu. "Try the Beef Wellington. It's their house special."

"But it cost so much," Raven whispered.

Eden waved away the protest. "Don't worry. My old roommate at UMich used to talk about this place all the time. She and her family came here often. I've always wanted to try it, so enjoy it with me."

"Would you like to order a drink while waiting for..." The waitress trailed off as Tate appeared in the wide doorway of the Library room.

Wow. He looked tastier than anything on the menu. The man could wear a suit. It was navy, paired with a white button-up and a lighter blue tie. The color combination was perfect with his auburn hair. Eden waved, snagging his attention. He grinned, and, damn, she nearly swooned.

"Could you give us a minute? I'd like to give my boyfriend a chance to look over the drink menu," she said as Tate made his way to the table.

The waitress tore her gaze from him, blinked, and then smiled professionally. "Of course."

She left as Tate arrived. "I hope you two weren't waiting too long." He kissed Eden lightly. "You look stunning."

With him in mind, she'd bought the indigo off-the-shoulder maxi dress with the dangerous slit up the leg. The way his eyes drank in every detail was intoxicating.

"Not long." She picked up her menu. "We hadn't even decided what to order."

When she'd said 'we,' Tate's gaze shifted to Raven. "You look as pretty as your mom."

Raven was lovely in her green dress. She was a beautiful little girl and would be a gorgeous woman.

"Thanks, Uncle Tate." She smoothed her hand over the silky material of her outfit. "We went shopping this morning, and Mom got it for me."

He took the empty seat at the small round table. "Are you enjoying your girls' day?"

She nodded. "I love Detroit and Ann Arbor. Cities are so much more fun than our boring little town. When I grow up, I should go to UMich like Mom and Hope. Or here, in Detroit."

"Guess it depends on what you want to do when you grow up. What are you thinking?"

Raven held her hands out, palms up. "Maybe I'll be a surgeon, like Mom."

Eden covered her heart as lightness filled it. Her daughter saw her as someone to emulate.

"Speaking of that, I have exciting news." She set her menu on the table, hoping they wouldn't notice the tremor in her voice. "I've been offered the position at the hospital when my fellowship ends."

Raven jumped from her seat and hugged Eden so tight that she wheezed out a laugh. Her gaze swung to Tate, and his broad smile filled her with contentment so bone-deep it made her light-headed.

"They're lucky to have you," Tate said, reaching across the table and squeezing her hand.

"What about my great-grandma?" Raven let go and sat.

Eden's smile widened, joy coating her heart. "I spoke with her this morning, and she agreed to move here. She's excited to see snow." Eden shook her head. "Let's see how she feels come February."

Raven waved a hand. "I love winter. Ice skating, snowmobiling, better hair days."

"Maybe for your hair," Eden laughed, running a hand through hers. "Mine is a ball of static. Anyway, hopefully I can get everything ready over the phone and online. When my fellowship ends, I'll take a week off and go to New Mexico, help my abuela get ready to move here."

"I'm coming with you, right?" Raven asked. Then she looked at Tate. "You should come with us!"

He blinked. "To New Mexico?"

"Yeah," Raven leaned forward. "Me and Mom made a bet. If I beat her in pinball, she'd have to take me there. I won."

Oh crap.

Tate's brows rose, and he looked at Eden. "Damn. You're a high roller."

Her fingers ran along the leather encasing the menu. She glanced at her cell. Abuela had mentioned her mom had called again, asking for Eden's number. Why couldn't she disappear like Katrina had after Tate met with her those couple of weeks back? Trepidation crawled over Eden, quick and fast, creating a spider web of nerves. But there wouldn't be a confrontation. Eden would never call her.

She cleared her throat and looked at Raven. "I'll ask your dad if it's okay."

Raven squealed. People at nearby tables glanced over and smiled. "I'll talk him into it. This is going to be awesome. I can't wait to tell my friends I'm going to New Mexico! Can we go to White Sands?"

"If you don't mind a drive," Eden replied, hoping she appeared carefree. "It's about three hours from my your bisabuela's house in Albuquerque."

Raven grinned. "It's gonna to be so cool. Have you ever been there, Uncle Tate?"

"Uh, no."

"We're going to have so much fun!"

Tate scratched behind his ear. "Umm..."

"I can't wait to see where you grew up." Raven told Eden.

Yes, as long as her drunk of a grandmother didn't come around when they were there. Eden took a sip of water, her throat suddenly dry. That part of her life couldn't come near her new one. Maybe she should tell Raven and Tate that her mom was alive, living somewhere in New Mexico. The lie felt heavier each day she held it inside.

She looked at Tate. His face was unreadable. The truth refused to leave her lips. Instead, she asked, "Will you come too?"

The waitress returned and asked if they were ready to order.

While Raven asked about the menu, Tate took Eden's hand under the table. "Don't feel obligated to invite me because, um, Raven did."

A soft warmth filled Eden. Tate was such a kind, understanding man. She entwined her fingers with hers. "I want you there with us." At least she could speak that truth while holding in lies.

His radiant smile spread over his handsome face. It reflected the same hope and happiness flooding her chest.

And she wouldn't ruin this perfect day with her ugly past. She could tell them later, before they left for New Mexico. Or not at all. All the hurt her mom had caused was history, dead and gone in her heart. A trip home would be fine. The ugly would stay buried. She'd show them the places and memories that had made her smile, not cry.

Everything would be fine.

CHAPTER THIRTY-SEVEN

Eden's hands were steady as she slid the key into her lock, but her insides shook like ice in a blender. It took everything in her not to slam the door shut and kick it until the solid wood frame, or her foot, broke.

Stepping from her clogs, Eden dragged herself to the couch, flopping onto it. Her throat tightened, and her eyes stung. The final month of her fellowship had been challenging, but she'd floated on the happy clouds of her fantastic life. She had her daughter and all the time in the world to make things right, a wonderful man, and would soon be starting her dream job. But today—on the last fucking day of her fellowship—that dream was a nightmare.

Little girls shouldn't die. And not during a routine surgery.

She took a few useless, deep breaths. It didn't do shit. A ping from her phone pierced the silence. She ignored it. The message was probably from Tate or Olivia wanting to celebrate the completion of her fellowship. But talking to anyone wasn't possible.

She needed to be alone and put herself back together.

Groaning, she sat up, her feet hitting the thin, braided rug with a soft thud. Sitting still with her thoughts was torture.

She set the water near scalding in her bathroom and stepped inside the shower. Once there, her tears fell. Blood clots happened. Death happened. She knew this rationally. But logic refused to take hold because neither should touch kids.

Her fingertips pruned, and the hot water turned cold. She gave up. It was delusional to think a shower could wash away her sadness. Shutting off the levers, she grabbed her robe just as the doorbell rang. Her emotions ran in separate directions. One wept for comfort. The other shouted to be left alone.

A long sigh escaped her lips. If it were Tate, he wouldn't leave until he saw her. At the moment, his care exhausted her. She didn't have the energy to pretend everything was fine. Pretending was difficult with him. He saw too much of her and always knew when she was faking.

She opened her door, and he stood on her porch, holding a cloth bag and her favorite flowers, daisies and red roses. He looked like her true home. She wanted to fall into his arms. She wanted to close the door.

"Congrats…" His brows furrowed. "What's wrong?"

"Nothing."

The corner of his mouth tucked in with disbelief, but instead of contradicting her, he held up the bag. "In case you forgot to eat today, I brought dinner for us to eat together. To, um, celebrate…" He peered at her, a worry line appearing between his brows. "You still got the job, right?"

"Yes."

He nodded slowly. "Okay, to celebrate your last day as a fellow. I made your favorite Michigan meals."

She should eat. Her only bit of sustenance was a small bowl of oatmeal at five in the morning. Giving in to the comfort of his presence, she stepped aside. When he was next to her, he leaned down and kissed her lips. It was light and sweet and her damn tears returned. She blinked them away—along with her weakness and her desire to beg him to hold her. She couldn't break into a million pieces, expecting him to find them and put her back together. That would have to wait until she was alone.

Heading to the kitchen, she warned, "My last day wasn't so great. I'll be terrible company."

"Do you want to talk about it?"

"No." Her tone was sharp, and she regretted it. "I'm sorry. I'll tell you later, just not now. Will you tell me something light? Something to distract me. Please."

"Okay." He opened a container and handed it to her.

Her stomach growled at the scent of grilled fresh fruit and goat cheese. Michigan cherry salads were the best. He handed her another box. "Chili-cheese fries? As a doctor, I should eat what I preach," she argued aloud with herself. Her taste buds refused to listen, and a moan slipped from her when the ooey-gooey cheese, spicy chili, and fried potato hit her taste buds. "So good."

"I make them, so I know exactly what goes into them. You'd think it'd stop me," he said before eating ate a few. "Worth it. Okay, do you want to hear about the Karen couple that had my staff threatening to spit in their food?"

She nodded and settled into her chair. Tate was a talented storyteller. His calm, deep voice filled her small kitchen, soothing her and making her heart and body ache a little less. The hollow sadness stilled, comforted in his presence.

However, the empty abyss reopened when he finished his story and fries, with a satisfied groan. He'd be leaving soon. Her emotional tug-of-war resumed with a vengeance—push him away or hold him tight. Trust him to hold her and her ugly emotions or be safe and refuse to let him see her break.

Sitting still made her skin itch like ants crawled all over her. She shot up. Her chair screeched across the tile floor. The sound scraped along her nerves. Grabbing the near-empty containers, she turned, and one slipped from her hand, crashing to the ground. A muddy mixture of salad dressing, grease, and cheese splattered her robe and some of Tate's jeans and shoes.

"Shit." Her skin flushed hot as her pulse pounded.

Rage and impotence at her all shortcomings snapped and poured out. She slammed the remaining container on the floor, kicking both across the kitchen. They hit the cabinet by the sink, spilling more food.

"Eden." Tate's warm hand rested on her back. "Tell me what's wrong."

He couldn't see her like this—losing it, just like his ex. He'd leave her.

She sucked in a sharp breath and shook him off. Her throat hurt with a re-pressed scream, but she *wouldn't* let it out. Her ridiculous, useless fury had to be contained.

Tate moved around her, stooped to the floor, and began picking up bits of fries. "Leave them," she snapped.

"I got it. You go rinse off. I'll clean this."

His calm kindness sharpened her anger. "Why? It's my fucking mess."

Christ. She sounded like her mom.

Her chin dropped with shame. She pinched the bridge of her nose with her thumb and index finger. "I'm sorry. I shouldn't have yelled."

"It's fine." He threw everything in the garbage, washed his hands, then gently cupped her shoulders. He was so fucking gentle that it hurt. "Talk to me."

She pressed her hands against his chest. His heart was racing, probably nervous at what she might do. Hers was pounding for the same reason. "Go back to work," she said numbly.

"Let me help you."

"I'm not helpless."

"I never said you were. I care about you. I want to make your day a little better." He gripped her arms as if to pull her into a hug.

She stiffened. "You can, so leave." *Please don't leave me.*

His hands fell from her. "Is that what you want?"

"Yes," she whispered as her heart screamed, no. She kept her head down, waiting for him to stomp out, slamming the door behind him. Maybe to never come back. But that was better than looking into his eyes and seeing his belief that he was with another wreck of a woman.

"If that's what you need, I'll give you space." His words were quiet but laced with hurt and even a little anger.

Forever? Or just the night? She was too scared to ask. The answer could snap the frazzled rope of emotions holding her together.

She craved his warmth and needed his comfort, but she couldn't form the words and prevent her chaos and unhappiness from spilling all over him. Everything in her ached to call out to him. Beg him to stay.

Instead, she kept silent as he walked away from her. And as the door quietly clicked shut, the emotions she'd held in all day ripped from her, and her grief howled.

CHAPTER THIRTY-EIGHT

A ringing cellphone woke Eden from her nap, and she groaned, cursing for not silencing it before she'd drifted off. After her horrible day at work and the confrontation with Tate, she'd slept terribly and had needed the nap. However, seeing the call was from her abuela chased away some of her grouchy mood.

Sitting, she tucked a leg under her and answered the call. "How are you? I thought you'd be out with Fernanda."

"I cancelled. I don't feel well."

Eden frowned. "What's wrong?"

"I have a headache. I'm tired. Tranquilo. Mija, Let's talk about cosas importantes things. Like you arriving here in less than a week with your man and little girl."

Her man might not come. Her man might not be hers. It was late afternoon, and they hadn't spoken since she'd asked him to leave yesterday.

She pushed away that heartache and focused on Raven. Focused on the excitement of taking her daughter to New Mexico. "My girl isn't so little. She's eleven." Eden's heart ached. It had been almost five years since her abuela had been able to visit Michigan to see Raven.

"Well, I'm an old woman, so she'll always be a young girl to me."

Eden chuckled. "Fair enough. I'd like her to see Old Town. And she asked to visit the White Sands."

"I also want to take her where your papa is buried. I made her an album with photos of him. When he was a baby, a teenager. A few from the wedding." Eden's heart stopped.

"That sounds really nice," Eden cut in. "But, um…would you mind not mentioning my mom in front of Raven or Tate?" *If he comes.*

There was a long, weighted pause. "Okay. Why?"

Eden rubbed her brow. "They sort of think she's dead."

"Sort of? How is a living person, 'sort of' dead?" Her voice dipped low with disapproval.

"It's a stupid habit I've gotten into when people ask about my parents. It was easier to say they were both gone. I don't like the questions that follow when people learn I'm estranged from my mother."

"Your daughter deserves the truth."

Guilt crashed into Eden. "I know, and I'll tell her. I'm just waiting for the right time."

"There is no wrong time for the truth."

Eden didn't reply. Her abuela saw the world in black and white. She wouldn't understand Eden's reasons. Hell, she barely understood them herself anymore.

"Is this man you are seeing important?"

"Yes," Eden admitted. "But Mom is my past. She'll never meet Raven or Tate."

"That is your choice, but you should stop hiding from your past. And hiding it from those who care about you."

"I'm not. I don't." Eden huffed. "I'm choosing what to focus on and who'll be part of my present and future."

"They can't love you completely if you let them see only pieces of you—not your whole soul."

They don't need to see all of her. *Some parts aren't worth loving.*

Rare annoyance with her abuela simmered. "What good will come of Raven knowing her grandmother's a mean drunk? And I'm fine not knowing every single, little secret of Tate's to lov—" Her heart skipped a beat. "To care about him."

"We aren't talking about little secrets, Mija. We are talking about big lies that can bring big problems. If they find out, they will be hurt."

"Then don't tell them."

Abuela's loud inhale and exhale carried through the phone. "I won't, but the past doesn't always stay in the past. You are making a mistake."

There were a few times Eden was certain her abuela was wrong. This was one of them.

Abuela sighed. "My headache is getting worse. I will go lay down now."

"Okay. Feel better, and I'll see you soon. Te amo."

"Te amo mi nieta." Her abuela then repeated herself in English. "I love you, my granddaughter."

Hanging up, Eden was relieved the small argument had stayed small but feared the issue was far from over.

CHAPTER THIRTY-NINE

Tate bypassed the doorbell, hammering on Eden's door with his fist, needing the bite of solid wood against his knuckles. A cluster of moths hovering around the porch light scattered, then returned. He'd given her space to sort through whatever was bothering her, but twenty-four hours had passed. It was time to talk.

Yet, with each knock, Tate questioned if showing up at her house was wrong. There was no doubt in him that was falling for Eden. The problem was, he had no idea what was the right thing to do with her. He used to know, but Katrina's parting gift was to leave him unsure of how to handle love, when to help, and when to back off.

His knuckles barely whispered against the surface as indecision stole his resolve. Maybe he should go. As he turned to leave, the door's lock clicked. Eden stood before him in a threadbare T-shirt and faded leggings. The circles under her eyes were practically bruises.

Christ, he should have come sooner. "Are you okay?" he asked.

Her gaze held no emotion. "I'm fine. Why are you here?"

Her question was a punch to the gut. "Why wouldn't I be here?" He shoved his hands in his pockets. "Am I not allowed to check on my girlfriend?"

"Am I? I thought you dumped me." Her words, like her face, held nothing, not anger, hurt, or happiness.

He'd wanted to give her space, instead she'd felt abandoned. *Shit.* He was failing her. "You think I'd dump you because you had a bad day? Seriously?"

"I was incredibly rude to you and practically kicked you out. After I hadn't heard from you last night and today, I figured you wanted out."

"Eden, what I *want* is all of you. And that includes when you're unhappy and upset." He stepped closer and was relieved when she didn't move away.

Her lashes fluttered, and she frowned. "Why?"

He traced his thumb where her mouth dipped down. Would she ever believe him? "Can I come inside?" He kissed her cheek.

She wrapped her hands around his wrists and tugged him into her living room. He closed the door with his foot, pulling her into a hug. All his questions and worries faded in her embrace.

"I was wrong about something when we first began dating," she said against his chest.

"What's that?"

"I told you there was only room in my heart for Raven and my abuela." She nuzzled into him. "It turns out there's space for you there as well. But this new territory scares me. It terrifies me."

Her words shot into his heart, sinking into him to stay, even as he wasn't sure what to do with them. Was she telling him she might be falling for him? Or that she shouldn't because he was a shit boyfriend, too fucked up to care for her as she needed and deserved.

She squeezed him tighter. "Part of me believes I should let you go."

Fuck. His mouth went dry as his chest tightened. He was failing her, and she wanted out.

He leaned back, refusing to break their embrace. "I don't want to let go of you."

"But you deserve better."

Was she kidding? "*I* deserve better?"

"Yes." Her arms went slack on his waist. "I'm a mess."

"So am I." He kissed the top of her head. "We can be messy together."

"You don't want my chaos. Believe me. You only caught a small glimpse yesterday, but there is more. So much more."

"I don't care." He kissed her forehead, both eyelids, then her lips. "Somehow, I'll prove to you I don't need perfection. All I need is you."

Her deep and desperate kiss matched the ache that pulsed through him. He cupped her ass, pressing her against him. She moaned, and the sound made him forget everything but finding a way to keep her making it.

Walking her backward toward her bedroom, he pulled off her T-shirt, tossing it toward the couch. He kissed and nibbled along her collarbone. In the hallway, she removed his shirt and then unzipped his jeans, pushing them mid-thigh, restricting his legs. He made to take them off, but she swatted his hands aside. She slid to her knees, pulling his jeans with her, then taking him into her warm, wet mouth.

Pleasure engulfed him as she took him deep. He locked his legs to keep from buckling and buried his hands in her hair. Her hunger and rhythm had his orgasm reaching for him way too soon. He stepped away, nearly tripping on the jeans around his ankles.

"Where are you going?" She stroked him in a way that hit all the right places, and his eyes drifted shut as he thrust in her hand.

Before she could finish what she'd started, he gathered his crumbling willpower and gripped her chin, tipping it up. "I want to be inside you, your moans and hips making me come."

Her dark eyes dilated, and she stood. He'd show her how much she meant to him through touch and satisfaction. He kicked off his jeans and picked her up, carrying her the last few steps to the bedroom. Wanting more than a quick and dirty fuck, he laid her gently on top of the bed's down comforter.

Grabbing a condom from the nightstand, he put it on and returned to her. He unsnapped her front-clasp bra, then used his hands and mouth to make her writhe. He removed her leggings, caressing her warm, supple thighs. She was so fucking sexy. Leaning down, he kissed the side of her knee, working his way up to feast between her legs.

She hummed with need, begging him for release. Gripping his head, she rolled her hips, taking what she needed. And within minutes, she was moaning his name and coming against his tongue.

He slid up her body and inside her. They groaned in unison. The pleasure was perfect.

"Please," she panted. "Don't hold back."

That was a demand he was happy to obey. "With you, never," he grunted, thrusting with enough force that the headboard slammed into the wall.

She rocked up to meet him, digging her nails into his ass. "Oh, my...I'm...already, going to come again." Her moans filled him as her orgasm owned her. Raking her hands into his hair, she brought his mouth to hers, and the kiss pushed him over the edge. He fell into euphoric bliss, wrapped in the woman who held his heart.

"Stay with me. Stay the night," she whispered against his lips.

He nodded, hugging her tight and hoping it was enough to keep her from slipping through the cracks of his shortcomings and their mistakes.

CHAPTER FORTY

"**M**om," Raven called from the front of Eden's house.

She choked on her sip of coffee. *Crap.* Springing from her chair at the kitchen table, she knotted her robe tight, racing to the living room. Raven was kicking off her flip-flops and striding toward the nearest chair. So far, she hadn't noticed the line of discarded clothes from the couch to her bedroom from her and Tate's fun last night.

"Hey, hi! Where'd you come from?" Eden asked.

She kicked Tate's jeans into the bedroom, glancing at this naked body sprawled on the bed, sound asleep. She closed the door and snatched their shirts from the living room floor.

"Dad and I stopped at The Hill for breakfast."

"He doesn't mind you bailing on him?"

Raven sat, stretching out her gangly legs. "Nah. Jackson was there. He and dad started going on about boring stuff. And I saw Uncle Tate's truck there. The three of them will talk *forever*."

As if he'd heard his name, the bedroom door opened. Eden's heart dropped. *Please don't be naked.* "Raven's here," she said in a rush.

"What?" Tate stepped out, rubbing his eyes, his voice laced with sleep.

And thankfully, in his jeans. However, he was shirtless and had a pillow line on his cheek—also, a case of serious bedhead.

Raven blinked, looking from Eden to Tate. "Why were you sleeping in my mom's room?"

Tate froze. He opened and then closed his mouth. If Eden didn't feel how he looked, she'd have laughed.

"Um, hey, Raven." Tate ran a palm down his naked chest, scanning the room. Eden tossed him his T-shirt she was still holding.

She cleared her throat. "He worked really late last night. I let him stay here instead of risking him falling asleep at the wheel."

"Why'd he sleep in your room? You have an extra one."

Tate's cheeks were pink. Eden's were warm too. "Um…" Her phone mercifully rang from the kitchen counter. "Saved by the ringer," she said.

Passing Tate, he muttered, "I wish someone would call me."

She patted his shoulder. Her smile stayed with her until she saw the University of New Mexico Hospital flash across her phone's screen. She answered. "Hello."

"Is this Dr. Eden Perez?"

"Yes."

"I'm Connie Philly from the University of New Mexico Hospital. I have you as Esperanze Perez personal representative contact. Is that correct?"

Eden collapsed against the counter as a tingling exploded in her chest and stomach. *No. Abuela* "Yes, that's correct." Her voice was steady, even though it was hard to breathe.

"Esperanze Perez was brought in by ambulance. She's had an ischemic stroke," Connie said.

Eden's breath whooshed from her. "Is she okay?"

"She's stable but agitated. She is asking for you and her milagros."

Abuela always wore it as a necklace. "She should have it with her. It's on a turquoise beaded chain, has an arm, leg, and eye charm. Was it removed in the ambulance or at the hospital?"

"Let me check." Desolate hold music filtered through the phone. A minute later, Connie returned. "I'm sorry, she didn't have on any jewelry upon arrival."

Eden slumped against the counter as despair pressed into her. Abuela had moved to the US—left most of her family and friends—for Eden, and now lay alone and scared in a soulless hospital.

"I'm in Michigan but will be there as soon as possible. Could I have her room number?"

Connie gave it, and then they hung up. Eden choked on a deep breath. Her vision blurred, and she wiped away her tears. Abuela was stable. She'd be fine. She had to be fine.

But Abuela would be distraught without her milagros. She wouldn't be able to relax. They'd both held tight to that necklace during dark days. Eden had to get it to the hospital.

"Are you okay, Mom?"

Eden startled. Raven and Tate stood in her kitchen. "What happened?" he asked, stepping toward her.

She shook her head, unable to answer. The static worry in her head made it hard to think, and she didn't have time to answer questions. She scrolled through her phone contacts, finding Fernanda's number. Abuela's friend would find the necklace and get it to the hospital.

Eden clicked on the phone number. It went straight to voicemail, and she cursed when an automated message told her the box was full. She hit redial. The result was the same.

Dammit. Who could she call? Her abuela had a lot of friends, but Eden didn't have their numbers. There had to be someone to call.

Raven moved closer. "Mom?"

The name sparked an idea. Eden licked her suddenly dry lips. "Your bisabuela is in the hospital. Let me make a quick call, then I'll explain what's going on." *I need to do it before I lose my nerve.*

She pulled open the junk drawer under the toaster oven as if in a thick fog. Rifling through pens, rubber bands, and other miscellaneous items, she found the folded paper pushed nearly to the back. Unfolding it, she stared at the phone number. Could she actually call her after all these years? Ask her for help?

For Abuela, yes. For her, Eden would do anything.

She dialed the number. Her heart pounded so loudly it thudded in her ears, muffling the phone's buzzing. After too many rings, but not enough, her mother answered.

"Hello," she said in a soft voice that was both familiar and unfamiliar.

"Mother." The name was ash on her tongue. "This is Eden."

"You actually called—"

The hope and wonder in her mom's voice pulled at some forgotten place in Eden. She talked over them. "Do you still live in Albuquerque?"

"Yes."

"I need a favor."

"Of course. What do you need?"

Of course? Who was this woman?

"Abuela is in the hospital. She has a necklace that's important to her—"

"The onyx and turquoise milagros?"

Eden's mouth fell open. Her mother remembered it. "Yes. Could you drop it off at the UNM Hospital?"

"Sure. I'll do it today after work."

"Could you do it on your lunch break? It's very important she has it."

"Okay."

Eden rested a hand over her throat, finally able to truly breathe. She told her mom where to find the hidden key, how to shut off the security alarm, and likely places where to find the necklace—all the while making a mental reminder to change the first two soon as she arrived in New Mexico.

"If you have any issues call this number," Eden finished.

"Could we talk more?" There was a note of pleading in her mother's voice.

The vise in Eden's chest tightened. "No. I have to go."

"My grandma's alive?" Raven's voice was barely above a whisper.

Eden squeezed her eyes shut as her deceit crashed around them. Then she looked at her daughter.

Raven's chin trembled. "Why'd you lie?"

Eden's glance crawled toward a silent Tate. His expression was unreadable. "My mom is dead to me," she said.

"But she isn't." Raven's bottom lip quivered.

Tate rested a hand on her shoulder. "Now isn't—"

Anger flashed in Raven's eyes. "She lied to me, Uncle Tate."

"I'm sorry." Eden said, knowing she had to say more, had to explain… but how could she? In the face of her daughter's pained disappointment, the lie looked so wrong, so misguided. "I'm so sorry," she whispered.

Raven shook her head. "Are you lying about staying in Michigan too?"

"No, of course not." Eden reached for her daughter, but she stepped back.

"No." She turned on her heels, slamming out of the kitchen and through the front door.

Eden chased after Raven, reaching her halfway up the long driveway. "Please, talk to me."

Raven brushed at her wet cheeks and kept walking. On the restaurant's porch, she turned to Eden. "Leave me alone. I just want my dad."

Hanging back at the entrance, she made sure Raven was safe with Asher. He looked from her to Eden, clearly worried. When he got up, she mouthed. "We'll talk later."

He nodded, and she left. She was surprised to find Tate still in her kitchen at her house, leaning against the counter.

Eden dragged herself to the nearest chair. She'd messed up. Pushed Raven away. Big surprise. Inevitable dread bit at her heart. She met Tate's gaze, waiting for his abandonment.

"Are you going to change your flight? Leave tonight?" he asked.

"Yes. As soon as possible."

"Your grandmother will probably need to come home with you now, instead of waiting until the spring."

"She can't. She had a s-stroke." Eden choked on the word and swallowed her rising panic. "Even if it's a mild one, flying's impossible for a few months. Long drives aren't a good idea either."

"I'll change my flight, and go with you," Tate said.

Her heart filled, only to drain empty seconds later. Leaning on him would make her break, and she refused to do that to him. She cared about him too much to become his burden.

"No," she straightened. "You have a restaurant to run. Who'll take care of it when you're gone?"

"I'll figure something out. This is more important."

"No," she repeated.

He took the seat across from her but didn't touch her. "Why won't you let me in? Why won't you lean on me?"

"Why do you insist I'm weak and need you?"

He jerked as if hit. The silence between them screamed. She hadn't meant to sound so cold and cruel, but she couldn't think straight. Everything in her was shouting to leave. Leave now for New Mexico.

She had to explain. Get him to understand. And quickly. "I'll be fine. I can do this on my own."

"I'm sure that you can, but why? I care about you. Your hardships are mine—if you'll let me in."

I've been a burden to everyone who cares about me. I won't be one to you.

She held tightly to her rational reasoning. "It's short notice. It'll be better if I go alone." Better for him. Better for his restaurant.

Tate held up his hands. "Fine. Do it. Do everything alone. I can't force my way into your heart."

You're already there. But admitting that truth aloud was too terrifying, so she clung to her logic. "This isn't about our relationship. It is about responsibilities. You have a business to run. I have my grandmother to care for." Her voice sounded frozen, but she was powerless to change. This was her. She stood. "I can't do this right now. I need to get to my abuela. I need to go."

Tate's shoulders sagged. "If that is what you want."

"That's what I want." There she went, lying to him again. But like all the others she'd told him, this was to protect, not deceive.

He would leave. She would fall apart. Then she would put herself back together, help her abuela, and then fix things between her and Tate—if he was willing to accept her stunted love.

Taking her hand, he kissed her gently. "If you change your mind..."

"I won't."

He nodded and left.

She broke.

CHAPTER FORTY-ONE

E den pressed the key fob for her trunk, and after placing her roller-bag in it, she checked the time on her phone. If she hurried, she could stop at Raven's, then Tate's house before heading to the airport for the unholy expensive red-eye flight she'd managed to snag.

"I thought you weren't leaving for New Mexico until Monday." Olivia called, stepping from her porch with her youngest, Luna, propped on her hip.

Olivia was kind and understanding, but Eden didn't want pity, endless questions, or the fake platitudes that usually followed when people heard bad news. So, Eden went with vague, saying, "Change of plans."

Olivia stopped in front of Eden. "Something tells me the changes aren't good ones."

The concern in her eyes freed Eden's tongue. "My abuela, she had a stroke."

Olivia laid her hand on Eden's arm. "I'm so sorry. How is she doing?"

"She's stable but might need to have surgery tomorrow because the drugs aren't dissolving the clot." The slight shake in her voice sounded as unsteady as her emotions felt.

"My mom had one a few years ago. Right after she was born." Olivia tilted her head toward Luna, who was wiggling in her arm. She set her daughter in the grass at their feet. "It felt like my world was collapsing."

"Is she—" She couldn't ask if her mother had died. Death wasn't allowed in Eden's thoughts. "How is she?"

"Good. She has to use a walker and has some difficulty with her right side. My mom didn't want to move in with us. Said we lived in the boonies. We found a fantastic assisted-living home in Dearborn. She loves it there. Or I should say, she loves kicking all her new friend's asses in poker and darts." Olivia chuckled. "It's a little sad that my mom has a better social life than me."

"She sounds happy. That's wonderful." Eden meant it and hoped the outcome for her abuela would be as positive.

Olivia squeezed Eden's arm. "How are you holding up?"

"Worried, but fine."

There was nothing else she could be; she couldn't fall apart. It wouldn't help, so she concentrated on the positive. She'd be in the recovery room before the surgery and with her abuela. And she had the milagros. Eden's mom had actually kept her word and dropped it off.

"How long are you able to stay with your abuela?" Olivia asked.

"I don't know." Eden glanced toward the calm lake, her insides roiling with indecision. "As you know, I was offered the job at UMich, and my abuela was supposed to move here in the spring. But her recovery time makes that impossible. It could be half a year or more before it's safe for her to move here. I don't know what to do."

"Shoot, that is tough." Olivia swooped down, picking up her daughter and opening her clenched palm. A beetle fell from it. "We don't eat bugs."

Luna glanced at Eden, her chin quivering and her bottom lip pushing out. She held out her arms for Eden to pick her up. After a slight hesitation, she scooped up the infant. Luna rested on Eden's chest and gave her mother what could only be described as a bratty victorious look. It made them both laugh, lightening some of Eden's gloom.

"Does your abuela have anyone who can help her in New Mexico while she recovers, and you get things ready for her here?"

"No. All of her family lives in Mexico. None are here right now and probably can't get a visa on such short notice."

"What about friends?"

Eden shook her head. "She's my responsibility, not theirs."

"You don't have to do everything alone. Others might want to help her—help you."

Olivia sounded so much like Tate that tears threatened to fill and fall from Eden's eyes. She looked at Luna, shifting so her hair hid her face.

"People who care about you want to help," Olivia continued. "Including me. Let me know if there's anything I can do."

Everyone said this, but rarely did they mean it. The only one who'd stuck by Eden was her abuela. And now Eden would stick by her, even if it meant losing the hospital position. She sighed, handing Luna back to Olivia, then closed the trunk.

"Thank you. But weren't you telling me the other day you're losing your mind with the kids, Elijah gone all the time, and an increase in baking orders?"

Olivia pursed her lips and shrugged. "Your point? I make time for my friends. Just as you stayed with Luna when I had to take Dasia to the doctor and Elijah was out of town."

Eden ran a finger along the little girl's chubby cheek. "That was no big deal. She slept the whole time. I was on my computer and got a lot done."

"Doesn't matter. You did it without question. Why can't I do the same for you?"

"Okay. Thank you for your offer of help. I'll keep it in mind." She'd never take her up on it.

"You'll never take me up on it, will you?" Olivia asked.

Eden offered a sad smile. "Probably not."

"Stubborn woman," Olivia muttered. "What about Tate? It's plain as the day that he'd do anything for you. Is he going with you? Or Raven?"

Probably not after today.

Their hurt and angry faces flashed through Eden. She'd managed to refrain from calling Tate. And when she'd tried Raven, her calls went unanswered.

Shame flooded Eden. She'd screwed things up between her and Raven. Her and Tate.

Eden inhaled deeply, letting it out slowly through her nose. "I should probably get going. I have a few stops before my flight." There wasn't anything she could say to fix her mistakes, but she couldn't leave without at least saying goodbye to Raven and Tate.

"Call me if you need anything." Olivia pulled Eden into a tight hug.

The connection was comfort but also pounded at the wall erected around her heart. She couldn't break down and stepped from her friend's embrace. She nodded goodbye and got in her car.

CHAPTER FORTY-TWO

Eden pressed Asher's doorbell, glancing next door to Tate's driveway. Just like at The Hill, his Bronco was absent. And he hadn't answered his phone when she'd called him.

She'd have to leave without telling him goodbye. It broke her heart, especially since she didn't know when she'd return to Michigan.

The front door opened, dragging her attention away from Tate's house to Asher. "Sorry, but Raven isn't home. She took off on her bike to Hope's house," Asher said, stepping aside. "Do you want to wait? I could call over there?"

Eden's shoulders slumped as she stepped inside the foyer, glancing at her watch. She didn't have much time. "Sure. Thanks."

"What happened this morning?" Asher asked, pulling his cell from his pocket. "Raven came back to the restaurant upset but wouldn't talk about it. And you're looking a little ragged."

She kept out the part about lying to their daughter and told him about her abuela.

"Shit, I'm sorry. How is she?" Asher asked.

"Stable, but her blood isn't clotting properly. I'm on the way to the airport now."

"She's lucky to have you."

Eden could argue the opposite. Abuela had been alone in that old house, probably terrified and hurting. *I wasn't with her. Yet, another person I let down.*

Asher placed his phone to his ear. He waited, then clicked a button. "Raven isn't answering. I'll try Hope. How long will you be in New Mexico?"

"Since I'm between my fellowship and possible hire date they were able to give me two weeks."

"Possible hire date?" Asher parroted. "I thought it was a sure thing."

"Yes, on their end. However, with my abuela ..." *And the mess I'm making here.*

"She's moving here, right? That's what Raven told me." He tilted his head, sliding his phone from his ear. "You're coming back, right?"

She shrugged, defeat slumping her shoulders. "What does it matter? I'm a terrible mother. A shitty girlfriend."

Asher's eyes hardened. It was odd seeing that look on him. He didn't wear it often. "Only if you run again. If you do, you are those things."

Her pulse skipped and heated. "That isn't fair."

"Life isn't fair. Get over it." He crossed his arms. "Be the strong woman I know you are."

"Taking care of my grandmother doesn't make me weak," she countered.

"No but using her as an excuse to run is."

"What the hell do you know?" She snapped. "You're my past. You know nothing of my present."

"Your future could be with Raven. You are her mother. You've built yourself into her life since moving back. You have something with Tate too. But you're so afraid you'll get hurt you'd rather lose them then risk truly committing to either of them."

"I don't care about getting hurt," she nearly shouted, then inhaled, rubbing her throat. Locking away her spiraling emotions, she said calmly, "I don't want to hurt them."

Asher lowered his hands to his sides, shaking his head. Lilith came around the corner as he said, "For someone so smart, you can be so stupid."

Lilith gasped, "Asher."

He glanced at his fiancé. "It's the truth." Returning his focus to Eden, he said, "If you leave, you'll hurt them more than anything you could do if you stayed."

"You're leaving? For good?" Lilith asked Eden. "But Raven…Tate."

Eden couldn't look at Lilith's disappointed face and kept her steady gaze on Asher. "You don't know that. The people we care about the most are the ones we hurt. You don't know the pain I could cause them."

Asher scoffed. "I don't know the suffering you cause others? Are you kidding me?"

His words cut her, and guilt spilled from the wound. "You know why I had to leave back then."

"But you're no longer that scared, damaged college girl who runs from her fears. Or are you?"

She blinked at the tears welling behind her eyes. "I have to go, or I'll miss my flight."

The cold in Asher's eyes turned arctic. "I won't give you another chance if you hurt Raven again." He turned, leaving Eden in the foyer.

Lilith stayed, and after a pause, she pulled Eden into a hug. She accepted it but couldn't relax into it. Not with her pain, fear, and heartbreak lassoed and tied tightly around her. She couldn't risk letting it loosen as she might unravel.

"I'm sorry about your grandma," Lilith said. "You'll figure this out and do what's right."

"I don't know what is right anymore."

"Listen to your heart."

CHAPTER FORTY-THREE

Tate checked his phone. There wasn't a missed call or text from Eden. He ground his teeth and shoved his cell into his pocket. Grabbing his thick garden gloves off the wheelbarrow, he stomped up the ladder to the top of his single-story house. At the gutters, he scooped debris and threw them roughly on the ground.

"Damn, man. What'd those leaves do to you?" Asher called from his porch.

Tate softened his next toss. "Just in a hurry to get it done," he lied.

"Because you're eager to finish yours so you can do mine?"

"No, thanks, man. I can see them from here. They're nasty." They weren't, but trying to goad Asher was a nice distraction. "Have some pride in your home."

"Fuck you, dick," Asher laughed. "I cleaned them in the spring."

Tate shrugged, returning to his task.

Asher cut across his yard, stopping next to the ladder. "Jackson and I are going to Jokers. His favorite local band is playing tonight. Want to come with us?"

"Go to a bar on my night off? No thanks." He got his fill with his restaurant. With the live music on Fridays and Saturdays, his place was more bar than an eatery.

"But you won't be working. Come on," Asher insisted. "There will be darts, pool...women."

Tate climbed down, wiping his brow with his sleeve. "You're going to the bar for the women?"

Asher snorted. "Me, no. Why the hell would I be looking? I have Lilith."

"Damn straight." Tate crossed his arms, giving Asher a steely stare that was complete bullshit. They both knew since the day Lilith had become his neighbor, he saw no one else.

"Knock it off asshole. You know I love Lilith." Asher grinned. "She's the only woman for me."

"Stop with this sappy shit." Tate pretended to gag, though the tightness creeping into his throat wasn't fake. He was glad they found each other, but their blissed-out happiness shone a light and the dark, dank corner of his love life. "Now, leave me alone. I need to finish this and get started on the bathroom."

"What's wrong with it?"

"Shower pressure sucks."

Asher grinned. "I wonder if you'll find any interesting surprises during this home improvement project."

"Define interesting..." Tate had found nipple clamps in the far back of a storage closet that Lilith hadn't bothered to clean out before moving in with Asher. Until now, Tate had blocked it from his mind because nipple clamps and his sister shouldn't be in the same sentence.

"Did Lilith ever tell you about the present in the kitchen sink when she first moved in?"

Ah, yes. "And the first time she met you? She was so embarrassed." Tate cracked a small smile. "It was great."

"She's adorable. When I removed the butt plug stuck the sink's pipe, she thought it was some kind of kitchen tool." Asher chuckled. "Did she tell you about the dildo in the A/C and the vibrator in the heater?"

Tate choked on surprised laughter. "No."

She called the person who left these odd 'gifts' her naughty bunny. Tate wasn't sure if learning this made him want to do more or less home improvement projects.

Jackson's truck pulled into Asher's driveway. After parking, he strolled toward them and called out. "Tate, you coming with us tonight?"

"Nah. I need to get caught up on a few important things I've let go this summer."

And he needed to keep busy. Eden snuck into his thoughts in the silence, and he wasn't ready to confront them. He was at an impasse—walk away or try. She wasn't cruel like Katrina, but her easy lie fucked with his trust in her. She'd lied to him, to her daughter. He pushed them both away. When was enough, enough?

"Important? You were chopping wood this morning." Asher pointed to the pile at the side of Tate's house. "I don't think your fireplace is used much in the middle of the summer."

"Bonfires," Tate tossed back. Asher nodded as if giving him that one. "And, dude, stop watching me through the windows with your binoculars. Creep."

Asher snorted. "If I had had binoculars with me, I'd have strangled you with the strap. It's my day off. And you woke me up with your racket."

"Sleep with your windows closed, lazy-ass."

"It's the summer jack-ass." Asher tossed back.

Tate almost smiled. Why did tossing insults and jabs with friends improve a person's attitude?

Asher kicked at a pile of gutter leaves. "So...Eden left for New Mexico yesterday..."

Annnd, his improved mood plummeted as Asher's words punched Tate in the solar plexus. Eden had left without even telling him goodbye. He turned from his friends, so they couldn't see the damage the news had caused him.

Moving toward his ladder, he rested a foot on the bottom rung. "Oh, is that what this 'night-out-with-the boys' is about? Did Lilith tell you that Eden and I are arguing? Again." He dipped his chin and looked at the two men over his sunglasses. "So, what, are we going out to braid each other's hair and talk about our feelings?"

"Um, fuck no." Jackson looked so horrified Tate almost laughed. "Last I checked, I wasn't a little girl. Nor did we suggest a slumber party, dickweed." He glanced at Asher. "Maybe we should have Raven and Chloe invite him over instead."

Asher nodded. "Maybe."

"Asshole," Tate muttered, starting up his ladder.

"But, if you want to join the big boys," Jackson called after him. "We're going to drink, play pool... and if you're single, you can be my wingman while hitting on the ladies. I'm losing you all to *relationships*." He said the last word like it was a virus.

Tate had no interest in talking to women. Returning to his monk status suited him.

When he reached the top of his gutters, Asher asked, "Did you break up?"

Tate pressed his lips together, forcing air through his nose, then looked down at Asher. "Well, she left the state and didn't tell me, so I'd say, yeah, we broke up."

The other man cursed, then said, "I asked how long she was staying in New Mexico. She might stay. Not come back."

Tate's heart clenched. He laid his hands on the hot shingles. "In New Mexico?" he asked through numb lips.

"Christ," Asher grumbled. "She didn't tell you?"

Tate shook his head. Well, at least he'd gotten his answer about his worth. He was without value to her.

"That could be a good sign. Maybe she didn't tell you because she isn't staying there," Jackson reasoned.

"Or she doesn't give a shit about me," Tate snapped, then drummed his fingers against the roof, counting out a tap of five.

Asher's jaw flexed as he ground his teeth. "I swear, if she bails on Raven again—"

Jackson made a patting motion in the air. "Just wait and see. The granny who raised her just had a stroke. Give the woman time to figure things out."

Asher shook his head. "You sound like Lilith—so convinced Eden will make the right choice."

"Is there really a right one?" Jackson asked. "Leaving behind her ill grandma or leaving behind her daughter. Both suck."

Asher sighed. "You're right."

Jackson grinned. "I'm always right."

"You fucking wish." Asher turned to Tate. "Come on, man. We could all use a beer, food, and music."

"Nah, I need to finish the gutters and knock a few other things off my list."

"They'll be there tomorrow," Jackson said, doing a slick shuffle. "The band Smooth Sea will be playing at Jokers. Let's listen to some good music, get our beer buzz on, and forget about work and women tonight."

Tate cocked a brow. "You're going to forget about women?" Jackson loved the ladies, and they loved him.

"Ah, fuck no. But you can. Drown your shit with Eden in liquor or women—you can choose when we get there."

Tate grumbled but admitted that getting drunk enough to fall asleep without thinking about Eden was a plus. Then he could get up, work on the retaining wall, and then go to the restaurant. Keep busy until life returned to normal—without Eden in it.

"Fine. I'll go." He scooped some leaves and twigs from the gutters, tossing them on the opposite side of Asher and Jackson. "After I finish this."

CHAPTER FORTY-FOUR

Tate groaned as his pounding headache woke him. He was lying on his side in a pitch-black room, his head resting on the arm of a leather couch. "Where..."

Unhurried, heavy footsteps came toward him. There was a click, then dim light from a lamp pierced Tate's eye. "You're at my place," Jackson said, handing him a glass of water and two pills.

"Thanks." Tate sat, the soft leather creaking, and took the offered items.

The slamming sledgehammer in his head increased, as did the metallic taste in his mouth. The combination had flashes of the night returning. There was good music and lots of drinks—a woman with too much perfume sitting uninvited in his lap, propositioning him and Asher as Jackson danced with her friend.

"How did I get here?" He took in the neat and sparse living room. Jackson's home was immaculate, unsentimental. Tate could've mistaken the place for a hotel suite if it weren't for the three photos—his mom, another of him and Hope, and a group shot from last year's Halloween party.

Jackson chuckled. "You had it in your drunk brain that you'd walk home. Since my place is down the street from Jokers—a forty-five-minute drive to your place—we decided to let you sleep off your liter of bourbon instead of walking off.

Tate nodded, then stopped. His whole body didn't like that move. "What time is it?"

"After three." Jackson relaxed into a matching recliner across from Tate. "We dumped your ass here a little after midnight."

"Have you been watching over me that whole time?" he teased, then held up the water. "I don't mind since your weirdness came with life-support items."

Jackson snorted. "I'd just walked in the door. You started groaning and grunting like a troll. I figured you'd need the hangover supplies."

"I did. I do. Thanks."

Jackson bobbed his head once.

"After three, huh? That's a late night. Did you find the love of your life?"

Jackson ran a hand through his short dreads. "More like the love of my night."

Tate chuckled. Jackson never left alone and didn't seem the least bit interested in anyone for more than an evening, except for maybe Asher's sister, Hope. When she was around, Jackson never left her side.

Thinking of her made Tate ask. "What's up with you and Hope?"

Jackson leaned back into the recliner, and the leg rest popped up. "Are you still drunk?"

"Probably. Were you two always friends?"

Jackson sucked on his bottom lip, then released it. "No, but that was a long time ago. We dated back in high school."

"What happened?"

Jackson rubbed his hands up and down the chair's arms. "What's going on with you and Eden?"

"Nice topic change."

Jackson grinned. "Smooth, huh? Are you two done?"

"I think so."

"What the fuck does that mean?"

"She keeps pushing me away." He rubbed his dry and scratchy eyes. "I took the hint. I'm staying away."

"Hope's like that. Doesn't like people to get too close."

"Is that why you stay away? To save yourself the aggravation." *The pain.*

"I stay away because that's what I deserve." Jackson crossed his legs at the ankles.

He stared out the large living room window. The curtains were open, but there weren't any streetlights on this stretch of road, so outside was like looking into a void.

"What do you mean?" Tate asked.

Jackson looked at Tate. There was pain and regret in his eyes. "I wasn't there when she needed me."

"Everyone's let someone down at one point or another."

"Sure, but sometimes the consequences are unforgivable." Jackson waved a hand. "Besides, she doesn't bother much with boyfriends. If she happens to have one, they never last. She leaves them after a week, a month at the most. I don't want that to happen with us, so I settle for friendship. It's better than not having her in my life."

Damn. Tate heard Jackson's silent admission in every word he spoke. He was in love with Hope. No wonder he never had more than flings. He refused to go after what he wanted, relegating himself to a half-life, meaningless sex, and watching the years pass between him and Hope.

"Is that really better?" Tate asked.

Jackson shut off the lamp and stood. "Hell if I know." He patted Tate's shoulder as he left the living room. "Night, man"

"Hey, Jackson..." Tate called.

"Yeah?"

He smiled in the dark. "Since I'm staying at your place and we talked about our feelings, this could be considered a slumber party. So, do you want to braid my hair, or should I do yours?"

"Dude, fuck off." Tate heard the smile in Jackson's voice.

It took a long time for Tate to fall back asleep. It was as if his and Jackson's discontent stayed in the room talking. Tate felt for Jackson and wondered if he was doing the same. Was he giving up, not really going after what he wanted? He could hold on instead of letting Eden go when she pushed him away. He could refuse to leave—show her she could trust him, that he wouldn't go.

But could he trust her with his heart?

"Fucking drunk ramblings," Tate muttered, rubbing his face and stretching out on the couch.

He sure as hell didn't have the answers.

CHAPTER FORTY-FIVE

Eden studied her abuela's beautiful, wrinkled face. Each line was a map of years, joyful and painful.

Her tired eyes opened. "Mi dulce nieta."

Eden grasped her hand. "How are you?"

"Better now that you are here," she said in her lilting English that Eden adored. It was as comforting as her favorite childhood blanket. Her abuela shifted and lifted her arm with the milagros necklace wrapped around it. It clanged against the hospital bedrail. "Thank you for making sure this got to me."

"Of course. I know how important it is to you."

Her abuela squeezed Eden's hand. It was weak but strong on comfort. "And you too."

That was true. That necklace and its charms had been her talisman too. On the fifth anniversary of Papa's death, her mother had left in the morning, returning late at night in a terrifying drunken rage. The end result was Eden in the hospital's burn ward.

The next day Abuela gave Eden the necklace and told her to tell the talisman all her fears and wishes because it'd help her find a solution. It had. After a week in the hospital, her abuela, not her mother, came to take her home. To her home. When the court awarded her custody, Eden returned the necklace.

Abuela held it up. "I was groggy, but I think it was your madre who dropped it off."

"It was." Eden frowned and drew back but didn't let go. "I called her when I couldn't get ahold of anyone to bring it to you."

Tears glittered in her abuela's eyes. "You must love me."

Eden's throat clogged, and she cleared it. "Very much."

"She has been sober for five years."

"Good for her."

Her abuela tsked. "She sees a—psiquiatra."

Eden gave a slight shake of her head. "I don't know this word."

Her abuela looked to the side as if searching for the word. "Um, head-shrinker."

"A psychiatrist." Eden's mouth twitched. Then she tilted her head. "How do you know these things?"

"She told me one of the times she called for your number. We talk a little."

Eden stiffened. "How can you talk to her? After all she's done."

"I hate what she did to you. It broke my heart. But she loved my son, truly loved him, and when he died, she fell apart. Drank too much."

"That isn't an excuse for the person she'd become."

"No, but I should have helped her."

"She was an adult. She didn't need a mother. She should have been mothering."

Her abuela's eyes drifted shut. "Even adults need mothering—need help. She had no one. And my forgiveness is not for her, but for you, for my son, for me. I don't want to hold on to the anger. It eats at my soul." She tapped the left side of her chest, opening her eyes. "Does it you?"

"No. Because I keep her out of here." She touched her heart and then her head. Though imagining her mother alone and grieving softened a sliver of something in Eden.

Her abuela sighed, sounding tired. "My doctor told me I will be able to go home in a few days."

"That's great. I'll make sure the fridge is full, and the house is ready for your return."

"How long are you able to stay?"

"As long as you need me."

Abuela mouth pressed together, her lips nearly disappearing. "No. You have to return to your life. I'm sure that fancy hospital will not hold that new job forever."

Eden ran her fingers along the bed's cold metal railing. "Maybe I don't take the job and stay here with you. I could apply to this hospital."

"No. Your home is in Michigan."

"You're my home."

"And you are mine, but I will move to Michigan soon."

"You just had a stroke caused by a blood clot. You can't get on an airplane or go on a long car ride for at least three months. Who's going to take care of you?"

"I have three sisters and two brothers."

"In Mexico."

"They are applying for emergency visas."

A smile tugged on Eden's lips. "All of them?"

"Of course. Luis called this morning. His was approved." She huffed out a breath, folding her arms over her ample chest, using her left hand to situate her right arm. "Not that I need them to come here. It was a little stroke."

There was the stubborn woman of Eden's childhood.

"Little. I see you struggling. And you're holding your Milagro in your left hand. It's because you can't with your dominant one, right?"

"I'm good." She glanced away, telling a different answer.

"Listen." Eden ran a palm over her abuela's soft white hair. "The first three months are very important to your recovery. I can't risk you missing appointments."

And more distressing, she was twenty percent more likely to have another stroke within that time period. Someone had to be with her at all times.

"Muy bien! Fine. My family will come. Or I'll hire help. You don't need to uproot your life. I will get better, then come to Michigan."

"But—"

"Your daughter needs you. And what about that new man? Every time you mention him, I hear a smile in your voice." She pressed a side button on the bed, raising it into a near-sitting position. "They will miss you."

"They will be fine without me." Eden's gaze shifted to the window. The relentless New Mexico sun pressed into everything outside. "When's your physical therapy?"

"Mija, look at me."

She turned from the window. The soft kindness in her abuela's eyes hammered at the walls Eden had cemented around her heart.

"What happened?" she asked, placing a hand atop Eden's.

She told her how Raven and Tate learned she'd lied about her mom's death. Then, despite it, Tate had tried to comfort her, and she'd pushed him away—probably for good this time.

A nurse's soft steps shuffled past, and monitors continued beeping. After a moment, her abuela spoke. "You made a mistake. Fix it."

"I keep making mistakes. They're better off without me."

"Do you really believe this? Do you think Raven will be happier without her mother?"

Eden gave a heavy one-shoulder shrug. "She has a fantastic father. And wonderful stepmother."

"So?" Abuela scoffed. "There is one thing a child can always use more of—family who loves her."

"What if my love is destructive?"

"Is it?"

"It could be. Sometimes the rage and sadness I feel are so intense, it scares me. I don't want to hurt them like my mom did me."

She'd buried this fear so deep, hoping it'd stay hidden if she never spoke it aloud. So the sudden weight that lifted after admitting her fears nearly stole her breath.

"Eden, you are not your mom."

"But I could be. If I let out those emotions."

"No. And if you must compare yourself with her, remember she was a monster when drunk. Not sober. Do you drink?"

"No, but that doesn't matter. I learned violence young and often." She drooped in her stiff visiting chair, making it creak. "I've read that data, the papers on the cycle of abuse from generation to generation."

"It started with your mom but will end with you."

"Why are you so certain?"

"I know you. Your heart. You will *make* sure it does not happen." She tapped the bed's metal bar. "Move this." When the railing was down, she opened her arms. "Ven."

Eden wrapped herself in love and comfort. They stayed like that until some of her heart was soothed.

"Trust those who love you, to hold you." She squeezed Eden. "Trust yourself, your feelings."

"I might be too late. I really messed things up with Raven. With Tate."

"If they love you, they will forgive. If you love them, you will fix your wrong."

She made it sound so simple.

Could it be that simple?

CHAPTER FORTY-SIX

E den's constant pacing between the living room and kitchen of her adolescent home was going to wear away the threadbare carpet. She had messed up. Big time. It was time to fix her colossal mistakes. *Woman-up and make the damn call.*

She'd tossed and turned all night as the truth of her abuela's words crashed and tumbled through her. They finally penetrated. Eden *could* have the life she wanted—one with love, friends, and a big family.

Enough hesitating. She called Raven, but it went straight to voicemail. Scrolling through her contacts, she tapped Tate's number before losing her nerve. Her heart sank lower as it also went to voicemail. Should she leave a message or keep calling? He might never answer.

No more hesitating.

The voicemail beeped. "Tate, this is Eden. I'm sorry I pushed you away. I want you with me during good and bad. Please call me."

Her chest constricted as she counted all her mistakes. Her five-second message might have come too late. It should have happened days ago when he'd offered his support. Or the countless other times he'd given it to her, and she'd turn her back on it and him.

Right now, she could only hope he didn't delete her message without listening. If he didn't return her call, it didn't matter—she'd keep calling, keep trying until he heard her.

Knocking her knuckles to the rhythm of her heartbeat, she waited for it to slow, then pressed another number in her contacts. Luck was finally with her. Asher answered on the second ring.

"Hi, Eden." He sounded weary. "How's your grandmother?"

"Good. I'm optimistic."

"That's great." Silence hummed, filled with the question she was sure he wanted to ask.

"I'm sorry for constantly throwing my insecurities at you," she blurted.

"I can handle it." His heavy sigh carried over the miles. "It's Raven I'm worried about. You can't come and go from her life as you try to figure out yours."

"You're right."

Another loaded pause fell between them. "Are you staying in Albuquerque?"

"No." Her home was no longer here. It was in Michigan. "I will make sure my abuela has the care she needs until she's able to move to Michigan, and I'll figure it out before my job at UMich starts."

"Thank, Christ." Asher muttered.

His relief was a shot of serotonin. He truly believed she was a positive influence in their daughter's life. It boosted her belief in herself.

Eden stopped pacing. "Is Raven home?"

"She is. I'll get her."

"Asher?"

"Yeah?"

"If she agrees, is it okay if I fly her out here?"

"Sure. She's talked of nothing else, before...well, before." Asher chuckled. "Even if she's still pissed at you, she'll come."

Eden laughed. "Good to know." An overwhelming urge to see her daughter squeezed Eden. "I'm going to hang up and do a video call, okay?"

"Sure."

They disconnected, and she called back. Raven's beautiful face filled the screen, though her expression fit squarely in the sullen category. Eden didn't care. She was so happy Raven had answered.

"Thank you for taking my call," Eden said.

She shrugged. "Dad made me. How's New Mexico? How's great-grandma? And my grandma." Eden could see Raven was aiming for tough but had hit on hurt instead.

"Raven, I'm so sorry for letting you think your grandma had died. She wasn't a very good mother and when I moved in with my abuela, I cut my mom from my life, told everyone both my parents were dead."

Raven frowned. "But I'm not everyone."

Eden rubbed her throat, forcing down the lump. "No, you aren't. But that's the thing with lies. Tell them enough, they start to feel like the truth." Just like the one she'd been telling herself for years; that she didn't deserve love or forgiveness.

"Why don't you want your mom in your life? I always wanted you in mine." Raven's gaze fell from Eden. "Even when you didn't want to be in it."

"Look at me." Eden waited until their eyes locked. "I always wanted you in my life. But I was scared. Terrified. And that is my shortcoming, never yours. Please believe me."

"Scared of what?"

Eden's doubts and old ghosts tried to haunt her, but she was ready to exorcise them. "Hurting you. Like my mom hurt me."

Raven's eyes widen. "Why..."

"She wasn't always that way. My dad was in an accident at work—"

"So, he died? For real?"

Her daughter's doubt hurt, but Eden deserved it. "Yes, for real. He was a fire lieutenant. There was an apartment fire, and the roof collapsed."

Raven covered her mouth. "I'm sorry."

"Me too." Eden pulled in a shaky breath. "Anyway, after he died, my mom started drinking. A lot. And she's what people call a mean drunk." Eden halted, stuck on what to say. Not because she wanted to hide her past from Raven. It was more that she was only eleven. Eden wasn't sure what was too much for a kid. "Things got bad. Eventually, the state took me from her. That's when I moved in with my abuela. Anyway, when I found out I was pregnant, I freaked out. A big part of me feared I would be like my mom. So, I fell back on the one thing I was certain of in my life—becoming a surgeon. I'd already been accepted to Stanford. It felt like the safest path for us had already been paved."

"How was is safe for us? I love my aunt and grandparents but wanted you too. I'm sure Dad needed you too."

Eden heard the hurt in her daughter's voice, and it tore at her soul. "Raven, the minute you were placed in my arms, I loved you. All I wanted was the best for you. I'd believed that was without me in your life."

"Because you *are* like your mom?" Raven asked, her lower lip trembling.

Eden hated the weariness she saw in her daughter's eyes. "It was my number one worry. Part of me argued that I'd be fine. My mother wasn't cruel unless she drank, but her violence was all I knew for far too long. It was all I understood. When I moved to my abuela's, I struggled so much with my emotions. It took me years to get them under control, and even then, I couldn't contain them all the time. I wanted to be with you so badly, but I couldn't risk it. If I hurt you, I wouldn't have been able to live with myself."

Raven wiped her eyes with her sleeve. "And now you're not afraid you'll be like her?"

"No, not as much. And I'll do whatever it takes to make sure that doesn't happen. I saw a counselor in California, and I'm going to start seeing one again. I want you in my life. I'll do whatever it takes to make it happen." She leaned against the wall and slid to the floor. "Will you forgive me for lying to you? Will you give me another chance?"

Raven smiled and nodded. Both were a gift that made all the painful honesty worth it. She'd take the agony of burning all her demons for her daughter.

Eden slid her knees up, resting the phone on them. "Would you like to meet me here this weekend? See where I grew up?"

"Really?" Raven sat up so fast the screen blurred. "Yes!"

The doorbell chimed behind Eden, and she glanced toward it. "That might be one of the in-home nurses I'm interviewing." She checked the time. "He's early. Really early. Let me call you this evening. We'll get everything figured out."

"Okay!"

Eden waved goodbye before they ended the call. Standing and nearly skipping down the hallway, she opened the door, then froze.

Tate stood on her porch.

CHAPTER FORTY-SEVEN

Shock was written all over Eden—from her wide eyes to her frozen stature. Tate couldn't tell if his appearance was a good or bad surprise.

She took a step back and covered her mouth. "How..." Her gaze dropped to her phone. "I left you a message, like ten minutes ago..."

Tate rubbed his jaw, his breath squeezing in his chest. He'd missed her so damn much. "Sorry, I didn't answer. I was driving here."

"Did you listen to the message?"

He shook his head. "I hope you don't mind me answering it this way."

"No, I definitely don't." She slammed into him, wrapping her arms around him and peppering his lips with quick kisses.

The tightness in him released, making him nearly weightless. "I had this big speech prepared about how I trust you with my heart, and that I'm here to prove you can trust me with yours. Do you want to hear it?" he said against her mouth.

"I don't need a speech. You're here. I can't believe you're here." Taking his hand, she brought him inside. The house opened directly to a small living room, and she led him to the light-brown sofa. When he sat, the old springs squeaked in protest. She straddled his lap.

Her body against his was heaven, as were her exploring lips. However, he didn't want to fall into their pattern of using sex to ignore issues between them. It was a temporary fix and— Eden pressed her breasts against his chest while rocking her hips, and for half a second, his mind shut off as more of his body came alive.

"Eden." He gripped her waist to stop her from moving.

She stilled. "What?"

He ran his thumb along the worry line between her brows, staring into her deep, beautiful brown eyes. "I'm sorry I pulled away when you needed me."

She shook her head. "I pushed you away, even though I wanted to hold you tight."

"And I knew that, but I couldn't quite believe it. A small part of me was convinced you were playing games, manipulating me. I let it dictate my bad choices—to not be there when you needed me."

"I'll forgive your mistakes, if you'll forgive mine," she said.

He trailed his fingertips from her cheeks down her neck, tracing her collarbone. "Is it that simple?"

"Yes. And that hard."

He smirked, and she laugh-groaned. "I swear, if you make a dick joke right now."

"Only one? A few"—He wiggled his brows—"*sprang up* in my mind at the word hard."

She giggled into his neck, and it made his heart float. This light moment seemed impossible yesterday but was reality today. He smoothed his palm down her spine. A clock ticked somewhere in the house, keeping time with their buoyant heartbeats.

He brought them back to the conversation they needed to have. "Why's forgiveness hard if it has already been given?"

"Because we'll have to do it repeatedly. This isn't our happily-ever-after. We have to be willing to create it over and over as we stumble. And, Tate, I'm afraid I'll stumble a lot."

"If you fall, I'll be there to catch and hold you. I promise." He hugged her, meaning it.

"I believe you." She rested her forehead against his. "I love you."

His heart expanded, caressing those three words. "I love you too."

Unfolding herself from his lap, she stood, tugging him to stand. She guided him out of the living room and into the narrow hallway. They passed a small, sunny kitchen, and turned into a bedroom.

The room was painted a cheery blue with miscellaneous posters of old bands and art prints. There was a squat white dresser with chipped paint, a bed with a simple wood frame under a gauzy white curtain, and a steel desk in the farthest corner. It was the kind seen in offices, not homes. On it, old books and folders were neatly stacked around two framed photos.

He let go of her hand and went to the desk. "This room is like peeking into past pieces of you."

She laughed. "It's a time capsule. My abuela refused to change it into a guest or craft room when I left for college. She kept everything as is, and I never added anything during my visits home." She ran her hand along the bed's frame. "I should get it ready for when my Great-Uncle Luis arrives to help."

Tate touched a frame with a photo of a man who had to be her father. He had Eden's thick black hair and warm brown eyes. Next to it was a picture of an older woman wearing a wide-brim hat, standing in front of a temple he recognized from geography and travel books but didn't know its name.

He pointed at the photo. "Is that your abuela?"

Eden came up behind, wrapping her arms around him. "Yes. The other one is my dad."

Tate noticed there was none with her mother. He tapped a small pile of old textbooks. "This desk looks out of place with the room, but I bet it was your favorite spot."

She nodded between his shoulder blades. "This probably won't surprise you, but I adored studying. Especially science and biology. My abuela worried hunching over books on my bed wasn't good for my back, so when the office she was working at was remodeled, she asked for one of the desks and chairs they were replacing."

"She sounds like a thoughtful woman." He twisted to face Eden. "I can't wait to meet her."

"Will you come with me to the hospital today?"

"I'll go wherever you need me."

She kissed him, and he could taste her love alongside her desire. Taking his hand, she walked them to her bed. He sat on it, and she straddled his lap again, removing his T-shirt.

She hugged him tight, whispering, "I love you."

He could listen to her repeating those three words until the end of time. "I love you too," he replied.

Rising to her knees, she slid off her green sundress. He held her waist, keeping her simple cotton bra level with his face. He nuzzled her gorgeous breasts through the thin material until her nipples peaked. She unclipped and removed her bra. *Even better.*

She slowly rocked, her eyes full of seduction. Even through his jeans, her touch made him harder. Running his palm up her chest, past her collarbone, he lifted her chin to kiss and nibble a trail from her neck to her shoulder. Reaching the scar tissue, he paused. Part of him wanted to test the honesty they had sworn to give each other, but he feared breaking the hope and possibilities flowing between them. If he asked, and she refused to share the darker parts of her past, he'd know they were heading down a dead-end street.

"The tattoo covers a burn scar," she said. "My mom gave it to me when I was eleven. It was what finally prompted the state to remove me from her home."

"Jesus." He breathed through the ache her words caused and brushed his fingers over the puckered skin. "I'm sorry."

"Why? You didn't give it to me."

He held her tight against him. The steady thump of her heart against his chest was his home. "I'm sorry it happened. Especially by the person who was supposed to protect you."

Silence fell between them, calm and slightly haunted with the past. A car with thrumming bass drove by. The air-conditioner clicked on, rustling the curtain.

"What if her temper is in me?" Eden whispered, but her words screamed with fear.

He leaned back to look into her eyes. "What makes you think that's possible? You are one of the most controlled people I know."

"That's because I keep a tight hold on my emotions. You've only seen me lose it a little, that last day of my fellowship. But when I was a kid, when I first came to live with my abuela. I threw awful fits. Shrieked, raged, broke stuff, ran away."

Tate wasn't surprised, though it hurt to picture that lost, drowning girl. She was finally able to let lose all the fear and anger that she'd buried while living with her unstable mother.

"I taught myself the importance of suppressing my strong emotions—for my safety and others," Eden said. "But that part is probably still in me. It could get out, and I don't want to burden you with it."

"You will never be a burden to me. And you were abused." Tate ran a hand up and down her back. "You should have seen someone to help you learn how to manage, not suppress your emotions."

She tensed in his arms. "Your ex was violent. Did you seek help?"

"No." But maybe he should have. He would have stumbled a lot less with family, friends, and Eden.

Taking a deep inhale, Eden let it out slowly. "I'm sorry. I'm uncomfortable and lashed out."

He one hundred percent understood her reaction. Confessing exposed wounds hurt. For him, it had scraped against what he had been taught it meant to be a man.

"It's fine." He kissed her shoulder. "And you're right. I'm giving advice I never considered for myself. Hell, after leaving the hospital, I actually googled if domestic abuse toward men was even a thing. It is and happens more than I realized. Something like one in three men experience it. It shocked-the-hell out of me, but I still kept it to myself, like it was my dirty secret."

She held him tighter. "I told you that I did see someone to help me after Raven was born." She slouched, burying her face into his neck, making her words muffled. "But I've always been a terrible person. No counseling will change that."

He shook his head. "I might not know much of your past, but what I see of you now is the opposite of terrible. Sure, you're stubborn. Incredibly stubborn. Like, really, really stubborn," he joked.

She laughed and bit his neck lightly before kissing it. "I'm not that bad."

He snorted. "If we ever start calling each other pet names, yours is going to be Donkey."

"Only if yours is Ass."

"Okay, scratch the nicknames." He tickled her waist, and she wiggled, reminding him she was only in a pair of panties. "You are stubborn. And beautiful." He kissed her mouth, then bent to savor her breasts.

She leaned back, giving her more access, her hips undulating, making his cock rock-hard. He stood, and she locked her legs around his waist. Laying her gently in the center of the bed, he kissed her until she unzipped his jeans. He pushed them off and to the end of the bed. After sliding off her panties, he kissed his way up her gorgeous body, stopping at all his favorite places. By the time he was flush against her, leg to leg, chest to chest, she was panting, and her eyes were dilated.

"You are stubborn and beautiful." He looked into her eyes. "But also, kind and caring. A good person. A wonderful person."

"I'm a mess."

"You can be a mess, and still be all those things, Eden."

They kissed until she moaned, "Make love to me."

He retrieved a condom from his wallet in the back pocket of his jeans. He put it on under her watchful, hungry gaze. Then achingly slow, he pushed inside her. Being connected with her was always paradise, but this time was different. The link was deeper.

Her gaze locked on his, and she never looked away, not even when, sometime later, her body shook with the power of her orgasm. The force of her pleasure, the intensity, and love in her eyes, had his release chasing hers. He found euphoria and contentment he'd never experienced, and now he dared to believe it would last.

CHAPTER FORTY-EIGHT

Eden lay tucked into Tate's side, naked, satiated, and content. She wanted to capture the perfect afternoon and hold it between her heartbeats—wrap it around her soul where the memory would never dim.

She ran her palm over the light dusting of hair on Tate's chest, stopping on his heart. "I still can't believe you're here."

"I couldn't let us go without trying. I had to talk to you face to face and see if things were truly over. Or if you'd pushed me away because you're afraid of letting me in. Afraid I'd let you down."

"But *I've* let you down over and over."

"We've both made mistakes. We'll make more, but I can't give up on you—I can't give up on us." He kissed the side of her head. "I love you. And not just the easy parts, but the complicated, messy ones."

This kind of happiness had a weightless quality, even as he kept her grounded in his perfect embrace. Rolling on him, she ran her hands through his hair and looked into his beautiful eyes. "I'll do my damnest to be worthy of your love."

"You are worthy."

She kissed him, softly and gently. His arms wrapped around her, and serenity settled into her. As their embrace and touches turned to heat, her stomach let out a monstrous roar.

"It sounds like I have a tiger in my belly." She laughed.

"Yeah, one that wants to be fed. When was the last time you ate?"

"I grabbed an overpriced sandwich at the hospital cafeteria yesterday afternoon." She dragged her leg higher on his thigh. "I don't want to move. My tiger can wait."

He squeezed her waist, then rolled them to their side. Sitting, he rested his feet on the floor. "You relax. I'll find us something to eat."

Not ready to let him go, she gripped his thigh, pulling him toward her. His gaze crawled to her breasts. Leaning down, he took one into his mouth, playing and teasing until her stomach let out another roar.

He chuckled, flicking her nipple with his tongue. "I better get you food before that tiger escapes."

"You stay, I'll go." She made a lazy, half-hearted effort to get up, looking for her dress.

"I don't mind. I need to stretch my legs more. The flight was a long one, and I came here straight from the airport." Still sitting on the bed, he picked his jeans off the floor.

He was here. Actually here. Eden's heart was a bouquet of wildflowers blooming in her chest. Tate had flown to the other side of the country after she'd fought with him, pushed him away. She wrapped her arms around his broad back and reached around, kissing his cheek repeatedly.

"What's that for?" He twisted and kissed her on the lips.

"Because I love you."

His eyes sparked with joy. Loving him was scary but also freeing. It uncovered dusty hopes she'd thought were buried and dead. Instead, it seemed they were waiting to be found. She dared to believe in them and Tate.

CHAPTER FORTY-NINE

Eden slid on her sundress as Tate finished dressing. It was a shame to have all his glorious skin covered, but her hunger for food nearly equaled having him back in her bed.

"Let me get you a key for the house and directions to a nearby Thai restaurant. Back when I lived here, it was my favorite," she told him.

A few minutes later, Tate kissed her goodbye on the porch. She waved to him as his rental pulled from the curb, then she flipped the switch to the outdoor ceiling fan. Settling into one of the rocking chairs, she stared out at the street but didn't really see the other houses or passing cars. Her focus was on the languid calm from fantastic lovemaking and having Tate with her again—and the knowledge she might get to keep him.

She considered going inside for her laptop. There was so much to do before her abuela was released from the hospital. Plus, Eden had called C.S. Mott to formally accept her job, resulting in a ton of prep and paperwork in her email inbox.

However, right now, she'd bask in the flawless day and the glow of pleasure from Tate. To let her guarded heart play with the possibility of a future with him.

A car pulled into the parking spot Tate's rental had vacated minutes ago. It was the same color and possibly the same model—she'd been paying more attention to him than what he was driving. Maybe he'd forgotten something.

She squinted. No, it wasn't him. The make and model were too old for a rental. Looking closer, she saw a woman in the driver's seat.

The engine cut, ticking as it cooled. Eden's heart did the opposite, thumping so hard and loud it pounded in her ears, blocking the street's noise. The woman got out, and Eden gasped before clenching her jaw shut.

Over twenty years had passed, and the woman's blonde hair was mostly gray now. There were wrinkles around her eyes, forehead, and mouth, but there was no mistaking her mother.

She reached the bottom step of the porch and stopped. "It's been a long time."

"Not long enough." Eden stood, hands on her hips.

Her mother fiddled with the strap of her oversized purse. "Will you give me ten minutes?"

Heat flushed through Eden's body. "No."

"Then five. Please." She pleaded with her eyes and words.

Anger washed over frustration, mixing with a childhood longing that refused to die. A cursed part of Eden that still craved her mother's love. And that strong-willed child won. Eden motioned for her to sit in the other rocking chair.

Her mother sat ramrod straight and gripped her purse tightly. "Let me start by saying I'm sorry."

Eden barely suppressed the urge to roll her eyes. "Abuela mentioned you were no longer drinking. Is this one of your twelve-steps in recovery?"

"Yes, but that doesn't mean my apology isn't from my soul."

"Don't you think it's twenty years too late?"

"For your forgiveness, yes. For you to hear it, no." She leaned into the arm of her chair, closer to Eden. She, in turn, shifted away. "I wish it hadn't taken me decades to get here—my sobriety and to apologize. I'm not making excuses, but I broke when your father died. Then...well, for a long time, it was easier to drown myself in alcohol than face what I'd done to you in those drunken rages."

And she'd done so much harm, caused so much pain. So why were rivulets of pity and sympathy tangling around Eden for a woman who'd hurt and haunted her?

"I want you to have this." Her mother reached inside her purse and handed Eden a delicate gold frame. "It's the last time we were all together as a family."

The photo was taken when Eden was around six years old—the year her papa had died. She was standing with her parents at White Sands National Park. The memory of that day struck her. There was a flash of laughter from her mother, hot sand between Eden's toes, and her father's large, safe hand holding her.

Loss lashed through her, and she tried to return the frame to her mother. "I don't want it."

She clutched the top of her purse to her chest. "Keep it. Hell, cut me out if you must, but keep it."

Eden gave up, setting it limply on her lap. "Your five minutes are up." She despised how a small part of her ached for her mother to stay. She ignored the loss welling inside her and stood.

Her mother nodded, blinking rapidly and getting up. "Could I call you? I saved your number when you called about the milagros."

Eden opened her mouth to say no but found she couldn't answer. She just stared at her mother.

"You don't have to decide now. But maybe one day you'll want too..." Her small, delicate hand, which had caused so much pain, reached for Eden but stopped before touching her. "And your grandma mentioned you had a daughter. I'd love the chance to talk to my grand—"

"No." Eden clutched the frame to her heart. "Never."

"Okay," her mother whispered, then nodded. "I'll go. But maybe think about it."

Eden didn't move as her mom walked to her car, got inside, and drove away. A million thoughts and feelings whipped around her as she opened the front door on unsteady legs and went inside the house. Her vision was blurry from tears that had no reason to fall. She didn't need nor want her mom.

Why did she have to show up in her life again and turn everything upside down when it had finally righted? Her heart was cracking, and every ugly, sad hurt and betrayal leaked out. Her toe caught on the corner of the inside welcome rug, and she lurched forward. The frame tumbled from her grasp, crashing and sliding across the hardwood floor. The frame bent, and glass shattered around her. Papa's smiling face stared at her from a few feet away.

Heaving sobs broke from her. She needed her papa and walked toward the photo. Dull pain radiated from her feet, but she moved toward her papa. Kneeling, she grabbed the broken frame and held him close to her heart, making sure her river of tears didn't ruin the picture.

The pain in her feet pulsed and throbbed as she lurched to the kitchen. She stumbled into a chair, knocking it over. Tripping over it, she fell to her knees. Shards of pain sliced into her, and she howled from internal and external agony.

She pulled her legs up and against her chest, her sobs becoming whimpers. It was inevitable she'd end up here—alone and falling to pieces as everything she'd held in for years hemorrhaged from her, breaking her at last.

CHAPTER FIFTY

Minutes, hours, days later—in a faraway reality—the front door squeaked open, then clicked closed. The old, tiny part of Eden whispered she needed to get up and put her pieces back together. But she was too broken.

And maybe, just maybe, Tate would hold her. Help her.

"Eden?" he called. Worry laced his question.

"What?" she whispered from her spot on the kitchen floor.

Crunching glass, heavy footsteps, and another, more panicked sounding, "Eden?"

His black Converse came into view. A different pain than the one that plagued her feet and legs spread from her chest to her throat. She refused to twist around and meet his gaze.

He hunched to her level and swept away the hair stuck to her face so gently that more tears leaked from her eyes. "What happened?" he asked.

"My mom stopped by."

"Did she attack you?" He slid one arm under her legs, the other across her back, lifting her.

A sad laugh escaped from between her numb lips. "Nope. I did this all on my own." She pressed her face into his chest, inhaling his comforting scent.

He set her on the kitchen counter, the Formica cool against her thighs. He kissed her lightly. "Don't move."

As he walked away, her chest tightened. She took quick, shallow breaths. Was he leaving? Would she beg him to stay?

Maybe. He owned her heart, and she wouldn't let him leave without a fight. "Where are you going?" she asked his retreating frame.

"To the bathroom. To get a washcloth and tweezers. You have glass in your feet and knees."

"Oh." She glanced down. No wonder her body hurt so much. She covered her face with a shaky hand, wanting to disappear.

He returned to the kitchen, setting tweezers and ointment next to her. "I bet you're wishing you stayed in Michigan," she said.

He cupped her chin, then repeated his words from earlier. "There's no place I'd rather be than with you."

She shook her head, not quite believing his words. "Even when I'm like this?"

"Especially when you're like this. I love you. I want to be the man you trust to hold you as you fall apart."

She closed her eyes, savoring his words, wanting to crawl into his heart. "You are that man."

"I am that man," he confirmed. After wetting the washcloth in the sink, he wiped her cheeks and under her eyes. Then he covered her nose with it and told her to blow. She did, feeling about five years old but also loving his care.

He tossed it in the sink, a smile tugging at his beautiful lips. "I'll get a new one for your knees and feet."

She reached for the tweezers. "I can do it."

He shook his head. "Let me." Taking them from her, he bent over her and began removing shards.

She couldn't look away. His careful, precise movements soothed her pulse and the ache pounding through her. His touch was so gentle she could cry from his kindness. She was completely exposed to him and expected to be overwhelmed with the urge to run and hide. Instead, she loved that he saw her, really saw her, and still loved her.

After he dabbed her glass-free knees with a new, warm cloth, she tried again. "I'll do my feet."

The pampering was amazing, but she was a strong, capable woman—a surgeon, for goodness' sake. She could tend to her wounds.

"No way." He dragged a chair from the table to the counter and sat. Tenderly gripping her ankle, he lifted it.

"Why not? I'm capable."

"I know. Because I like taking care of you." He wiggled his eyebrows. "And I can see up your dress."

Laughter burst from her, dispelling most of her misery. Her man was a dream come to life.

Her amusement dimmed when he began removing the glass from the soles of her feet. The slivers were embedded deep, and each tug scraped along exposed nerves. She white-knuckled the edge of the counter to keep from moving.

Sometime later, he set the tweezers next to her. He wiped her feet with a washcloth with a gentleness that brought fresh tears to her eyes. "All done."

Kissing her lightly on the lips, he left again. Seconds later, she heard water splashing into the bathroom tub. Returning, he removed her dress and panties. Then he cradled her again, ignoring her weak protests. Secretly, she was glad she didn't have to put weight on her feet. Carrying her sideways down the narrow hallway, he stepped into the bathroom, setting her smoothly into the water. She moaned as its warmth covered her.

He kneeled next to the tub, dipped the washcloth, then ran it up her arm. Damn, if it was like this to be cared for and looked after, she should've surrendered to Tate a long, long time ago. Like when she'd first met him at Raven's Halloween birthday party.

"Get in here with me." She ran her hand along the rim of the clawfoot tub. "In my teen years, I had lots of fantasies about a hot guy joining me during my nighttime soaks. And a body like yours was definitely what I was dreaming about when I touched myself."

He groaned. "Annnd there went all my pure thoughts of soothing my girlfriend." He stood, tugged off his T-shirt, and shucked his jeans.

She cocked a brow at his full erection. "That doesn't happen from pure thoughts."

"You're wet, naked, and mentioned touching yourself." He motioned for her to scoot forward. "I'll get in behind you."

"Are you sure that's what you want from me?" She eyed him, licking her lips.

"For now, yes."

She debated changing his mind. Losing herself in the pleasure of sex held a lot of appeal, but she needed his calm comfort more than an orgasm—for now. He settled behind her, and she rested into his broad chest, loving how his dusting of hair tickled her back.

He ran the washcloth over her torso, breasts, and arms. "Do you want to tell me what happened?"

To her surprise, she did. And talking about it became an exorcism of sorts, allowing her to release a few demons she'd been holding for way too long. It also made one thing certain; Tate had her back, and more importantly, he had her heart.

She had no reservations about him owning it; he'd always take care of it.

Of this, she didn't have a single doubt.

CHAPTER FIFTY-ONE

When stepping from the parking garage, Tate shielded his eyes from the glaring sun. His gaze traveled over the multi-color building. Starting at the light brown, moving to the cream, and finally resting on the top gray level of the UNM Hospital. It had that hushed quiet that seemed to hover around medical buildings.

Eden took Tate's hand. "I've never brought a man to meet my abuela."

His pulse jumped. "Shit. What if she doesn't think I'm good enough for her preciosa nieta."

She came around the car and looped a finger through this belt loop. "'Preciosa nieta', huh? Where'd you learn that?"

He rubbed a palm along his trim beard, heat warming his cheeks. "I might have downloaded a Spanish app when you invited me and Raven here to meet you abuela."

She pressed her body against his, giving him a smile that was all sex and sass. "That is so damn hot."

He kissed her, hard and quick, and lust battled with his nerves. "Don't turn me on. I'm already freaking thinking about all the things I did to you under her roof last night. What if she sees it in my eyes?"

"You're adorable when you're nervous." She laughed, squeezing his hand and heading inside the hospital.

They rode the elevator to the second level, checked in at the nurse's station, then stopped outside room two-twenty. Eden peeked her head into the room. "I'm awake. Entra," a woman said in a raspy, melodic voice.

His pulse tripped over itself. He'd never been this nervous about meeting any of his old girlfriend's parents. Then again, he'd never felt about them the way he did about Eden. Plus, her grandma was the only person—at least until now—that Eden trusted. Her approval mattered.

They entered the room, and after Eden hugged her grandma, she said, "Abuela, this is my boyfriend, Tate."

Eden's grandmother's thick white hair was tied into a braid, and her wrinkled face was a map of triumphs and tragedies. Large, dark eyes, exactly like Eden's, studied him. He wasn't sure what to do—wave, offer his hand, hug her. She turned to Eden and said something in Spanish.

"What did you expect?" Eden asked.

Uh-oh. That didn't sound good.

Her grandmother said something else, and Eden slipped an arm around Tate's waist. "Well, he's what I need. And I love him."

His worry fell away as her declaration and certainty behind it shot him in the chest, spreading through him. "It is nice to meet you," he said in Spanish. At least, that was what he hoped he'd said.

"You too. Come here." Eden's grandma opened her arms, and Tate went willingly. In her calm, accented English, she said, "I was not sure what to expect when meeting you, but I can tell you are everything my Eden needs."

"She's everything I need."

Eden's grandma smiled, and it held all the warmth of the New Mexico sun. "Perfect."

And she was right. He and Eden were perfect for each other.

EPILOGUE

One year and some months later.

Eden snuggled into Tate's side with her feet curled along the cushioned bench. The porch swing creaked as he moved it languidly back and forth. The moment was as cozy as her favorite sweater. Not that she needed one. It was an unseasonably warm day in October. The sun warmed the dry leaves covering the ground, creating an amazing smell. The scent alone made autumn Eden's new favorite season. There was nothing that'd make her leave this idyllic spot.

Uncle Tate," Chloe called from the dock of Eden's house.

Next to her, Raven shouted, "Mom! You've been lazing over there, like, forever. Let's go sailing. It might be our last chance. It could snow tomorrow."

Okay, maybe one thing—or, more accurately, one person.

Eden laughed and called, "Again?"

"Yes! Are you coming?"

Tate nuzzled Eden's neck. "Give me ten minutes. I'll make sure you *come*."

Eden laughed, pushing lightly against his chest even as desire pooled low in her stomach. "Tempting, but if Raven doesn't get in that sailboat to literally sail into the sunset, she'll be devastated."

"You created a monster buying that boat and suggesting she learn how to sail." Tate stood and offered his hand.

She took it. "True. Her enthusiasm is remarkable." And Eden loved how it gave Raven another reason to visit. There was nothing better than coming home from a stressful day at work and seeing her out on the water with Tate or her bisabuela.

"Oh, I have some good news," she said, leaning into Tate.

"Yeah?"

"Yup. Raven asked if her and Chloe could stay here with their bisabuela tonight. Alone. She wants us to stay at your place." Eden leaned back, diving into his gray eyes. "She says it's because they're tired of sleeping on the pull-out couch in the living room and want my bed, but I think it's because abuela will let them stay up as late as they want and will make churros for breakfast."

"I can't blame them. Abuela's churros are heaven… but if I get to have *you* for breakfast on my kitchen table, I'm all for it."

She hummed her approval. Having her abuela live with her was wonderful for Eden's heart and mind, but having some proper alone time with Tate sounded exquisite. Especially since things have been extra crowded with Raven and Chloe staying with them while Asher and Lilith were on their honeymoon.

"Mom," Raven called again.

"Uncle Tate," Chloe chimed in.

Eden stepped away from Tate's perfect embrace. "Okay, okay. Let me ask abuela if she wants to go with us."

Raven rocked on her feet. "Hurry. Dad and Lilith are coming home tomorrow. I need as much time on the water as possible."

Tate snorted. "Raven acts like Lil and Asher won't let her sail when they're home. Like she hasn't come over here and gone out on that boat almost every day since school let out."

"You won't hear me complain." Being in her daughter's life was a wish made reality.

He kissed her temple. "Stay and relax. I'll ask Abuela."

"You know she'll go. I think she loves being out on the water as much as Raven."

Tate nodded his agreement before slipping inside the house. While waiting, Eden checked her phone messages. Two were from Lilith. One was her and Asher at Edinburgh Castle. Eden sent back a quick text asking if they had visited any Harry Potter spots. The other photo was a group shot from the wedding.

The front door opened, then closed. "She'll be right out," Tate said, resting his chin on her shoulder. He pointed at Eden's phone. "Look at the way Hope and Jackson are eyeing each other. I thought for sure those two would finally get together."

"I doubt it. They've been making those eyes at each other since college, and it hasn't happened yet." She tossed her phone on the porch swing.

Chloe bounded up the porch steps. "Ready?"

Tate held up his index finger. "Bisabuela wants to go. Give her a minute." Chloe nodded and returned to Raven, probably updating her. He turned to Eden. "It's a good thing you didn't get a sailboat with sleeping quarters. They'd have probably moved into it. Or tried to talk us into taking off in search of treasure and adventure."

She slid her arms around his waist. "I'd go anywhere, as long as you're with me."

"Same." He kissed her. He tasted of desire and love.

"Ugh," Raven shouted. "No PDA. Gross."

"They are worse than my mom and your dad," Chloe added.

Abuela stepped onto the porch. "Leave them alone." She winked at Eden and Tate. "Love and affection should never be contained. Let it flow as the river does to the lake."

Eden smiled, relaxing into Tate's chest, his heartbeat soothing the stormy waters of her soul.

THE END

Thank you so much for giving Eden and Tate your time. I hope you enjoyed their story. If you'd like to share your thoughts and feeling about the story, I would appreciate it. Reviews help other readers and authors so much.

If you are so inclined, here are the links to some review sites for Stormy Waters:

Extras

Want to be in the know? Sign up for my newsletter, and you'll be the first to learn of upcoming books, giveaways, and more! And I'm working on a free Lake House Love novella just for my newsletter subscribers.

Sign up here:

Dear Reader

Dear Reader,

Whether you're a returning or new, thank you. It is wonderful to write, but a dream to share my stories with you!

When I started this journey, I feared I'd never finish my first story. After I did, I was afraid I couldn't write another one. Now, I'm on my second series – with many more to come!

I'll let you in on a secret because you've traveled so far with me. The next book will be Hope and Jackson's!

If you're not ready to let go of Eden and Tate's word, dive into *Make Waves*. It is set in the same Michigan town, but it is Lilith and Asher's story. I keep reading for their opening chapter!

Or if you'd like a city/urban romance set in Michigan Check out the Opposites Attract series Keep flipping for the links and more information about each book.

Thank you!

Also By DK

CHAPTER ONE

Lilith Brooks closed her laptop, cutting off the chipper voice of the plumber from the how-to video. She set the computer on the side table, then picked up the travel-size toolbox she'd purchased yesterday. Time to tackle the sink.

The clay-like scent of fresh paint followed her from the living room to the kitchen, where the pleasant smell was replaced by stagnant water and yesterday's dinner of perch. The stench wouldn't last. She'd googled enough tutorials on sinks with their clogs and P-traps that she was practically an expert.

Scooting under the kitchen sink, she turned off the water valves. Pride and satisfaction washed over her. Contrary to Marshall's belief, she could take care of herself and their daughter.

Wrapping her hand around the slip joint nuts, she twisted. Bits of rust from the ancient pipe fell on her, but it didn't budge. She tried again, grunting as it shifted a fraction of a millimeter.

"You okay, Mom?" Chloe asked from somewhere around Lilith's legs.

She slid out from under the sink. "I'm great. Just fixing a clog."

"When you're done, can we go next door? To the white house."

Lilith wiped her forehead with her arm. "Why?"

"I saw a girl my age. I want to meet her."

"They might be weekend renters," Lilith hedged, not excited to make idle chit-chat with strangers.

"But maybe not."

"We'll see. I have to get a few things off my to-do list."

Chloe rolled her eyes, tightening her ponytail. "That thing's longer than Santa's naughty list."

Lilith eyed her daughter. Did she still believe? She was ten now, about the age when kids let go of childhood magic.

"How about tomorrow?" Chloe bounced on her tip-toes. "Please."

Lilith wanted to put it off all summer. There was so much work to be done to get the house ready for weekend renters. Plus, meeting new people was never fun.

"Mom..." A little whine crept into Chloe's voice.

"What? Should we march over there right now, demanding to know if they're permanent residents and if the girl will be your friend?" Lilith joked.

"Works for me." Her daughter wasn't kidding. "And, of course she'd want to be my friend."

Lilith would love to have even an ounce of Chloe's confidence.

She accepted defeat. "Fine. If they're home when I'm done, we'll stop by," Lilith said, looking inside the toolbox.

"Yah! Chloe yelled as the doorbell rang.

"Will you answer that? It's probably Uncle Tate. Why he wouldn't just walk in is beyond me," Lilith muttered, selecting something the person at the hardware store had called tongue-and-groove pliers.

She returned under the sink and twisted hard on the valve. All thoughts of her brother and new neighbors were drowned as the part snapped from the wall, water spraying everywhere.

"No!" She tried blocking the rushing water with her palm, and it burst through her fingers, hitting her in the face. "Crap! Shit!"

"Do you need help?" came a deep voice that wasn't Tate's.

Scrambling from under the sink, she stood, facing a tall man around her age—which was dangerously close to thirty—in a gray T-shirt and dark shorts.

"Who—" she began, but the splash of water hitting the kitchen floor stole all her questions. He could be the neighborhood serial killer for all she cared. What mattered was his offer. "Yes, please. Help me. The water valve broke."

"Where's the main shut-off?"

She held up trembling hands, the need to cry pressing against her throat. "I don't know."

He took off, calling over his shoulder, "I'll find it."

She didn't have it in her tight budget for a flood. Sprinting to a nearby drawer, she yanked it open, pulling it clear off its tracks, dumping towels everywhere. She dropped it, pushing the pile toward the rapidly growing puddle. As she debated about grabbing more from the bathroom, the water cut off.

Heavy footsteps grew louder as the stranger returned from the basement. He appeared in her kitchen a few seconds later, filling up the archway with his broad shoulders.

His hazel gaze caught hers, and her heart jumped. Whoa. The man could have stepped off the cover of one of her favorite romance novels. Longish dark blonde hair, a stubble beard that couldn't hide a strong, angular jaw. And his lips—

Who cares? Definitely not her.

"How did you find the valve so quickly?" she asked.

"I got lucky. I looked where mine is. Yours is in the same place."

His explanation held no censure, but humiliation flooded her, washing away her earlier pride. She straightened. "I'm an idiot. I should have located it before I started this project."

What was I thinking? I can't do this on my own.

He waved away her mistake. "Most people don't bother. I work in construction and built my house. That's why I know where mine is." He offered his hand. "Anyway, I'm Asher Crowley. I live next door. My daughter Raven has wanted to race over since seeing a girl around her age here."

Lilith laughed, shaking his hand. "That's my daughter, Chloe. I'm Lilith Brooks. You must be the neighbor with the white house. Chloe is also eager to meet your daughter."

"I hope you don't mind that Raven went off with yours." He let go of her hand, his gaze following the downward motion of her arm. Around chest level, his eyes widened, then snapped toward her kitchen disaster. He rubbed the back of his neck and asked, "What's wrong with your sink?"

Wondering what caused such an odd reaction, she glanced down and choked on a gasp. The front of her cream tank-top was soaked. And she wasn't wearing a bra.

Her cheeks flamed hot as she crossed her arms over her chest. "It was clogged. I was trying to clean the P-trap." She pointed with her chin at the lower cabinet.

"I have a replacement valve at my house," he said. "I'll grab it and fix it for you."

Lilith rocked on the balls of her feet. He'd already rescued her once, and she didn't want to take advantage of his neighborly hospitality. However, she was afraid to touch the sink after the current disaster, and hiring a plumber was out of her budget.

As if sensing her hesitation, he said, "I've put them in and replaced a ton. It will take me less than ten minutes. Then you won't have to go without water while waiting on a plumber."

"Are you sure you don't mind?"

"Not at all." He nodded toward the stairs. "Do you mind if Raven stays here while I run to my house to get the valve? She went downstairs with your daughter."

"That's fine," Lilith replied, pointing to the hallway. "I'm just, um, going to change into dry clothes."

After he left, she trudged to her bedroom. She slouched on the edge of the bed, kneading a kink in her shoulder. Everything in her wanted to crawl under her comfy blue quilt and let its softness soothe her embarrassment.

Instead, she changed, and this time she made sure to put on a bra. Then made a quick stop in the bathroom to wash her face and brush out the wet tangles. She glanced in the mirror. Her red, chin-length hair stuck to the sides of her head, the wetness making it look almost brown. She poked at the faint circles under her eyes. They highlighted her sleepless nights—the worry, but also the excitement of being free.

Almost free.

Shutting off the light, she returned to the kitchen, stopping at the entrance. Asher was scooting out from under her sink, holding the P-trap. When he saw her, he held it up and said, "I hope you don't mind. Fixing the valve was quick, so I took this off."

She was impressed. "I don't, and thank you."

"Something's stuck in it. It's probably why your drain was clogged." He rose from the floor and shook the curved pipe over the sink.

A bright pink object made of hard rubber or silicone, shaped like a large acorn on a stand, rolled across the counter, stopping next to the drying rack.

"I think someone was playing a practical joke on the previous owner," Asher said, sounding like he was trying not to laugh. "Seems fitting."

"What do you mean?" Her chest tightened, feeling exposed but not sure why.

"Well, this couldn't have accidentally ended up in the pipe. The strainer body would have to be removed, then this dropped into it. And," he scratched his cheek. "The guy you bought this place from, was um, on the wild side. I could see a disgruntled guest doing this."

Bought the place from? It was her vacation home. Before that, it had been her dad's. He'd given it to her as a wedding gift. Who the hell had been squatting here?

"What did this man look like?"

"The owner? A white guy. Tall with black hair. Lean. Why?"

He was describing her soon-to-be ex-husband, Marshall. So, this was where he was during some of those supposed 'business trips.' There was no shock, only dull disappointment. He'd sullied her childhood summer home with his many affairs.

Not wanting to admit who the man was to her, she said, "I don't see the point of dumping this kitchen tool in the sink's pipes."

Asher snorted, and she looked at him. "What?"

His smile slipped a little. "It's not anything you'd use in a kitchen..."

Her brows furrowed, unease running alongside her confusion. "What is it?"

"Um." He shifted from side to side as if his feet ached to leave.

It made her more curious and anxious. Was it dangerous? Something to do with drugs? She repeated her question, needing to know. If it was hazardous and there were more in the house. She'd have to find them before Chloe.

"Please tell me."

He stared at the sink, and she held in the urge to ask again. Clearing his throat, he said, "It's, umm, a sex toy."

Double fists of embarrassment and humiliation sucker-punched her hard enough to make tears well in her eye."

"Oh," was all she could manage.

The desire to be alone rocked through her. This was why she didn't like to be around people. She was the last to get the joke. Or was the joke.

Inhaling her mortification, she exhaled sadness. She was supposed to stay at her vacation home for the summer while she figured out what to do with her disintegrating life. Now she'd see her shame and inadequacies reflected in her neighbor's eyes every time they spoke. The fastest way to get rid of him was through the truth. No one wanted to hang around in her messy life.

"This house has been in my family since I was a kid." She met his eyes. "That guy is my husband."

Asher groaned, the color draining from his handsome face. "I'm such an asshole."

"Hardly, and believe me, I'm an expert. I've been married to one for a decade."

Grabbing the dishtowel hanging on the stove, she picked up the offending item and tossed it into the garbage next to the sink's cabinet door. She wrapped the towel around her fist, staring at it.

The quiet became heavy. Oppressive.

He drummed his fingers on the counter. "My daughter. She's with yours. Is it okay if I get her?"

Her mortification deepened. He had at least one kid and was probably happily married with a perfect family. The poor man had just wanted to introduce his daughter, not get pulled into her mess.

"I'll see if they are in Chloe's room," she said.

"If you'd rather put your sink back together, I can find her," he offered.

"Sure. Sure." *Please anything. Just leave.* Remembering her manners, she added, "Thanks for your help."

"Anytime," he said, backtracking from the kitchen.

Reaching for her phone on the counter, she knew it was a bad idea, but perverse curiosity held her tight. She googled 'sex toys', then clicked 'images.' "Christ." She slumped against the fridge. "A butt plug."

It was official. She was going to hide in her house until the end of summer.

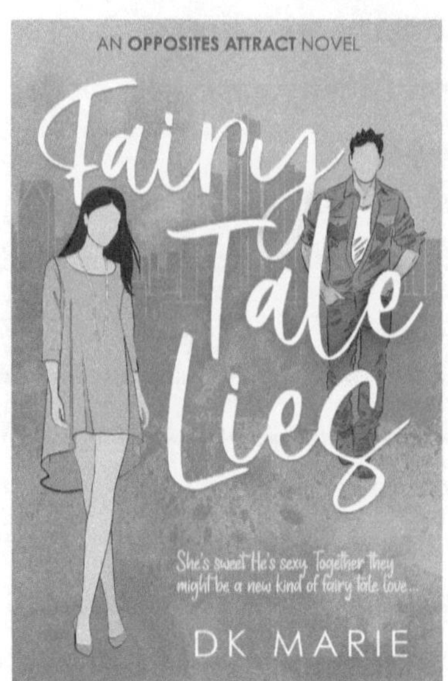
AN OPPOSITES ATTRACT NOVEL
Fairy Tale Lies
She's sweet. He's sexy. Together they
might be a new kind of fairy tale love...
DK MARIE

She's sweet. He's sexy. Together they might be new kind of fairy tale love....

Greta does everything that's expected of the prestigious Meir family—except for that one stormy afternoon of passion and pleasure where she took exactly what she wanted....

When the clouds parted, so did she and Jacob Grimm, certain they're only an erotic chapter in their vastly different lives. Weeks later, she finds him at her father's conference table, a real-life reminder of why risks aren't worth the reward.

Jacob should forget Greta. She'll never see him as anything more than a temporary indulgence who doesn't belong in her affluent world. And her family has the power—and desire—to destroy the life he's struggled to build.

Greta agrees—he doesn't fit in, and for them to try for more is a mistake. He'll cause upheaval and chaos in her orderly life. But for someone so wrong, he feels so right.

As tempers flare and passions deepen, will Greta and Jacob toss aside the worn-out concept of fairy tale love and find their happily-ever-after?

Fairy Tale Lies is the first book in the stand-alone steamy *Opposites Attract* contemporary romance series. If you like vulnerable, real characters who'll make you laugh, lust, and fall in love, you'll adore DK Marie's work-place romance.

Buy *Fairy Tale Lies* for a story that'll make your heart swoon!

She sings to the wild side of his heart, strumming his needs against his desires, disrupting his harmony.

Maggie Preswyck carries music in her soul; she lives and breathes melody. Nothing and no one can get in the way of her band's success. Including Tanner Reid—her sexy, temporary guitarist. His talent and quiet humor are irresistible. But mixing business with pleasure could destroy her heart and career.

Every time they rehearse, the chords of passion between them deepen. But Maggie will never give up on her music, and Tanner doesn't want the life of a musician—Her dream is his nightmare. With no middle ground, all that waits for them at the end of his time with the band is heartbreak.

Can Maggie and Tanner adjust their dreams, or will they become another sad love song?

Love Songs is the second book in the standalone, steamy Opposites Attract contemporary romance series.

If you like strong characters, intense and swoon-worthy scenes, then you'll adore DK Marie's passionate friends-to-lovers tale.

Buy Love Songs for a story that'll sing to your heart!

She has a taste for trouble. He craves more than her body. Together they could be a recipe for love or disaster...

Opposites, Cindy Meier and Will Grimm, have two things in common. They love to annoy each other, and their siblings are getting married. *That's it.*

Oh, and they have to plan the weekend wedding party. Will doesn't want to put up with the spoiled socialite who lives in a fantasy world. And Cindy could think of better ways to spend her free time with her hot but grumpy brother-in-law. The only way to survive the awful chore is with snips, sarcasm, and sparring.

When they're forced together on the sunny beaches of Lake Michigan, their annoyance and amusement morph into something neither expected nor wanted—desire. They give in, agreeing it won't extend past the weekend. *It can't.* Will had finally crawled out of the hell he'd created, and someone like Cindy would send him back into it. And while she might enjoy Will's body and what he does with it, she won't change to fit into his life.

As they struggle to keep their attraction and deepening feelings at bay, they'll have to decide if overcoming their differences is worth the passion they've tasted...

Taste of Passion is the third book in the stand-alone steamy *Opposites Attract* contemporary romance series. If you like vulnerable, real characters who'll make you laugh, lust, and fall in love, you'll adore DK Marie's friends-to-lovers romance.

Buy *Taste of Passion* for a delicious story that'll fill your heart!

His life has become gray and drab. Her vibrancy paints the dark shadows of his heart, turning them into shades of love.

Harper Marquette pours her passion into her art, not men. But Lucas Genezen had seemed different— her opposite in a way that was refreshing and gentle. Falling for his kind eyes and sensual smile, she landed in bed with him—only to wake to her mistakes and an empty hotel room.

Lucas royally messed up with Harper, and she's better off without his battered heart and life. Yet he can't forget her and wants a second chance. But when she learns he's a young widow, she knows it's foolish to date a man who'll never be able to love her in return—even if it doesn't feel reckless when she's with him.

They can't let go of each other or their pasts. Is it possible to embrace both and have a picture-perfect future together, or are they creating endless heartbreak?

Colors of the Heart is the fourth and final book in the standalone steamy *Opposites Attract* contemporary romance series. If you like vulnerable, real characters who'll make you laugh, lust, and fall in love, you'll adore DK Marie's love-after-loss romance.

Buy *Colors of the Heart* for a story that'll paint your world in shades of love!

About the Author

DK Marie loves to indulge in all things hot. Men, writing, reading, and coffee. The order of importance depends on the day.

Like characters in her books, she lives in Michigan, enjoying her happily ever after with her husband and kids.

When not writing, she loves the theater, concerts, and traveling.DK loves to hear from readers. You can find and connect with her at the links below.